Kelly Elliott is a *New York Times* and *USA Today* bestselling contemporary romance author. Since finishing her bestselling Wanted series, Kelly continues to spread her wings while remaining true to her roots and giving readers stories rich with hot protective men, strong women and beautiful surroundings.

Kelly has been passionate about writing since she was fifteen. After years of filling journals with stories, she finally followed her dream and published her first novel, *Wanted*, in November of 2012.

Kelly lives in central Texas with her husband, daughter, and two pups. When she's not writing, Kelly enjoys reading and spending time with her family. She is down to earth and very in touch with her readers, both on social media and at signings.

Visit Kelly Elliott online:

www.kellyelliottauthor.com
www.twitter.com/author_kelly
www.facebook.com/KellyElliottAuthor/

THE LOVE WANTED IN TEXAS SERIES

Without You
Saving You
Holding You
Finding You
Chasing You
Loving You

Finding You

Love Wanted in Texas
Book Four

Kelly Elliott

PIATKUS

First published in 2015 by K. Elliott Enterprises
First published in Great Britain in 2016 by Piatkus
This paperback edition published in 2016 by Piatkus

1 3 5 7 9 10 8 6 4 2

A CIP catalogue record for this book is available from the British Library.

ISBN 978-0-349-41348-8

Printed and bound in Great Britain by
Clays Ltd, St Ives plc

Papers used by Piatkus are from well-managed forests and other responsible sources.

MIX
Paper from responsible sources
FSC® C104740

Piatkus
An imprint of
Little, Brown Book Group
Carmelite House
50 Victoria Embankment
London EC4Y 0DZ

An Hachette UK Company
www.hachette.co.uk

www.piatkus.co.uk

WANTED
family tree

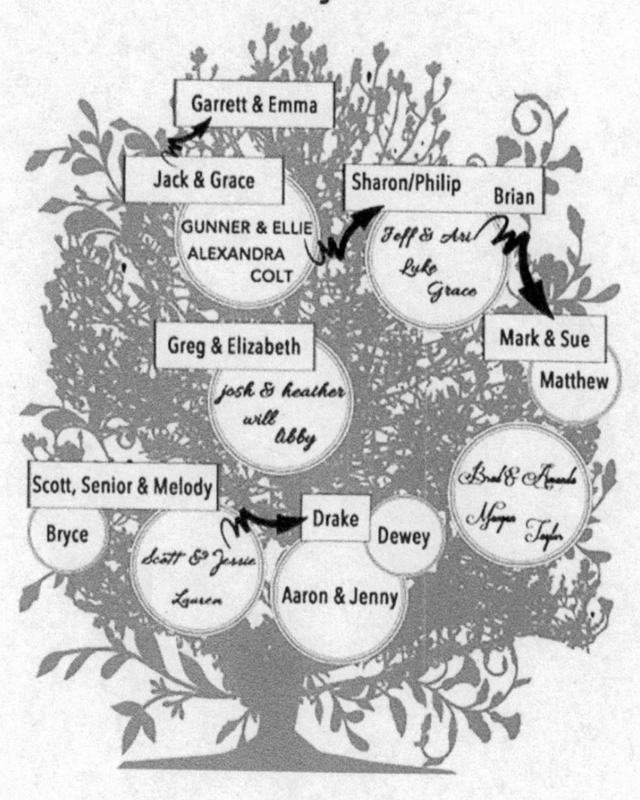

Finding You

Prologue

THE MEMORY OF Noah's lips lingered as I gently swiped my fingers across my mouth. Leaning my head gently against the door, his words flooded my head.

"You taste of honey, my sweet Grace. Your body holds my body captive."

Shaking my head, I quickly changed and crawled into bed as Libby slept a few feet away. Closing my eyes, the only thing I could see were caramel eyes looking deep into my soul. It was as if Noah reached a part of me I had successfully buried after Michael had betrayed me and brought it back to life.

"Grace? Did you enjoy your night?"

Snapping my eyes open, my breathing picked up as my heart pounded so loud in my ears, I was sure Libby would hear it.

"I'm exhausted, Libby. We'll talk in the morning, okay?" I said as I tried to sound as normal as possible.

Libby sighed. "Okay, Grace. Night."

Swallowing hard, I barely spoke back. "Night."

My insides were screaming at me to talk to Libby. I desperately wanted to ask her if she thought it was possible to fall in love with just one kiss. Rubbing my kiss-swollen lips together, I fought to hold back my tears.

It was only supposed to be a one-night stand.

That's it.

You cannot possibly fall in love with someone just from one night. One beautiful, magical night. It felt as if I'd known Noah my whole life.

"I want to make love to you all night, Grace. Please stay with me, baby."

Noah.

Rolling over, I pulled the covers up to my chin and pressed my lips tightly together as I tried to ignore the feelings rushing through my body.

I won't fall in love. I can't fall in love.

Noah's whispered words replayed in my mind. *"You truly are the most beautiful woman I've ever put my eyes on."*

Reaching up, I slowly wiped my tears away as I closed my eyes. No one had ever talked to me the way Noah did. The way he looked at me, as if I was the very air he breathed, had almost brought me to my knees more than once.

Noah.

Dare I open my heart to the one man who had ignited something so amazing, I felt as if I could hardly breathe? The man who held the power to completely destroy what little heart I had left.

No, I promised myself I would never open myself up to hurt again. This would have to be enough. One amazing night with Noah Bennet would have to do. I allowed myself to feel for one incredible night.

The hardest thing I had to do now was forget Noah even existed. I'd move on and keep the memory of tonight locked deep down inside.

Noah.

Who was I kidding? My body craved him just lying there. I'd forever crave the feel of his hands on my body. His tongue exploring my mouth. His words whispered against my lips.

"*You're mine now, Grace. I won't ever let you go.*"

One

GRACE

I SAT IN the library as I rolled my neck around and let out a sigh. My mind had been preoccupied and I couldn't afford to not be focused. I'd fallen behind in my classes when Lauren got sick.

Glancing back down at my book, I tried to read the words on the pages but my mind quickly drifted off to a memory of Noah and me.

SITTING BACK, I let the sun warm my face as Noah rowed the canoe.

"So, are you going to just sit there while I do all the work, Grace?" Noah asked in a teasing voice.

"Yep."

Keeping my eyes closed, I could tell he had turned directions. Trying not to smile, I asked, "Are you getting tired,

Noah? Was last night too much for you?"

Noah chuckled. It was the first night I'd stayed over at his apartment he shared with one other guy who also attended A&M. I wasn't sure why I was keeping how close Noah and I were getting away from everyone. Maybe it was my way of keeping this relationship distant from my real world. That, or I didn't feel like answering Alex, Lauren, and Libby's constant questions.

Whatever my reasons were, I pushed it from my mind.

"Baby, you could never be too much."

Opening my eyes, I tilted my head and gave Noah a sexy smile. As hard as I tried to keep from falling in love with him, I fell deeper every moment we spent together.

"Is that a challenge?" I asked as I leaned forward, making sure to squeeze my arms together so my breasts showed just the right amount of cleavage since I only had a tank top over my swimsuit.

Lifting his eyebrows, Noah glanced over to the shore. When I looked over my shoulder, there was a small path. Noah paddled us over and jumped out. Reaching his hand out for mine, I placed it softly in his. The rush I got just from his touch about caused me to let out a moan. Stepping up onto the shore, I watched as Noah pulled the canoe up and grabbed my hand.

Leading me down the path, he pushed me against a tree and smiled at me.

"That is indeed a challenge. Let's see if you can keep up with me now, Grace."

My heart dropped to my stomach as I fought back those three words.

Lifting me up, Noah pushed his hard dick into me as I gasped. Desire pulled in my lower stomach and I was ready for anything Noah was going to give me.

Except for the three little words he was clearly not afraid to say.

"I love you, Grace."

My mouth parted open slightly as I whispered back, "I love you too, Noah."

MY PHONE BUZZED on the table, pulling me from my memory. Glancing down, I saw it was Alex.

Alex: Hey. I'm finished with classes today. Want to go grab some food?

Me: Where's your hubby?

Alex: Sleeping. We both have been trying to get caught up on classes.

Letting out a laugh, I nodded my head at my phone.

Me: I love Lauren, but she screwed this semester up!

Alex: Right? So food or not? I'm starving and my baby wants food.

Me: I'll meet you at Fuego's.

Alex: Yes! I was hoping you'd say that. See you there in a few.

Smiling, I stood and gathered up my books. Turning to head out of the library, I came face to face with Doug Richards.

"Hey, Grace."

My eyes traveled over his body as I suppressed the moan I wanted to let out. Damn he was fine as hell and it had been to long since I'd had sex. My mind had been filled with memories of Noah and I was horny as hell.

Noah.

Pushing all thoughts of Noah away, I smiled as I quickly

gave my lower lip a seductive bite and purred, "Hey, Doug."

Doug's eyes lit up. I'd always been friendly with Doug, but this was the first time I'd ever put a little bit of something more into my normal *Oh hey, Doug, how's it going*?

Seeing Noah at the hospital with his new wife only proved to me that I needed to move on. I couldn't shake the way Noah had looked at me, though. I swear I saw the same look in his eyes as I saw the first night he made love to me. Actually, the first time he ever looked at me, I saw the passion.

"Plans for tonight?" Doug asked as he ran his fingers lightly up and down my arm. My body shook with the idea of being with someone. I needed a good hard fuck to pull me out of this funk. *What would one mindless one-night-stand do?*

It would at least ease the throb between my legs. I'd gone through too many vibrators. I was ready for the real thing.

Licking my lips, I winked. "I believe you're picking me up around eight? Taking me to dinner and then a little bit of . . . dessert afterward."

The smile that spread across Doug's face caused me to smile. "I like that plan."

My eyes roamed his body as they landed on his lips. Hopefully he was a good kisser. He had big shoes to fill.

Reaching into my purse, I took out a pen and grabbed Doug's arm as I wrote down my address. "See ya at eight, handsome."

The second I turned to walk away, I wanted to spin around and tell him to forget it. That I forgot I had plans with a friend. Worrying my lip, I continued to walk toward the exit door.

No, Grace. It's time to move on. What I needed was one evening of pure fun, and Doug was the one who was going to provide it. Noah was married and I needed to stop feeling sorry for myself. What we had shared was amazing and I let it spook me. I pushed away the only man I'd ever truly loved.

It was time to move on.

Tonight I was getting laid.

"WHAT DO YOU mean you have a date?" Alex asked with a stunned look on her face.

I took a bite of my taco and shrugged my shoulders. "You know, Alex. That thing you do when you're single and haven't had normal sex in I don't know how long. Even my vibrator wants me out of the house."

Alex giggled as she quickly looked around. "You're terrible, Grace Hope Johnson."

Shrugging my shoulders, I said, "Hey, you're getting dick every night. I wonder if I should get a Brazilian wax?"

Laughing, Alex shook her head. "That was random as hell."

"I just got to thinking, I think I want my hoo-ha to be smooth for tonight."

Alex started choking on her taco. "What? Grace, you can't do that today and then have sex tonight!"

Pulling my head back in a shocked expression, I asked, "Why not?"

"Have you ever had anything waxed on your body before?"

Tilting my head, I thought about it. "Nope, I can't say that I have."

Leaning in toward the table, Alex motioned for me to come closer. "Grace, it hurts like hell to get waxed for the first time. I don't think you want your hoo-ha to be tortured before you dive back into the whole sex thing again. I mean, I get the whole, *I just want mindless sex* thing, but do you really want to mistreat her like that all in one day?"

About to state my case, I heard someone clear her throat. Alex and I both turned to see a mom staring at us with her daughter sitting there with her mouth dropped to the table. Smiling, I said, "I'm not going to have mindless sex tonight . . . well actually I am, but I always use protection and . . . ouch!" I called out as I felt a stabbing pain in my shin from where Alex kicked me. Turning back to her, I yelled, "What the hell, Alex?"

Alex's eyes were widened as she shook her head. "Grace, stop talking."

The mother stood and motioned for her daughter to follow as Alex sat back and moaned. "Great, some mother I'm going to be."

Letting out a laugh, I shook my head and said, "You're going to be a kick-ass mother. Just like Ellie. Hey, so we never really got to talk about how your parents and Will's parents reacted to the big baby news."

Alex shrugged her shoulders. "I think they were all in shock. My father's biggest worry was school. I'm so glad we're all graduating this December."

Taking a bite of my taco, I nodded my head. "Yeah, I'm glad too." After swallowing the taco, I worried my bottom lip. I had been trying to figure out how to ask Alex if she had changed her mind about our plans.

Alex reached across the table and took my hand in hers. "The baby doesn't change anything, Grace. I want to still follow our dream of opening up Wild Flower. We've been dreaming of opening a flower nursery for years. Nothing is going to change that."

I instantly felt my body relax. Our whole focus throughout school had been to open a nursery between Fredericksburg and Mason. The news of Alex having a baby had scared the piss out of me. Smiling, I said, "I'm not going to lie, I thought I might be doing this on my own and I was scared as hell."

Letting out a chuckle, Alex shook her head. "No way.

Will and I have already talked about it. I fully intend on pursuing our dream, Grace." Shrugging her shoulders, she said, "Besides, we will own the place! I can bring the baby. She'll learn to dig in the dirt probably before she learns to walk."

Sitting up straighter, I let out a gasp. "Oh my gosh! We can build a little baby nursery beside your office. I mean, I'm sure y'all will have more kids in the future. I bet my dad or your dad could easily add that into the design. Move the storage space somewhere else."

Alex's eyes lit up as she nodded her head. "Grace, that's a great idea! This will be perfect for both of us."

Narrowing my eyes, I let out a confused chuckle. "How is a baby room perfect for me?"

Giving me a sly smile, Alex said, "For when you have kids."

Nearly choking on my tea, I held up my hands. "Whoa! Whoa! Holy hell, woman! Don't even speak such words. This girl has no plans for kids in the near future. Fuck, I'm not even having sex and the last time I checked . . . you can't get knocked up from a vibrator."

Alex looked around as she put her finger up to her lips. "Why do you have to talk so loud?"

"Why do you have to say such things? My God! There is already something in the water with you and Libby both getting pregnant. I'm sure Lauren is probably going to be announcing something in the next few months. Well . . . no thank you. I'm not having kids anytime soon."

Alex's eyes looked sad. "Grace, do you not want kids?"

My heart instantly hurt as I plastered on a fake smile. "Someday I'm sure I'll want kids. Right now, it is the furthest thing from my mind. All I want right now, Alex, is to move on and have a good time."

"Grace, I talked to Noah the day Lauren got out of the hospital. He desperately needs to talk to you."

Swallowing hard, I fought to hold back my tears.

"W-what did he say?"

Shaking her head, Alex said, "He asked how Lauren was and then for your number. I gave it to him. He said he needed to talk to you."

Feeling my entire body start shaking, I quickly stood up. "Why would you give him my phone number, Alex? He's married for Christ's sake! Besides, it's been over two weeks since Lauren left the hospital. He must not be that desperate to talk to me. Damn it, Alex. Why did you give him my number?"

Alex motioned for me to sit down. "Grace, just give me one second to explain."

Grabbing my food and drink, I glared at Alex. "I have to go; I have to head home and grab a book a forgot and head to class."

"Grace! Let me finish talking!" Alex called out.

Racing to the door, I pushed it open and quickly dragged in the fresh air. Glancing at my watch, I sighed. I was going to be late for class now. Quickly making my way to my car, my phone buzzed. Pulling it out of my purse, I saw it was Alex.

Alex: I didn't mean to upset you. It's just he seemed desperate. You really need to talk to him, Grace.

Rolling my eyes, I threw my purse and phone onto the passenger seat and headed back to the house I shared with Alex and Will. Now that Luke, Libby, Lauren, and Colt had moved out, it seemed cold and empty all the time. Even when they did live there, I spent more time at Noah's place than I did at home. Well, at least I did until I freaked out and pushed him away.

Wiping my tears away, I concentrated on thinking about nothing but my date tonight with Doug. I'll deal with Alex later. Right now I needed to push Noah Bennet far from my memory. I needed to move on and this date tonight was long overdue.

Two

GRACE

RUSHING INTO THE house, I looked for my book before heading upstairs to my room to check my makeup. Alex just talking about Noah had my emotions all over the place. Closing my eyes, I thought back to the day I ran into him at the hospital. His beautiful smile that about dropped me to the ground replayed over and over in my mind.

Then I saw her. His wife. Standing next to him. She didn't seem at all like his type, but hell, maybe I was the one who wasn't his type.

Sitting down on the bed I thought about all the things he had said to me. Had he meant a word of it? He sure moved on fast after I told him I needed some time. Shit. He even left A&M.

Dropping my head into my hands, I cried. "Jesus, Grace. It's your fault. You pushed him away until he had no choice but to fall into the arms of another woman."

With a sinking feeling in my heart, I fell back onto

the bed and let out a scream as I stared up at the ceiling. Sitting back up, I shook my head to clear my thoughts. "What's done is done. It's time to move on."

Picking up my phone, I sent Doug a text. We had exchanged phone numbers the other day for a project we were working on.

Me: Let's skip the date part and move straight to dessert.

It didn't take Doug long to respond back.

Doug: Sounds like a solid plan. My place or yours?

My hands started shaking and I fought the urge to tell him I suddenly got sick and had to cancel.

Me: Yours. Pick me up at seven.

Doug: Be ready to have your world rocked.

Rolling my eyes, I let out a sigh. "Ugh. Jesus H. Christ. Why do all guys think their dicks are the greatest thing since apple pie?"

Finding my book, I shoved it in my backpack and headed downstairs. Feeling guilty about ignoring Alex, I hit her number and called her.

"Hey, Grace," Alex said softly over the phone. "I wasn't trying to hurt you by giving Noah your number. It's just . . . well . . . he seemed so desperate to talk to you. He was practically begging me. I really think you need to talk to him."

Opening the refrigerator, I let out a fake laugh. "Maybe she sucks in bed and he wants out of the marriage."

Alex sighed loudly through the phone. "Grace, please don't go on the date tonight until you talk to Noah. Please listen to your heart."

Closing my eyes, I nodded my head as I whispered, "Alex, it's been two weeks and he hasn't called." Taking in a deep breath, I decided I needed to be honest with Alex and myself. "It's just . . . Alex, I'm so afraid to talk to him. My feelings for him . . . they're still so strong even knowing he's married. What if he wants . . . I mean what if I—I'm not that girl, Alex. I won't be with a married man."

Alex sighed. "I know you wouldn't and you don't have to be. Listen, just talk to him when he calls, Grace. I don't think Doug is truly who you want to move on with, but I understand your thinking behind that."

Grabbing my upper lip with my teeth, I bit down hard and nodded my head as I looked at the time on the microwave. "Hey, I've got to go. I'll see you tonight."

"Grace?"

"Yeah?" I asked as I put my backpack over my shoulder.

"Don't go tonight," Alex whispered.

I knew this wasn't a healthy way to live. Sitting around moping about a man whose lips I'd never feel on mine again. I also knew I didn't really want to have a mindless one-night-stand with Doug. "Great minds think alike, Alex. Doug isn't who I want to be with. I've got to run. See ya later. Love you."

"Love you too, sweets!"

I quickly sent Doug a text telling him something important had come up and I couldn't make tonight. I prayed like hell he didn't call me back and just took the rejection and moved on. Grabbing my keys, I dashed out the front door, cursing myself for being late to class. I was already so far behind in all my classes. Turning, I pulled the front door shut and locked it. Spinning around on my heels, I went to walk down the stairs and was stopped dead in my tracks as I sucked in a breath of air.

Oh. My. God.

Noah.

"W-what are you doing here?" I asked in a weak sounding voice.

Staring back up at me were those beautiful caramel

eyes I found myself lost in on more than one occasion.

"I never got to finish talking to you. I'm glad Lauren's okay."

Fumbling over my words, I asked, "H-how did you know?" Remembering Alex had *just* told me she talked to Noah, I swallowed hard and attempted to talk again.

"I mean, yeah, Lauren's actually in Vegas with Colt. They're . . . um . . . they're getting married."

Noah smiled and my world rocked on its axis. *Lord help me, for his smile does things to my body even still.* Swallowing hard, I smiled back.

"That's wonderful. I'm really happy for them both. I haven't had the pleasure of meeting Lauren yet, but Alex was talking to me at the hospital and filled me in on Lauren's progress."

Yet? He hasn't met Lauren—yet?

Shaking my head to clear my thoughts, I asked, "Noah, why are you here? I mean you're . . ." My heart hurt as I tried to speak the words that wouldn't form in my mouth.

He's married now. Just say it, Grace. You need to move on.

Noah took a step up as I instinctively backed up. *No. Please don't come closer to me.* I wanted to beg him to stop. If he came any closer, I'd feel his pull and my heart couldn't take another break.

"That's what I wanted to come and talk to you about, Grace. You mentioned me being married."

Swallowing hard, I looked away so he couldn't see the tears forming in my eyes. It was my fault. I pushed him away. It was no one else's fault but my own.

Noah reached the top step. Taking in a deep breath, I smelled that familiar scent of his cologne and I whimpered silently inside. My eyes stung as I forced myself not to look at him.

Another step closer. My chest was rising up and down so fast as I dragged in breaths of air.

Noah stopped right in front of me. My body shook as I attempted to push away every memory of him. Every touch. Every kiss. Every romantic word he whispered in my ear as he made love to me.

My skin exploded when his finger touched my chin. Turning my face to him, his eyes locked with mine. "I've missed you so much, and I thought I'd lost you forever, Grace."

My mouth parted open as a single tear fell from my eye. "Noah, you're married and I can't . . ."

Leaning in closer to me, I sucked in a breath of air as his eyes landed on my lips. "Grace, my sweet Grace. I'm not married."

Alex's words flooded my mind. *" . . . he seemed so desperate to talk to you. He was practically begging me."*

Widening my eyes, a sob escaped my lips. "You're . . . you're not? Are you sure?"

Noah laughed softly and nodded his head. "I'm positive, baby."

Baby.

Jesus, Mary, and Joseph.

He called me baby.

My mind drifted back to the girl. *Who was the girl he was with at the mall and hospital?* "But, I saw you with her. You were registering for your wedding." Placing his hand on the side of my face, Noah looked into my eyes as he gently moved his thumb across my skin. "That's Emily, my sister, Grace. She's the one who got married. When I lost my phone, I lost your number; I didn't know what to do. There were so many times I wanted to get in my car and come here. The last thing I wanted to do was show up on your doorstep and find you were with a guy. Looking back, I could kick my own ass for not just coming to you."

I slowly shook my head and whispered, "There's no one but you, Noah."

Smiling, Noah spoke softly. "Please don't push me

away again, Grace. I need you. I need you so much."

My whole world stopped as I stared at Noah.

I need you so much.

Holy shit. Closing my eyes, I dropped my head back against the door and let out a sigh. His sister. All those texts I ignored. The phone calls I sent to voicemail because I thought he was with another woman. If I had just given him the opportunity to explain to me what I saw, I could have saved myself so much heartache.

My body jumped when I felt his lips against my neck. "Grace, I had to come find you. I needed you to know the truth."

Oh God. He came for me.

Noah came for me.

Three

NOAH

GRACE WHIMPERED AS I brushed my lips across her neck. I'd never really known why Grace had decided to stop seeing me. I figured it had to have been because of what happened with her high school boyfriend. She had shared with me how deeply she had been hurt. She even shared her fear of falling in love with me. But I was sure we'd be able to withstand anything as long as we were together. The second I figured out why she had stopped communicating with me altogether, I fought like hell to get to her. She had mistakenly thought I was married. Everything made sense; the short conversations when I ran into her, the ignored phone calls and text messages. Alex had finally broken down and given me Grace's phone number at the hospital, but my sister Emily said I needed to talk to Grace in person.

Placing my hands on the sides of Grace's face, I looked into her eyes. "Grace, I've been going insane since we broke up. It's been pure hell for me in more than one way. I've never in my life felt the way I do for anyone like I do for you."

Placing her hands on my arms, Grace whispered, "I'm scared, Noah. You have no idea how scared I am."

Grace had put up walls the very first time we were together, but I saw the same look in her eyes that was in mine. I never believed in love at first sight until Grace Johnson ran into me one rainy afternoon.

Leaning my head against hers, I spoke softly. "Me too, Grace. Me too. But I can't forget what we've shared. Grace, I think about you all the time. Do you remember the guitar?"

Grace giggled as she whispered, "I'd never forget that day. I told myself all I would ever need is you with a guitar and a sunflower and my life would be complete."

My mind drifted back as I remembered that day we spent together months after we first started dating.

WALKING UP TO Grace, I held the teal guitar in my hand as she covered her mouth and laughed. "Man oh man. I didn't realize you were in a girl band, Noah."

Winking, I sat down in front of the little bench Grace was sitting on and I handed her a giant sunflower. Smiling, Grace took it and brought it up to her nose as she inhaled deeply. I positioned the guitar I had just bought from a street vendor on my lap.

"Don't be jealous of my good taste, Grace. Be ready for me to rock your world, baby."

Rolling her eyes, Grace pulled her knees up and rested her chin. "Let's see what you got."

The way Grace was looking at me had my heart racing with anticipation. I'd taken guitar lessons for years, but I'd never actually sung in front of anyone, and the only people who even knew I played the guitar were my mother and sister.

Knowing how much Grace loved Sam Hunt, I picked one of his songs to cover. Starting the first cords to "Take Your Time", I watched as Grace's face lit up and her eyes danced with excitement.

Clearing my throat, I started singing to the one and only girl I'd ever dreamed of spending the rest of my life with.

When the last cord was played, I smiled and watched as Grace slowly stood up.

"Oh, you're good. You totally just secured yourself one hell of a night, Mr. Bennet." Lifting her eyebrow, she said, "Smart thinking pulling the Sam Hunt card."

Throwing my head back, I laughed as I drank in the moment.

PULLING HER HEAD back, her eyes widened with panic. "I'm so late for class!"

Laughing, I took her hand and led her to my car. "I'll wait for you."

Slipping into the front seat of my Nissan GT-R, Grace looked up at me and winked. "Sexy car."

Feeling my heart drop, I attempted to play it cool. I'd never had someone affect me the way Grace has. "Ya think so?" I asked with a playful tone.

Grace's mouth parted slightly and I imagined her lips on mine. Letting out a quick breath, I shut the door and jogged around to the driver's side. Getting in, I turned and said, "Where to?"

Grace stared at me as her eyes looked deep into mine. For a quick moment I panicked. Would Grace get spooked again, or were we done with the push and pull game? What came out of her mouth caused me to totally get my hopes up that we were finished with the games. "I've never had sex in a car before . . . let alone a sports car."

Swallowing hard, I whispered, "You won't make it to class if you keep talking, Grace."

Licking her lips, Grace smiled. "What class?"

Closing my eyes, I moaned as I adjusted my hardening dick. Snapping my eyes back open, I cranked the car on and pulled out of the driveway. "Damn it, Grace. It's been too long since we've been together. Let's get you to class then we'll talk more."

"Killjoy," Grace whispered as she smiled and looked out the front window.

SITTING IN MY car, I waited for Grace to finish up her class. There was no way I was leaving from this spot after being away from her for so long. I had to stop going over and over in my head the fact that I didn't come after her when I knew I should have. I let her walk away when I knew we both loved each other and belonged together.

Never again.

Picking up my phone, I sent my sister a text.

> *Me: How's mom?*
>
> *Emily: Okay. Sleeping. She kept asking where you were. Today's treatment was bad. The doctor wants to talk about stopping the treatments. He said it's not improving anything. He mentioned moving Mom to the Christopher House.*

Letting out a sigh, I dropped my head back. *Hospice.* My mother had been fighting invasive epithelial ovarian cancer for the last year. We thought she had won the battle, but the cancer returned. This time with a vengeance.

Me: Tell her I'll be back tonight.

Emily: No! I told her you would be back tomorrow night or the next morning. Noah, you need to talk to Grace. Please. You've been miserable since you left A&M. Stay and make things right.

Feeling the tears threaten my eyes, I closed them and did what I always did when I felt like breaking down. I counted to ten. Opening my eyes slowly, I inhaled a deep breath and slowly blew it out.

Me: I feel guilty being away from her.

Less than thirty seconds later, my phone rang.

"Hey," I said weakly.

"Noah, you have got to stop beating yourself up for wanting to have a somewhat normal life. How do you think I feel? I'm moving to Virginia and leaving both you and Mom. But, I have to go where my heart is. Boo Bear, I know you don't like leaving Mom's side, but you need to think of your own life as well."

Smiling, I shook my head. My little sister had been calling me Boo Bear for as long as I could remember. I had a love-hate relationship with that damn name.

"After you leave, Emily, I'm all she'll have and I don't think . . . I'm not sure . . ." My voice cracked as I stopped talking. Reaching into my bag in the back seat, I pulled out my prescription pills and took one for anxiety. The pills calmed me down and took the edge off.

"Noah, listen to me. I know you don't want to hear this, but our mother is dying. The doctors told us she only has a few months, if that, to live. I see how you're slowly falling apart. I also saw how happy you were when you ran into Grace. It was as if a new energy surged through your body. Please, stay there a couple days with Grace. *Please.*"

Nodding my head, I glanced up and saw Grace walking

toward the car with a huge smile on her face. My heart instantly felt light; the pressures of my home life melted away. "All right, Emily. I'll stay a few days, but you have to promise me you'll call if anything happens."

"Of course I will, Noah. I love you."

"I love you too."

Hitting End, I smiled as Grace got closer to the car. This girl shattered me the moment she looked into my eyes the first time I made love to her. The endless phone conversations and text messages furthered my feelings for her. My mother always said love was a powerful thing. She believed in love at first sight. I didn't until Grace's eyes lit up the first time I ever touched her. When she stopped responding to my phone calls and text messages, it felt as if my world had been turned upside down.

Opening the door, Grace slid in. I felt like a kid in high school taking my high school crush out on our first date.

"Hey! I'm so sorry you had to wait. You didn't have to, you know," Grace said as her eyes searched my face. "Noah, what's wrong?"

Giving her a weak a smile, I asked, "Is there somewhere we can talk?"

I could see the fear in her eyes as she blinked rapidly. Taking her hand in mine, I gently kissed her wrist. I could feel her heartbeat and I needed to calm her down. "I need to tell you about my mother and why I had to leave A&M."

Relief washed over Grace's face. "Oh . . . um . . . how about Bee Creek Park? We can walk along the river trail."

Smiling, I nodded my head. "Perfect." As we headed off of campus and to the park, I tried like hell to shake off the nerves building up. Grace sat quietly next me as I stroked my thumb over her soft skin. Taking a quick peek at her, I made a vow to myself that I would never let her walk away from me again.

Grace Hope Johnson was mine.

Forever mine.

Four

GRACE

THE FIRE IGNITING across my skin was almost too much to take. Noah's touch about sent me into a frenzy. It had from the first moment he helped me up after we ran into each other.

Parking, Noah jumped out of the car and ran to my side. *Jesus H. Christ, why is my heart pounding so hard? Calm the hell down, Grace.*

Holding his hand out for me, I gently placed my hand in his as he helped me out of the car. Pulling my hand up to his lips, he smiled as he placed a gentle kiss against my skin. Fire exploded with the touch and I wanted to beg him to kiss my lips. I wanted to feel him against my body. His hands exploring what clearly belonged to him.

Noah guided me to the trail in silence as he held onto my hand tightly. The fear of him walking into my life only to walk out again was an overwhelming feeling I was trying to keep under control.

After a few minutes, Noah started talking. "My mother found out almost two years ago she had cancer. The news devastated our family. My mother is the rock—the center of all of us. She fought like hell and we thought she had won. The cancer came back last year. My father claimed he couldn't take watching his wife slowly die and he took off."

My heart dropped to my stomach, and in that moment I felt Noah's pain. "What?" I whispered in disbelief. "He left her?"

Slowly shaking his head, Noah said, "He left all three of us. My sister had been planning her wedding in the middle of all of this, and I honestly don't know how she did it all. Good ole daddy left both of us what I like to call his going away gifts. A car for me and he paid for Em's honeymoon."

Placing my hand over my mouth, I tried to imagine my father doing that to my mother and I couldn't. "Your poor mother," I said as Noah squeezed my hand.

Stopping, Noah looked out over the river. "When the doctors told us she only had four to six months to live, I lost it."

Placing my hand on his arm, I asked, "What do you mean?"

Swallowing hard, Noah closed his eyes. "I went out and got drunk. For days I drank myself numb and popped anxiety pills. Anything to make me forget. My poor mother and sister had no idea where I was. It was like I was losing everything . . . you . . . my father . . . my mother. My sister was getting married and moving across the country. My world fell apart. Then I realized my sister and mother needed me. I pulled myself out the slump and got my shit together."

Guilt immediately swarmed my body as I let Noah's words sink in. "Noah, I didn't know, and looking back I realize how stupid I acted by pushing you away. I was falling so in love with you and that scared me. I've been hurt before and when I saw you with your sister, I let my imagination get the better of me."

Turning his body to me, Noah smiled. "When I saw you at the hospital, I knew."

Tilting my head and giving him a questioning look, I asked, "You knew what?"

"I knew I couldn't ever let you go, Grace. Seeing what my mother was going through, I needed to tell you I loved you. I want us to be together, Grace. I don't want hookups and text messages. I want to wake up every morning with you wrapped in my arms. I want to see your beautiful smile each night when I lay my head on the pillow. Hear you breathing next to me."

Tears burned my eyes as my head spun. "I want that too." Looking down, I closed my eyes. "But . . . I'm here and you're in Austin, and then when I graduate . . . I . . . well I was . . . um . . ."

Jesus H. Christ, how do I tell him I want him and my dreams?

Placing his hands on my arms, Noah gazed into my eyes with so much love it felt as if my heart was going to combust at any moment. "Grace, I would never ask you to walk away from your dreams. I only ask you let me be a part of them."

"Noah," I whispered as he gently brushed his lips across mine.

Pulling back slightly, Noah's eyes searched my face. "I'm not going to lie to you, Grace. I'm not sure where I am in this world right now."

Smiling, I said, "You're with me."

Closing his eyes, Noah spoke softly as he opened his eyes and looked at me. "Please don't leave me again, Grace. Please." This thing between us was real. I could see it in his eyes, and I knew Noah would never hurt me.

Placing my hand on the side of Noah's face, I made a promise to him that scared the piss out of me. "Never. I'll never leave you again, Noah."

"Do you know what I really want to do right now?" Noah asked.

Giving him a naughty grin, I said, "Have sex in your sports car?"

Laughing, he shook his head. "Eat. I haven't had a real meal in I don't know how long."

"I'm going to take that as a challenge. Come on, let's go back to my place and I'll cook you up something good."

Noah gave me a loving smile and said, "That sounds like a plan."

Giving Noah a wink, I said, "First thing we need to do is go to HEB . . . I need frosted corn flakes."

Noah's face dropped. "Wow, sounds like you're going all out with this dinner, Grace."

Chuckling, I turned and looked over my shoulder. "Oh, I promise you won't be disappointed, Mr. Bennet."

STANDING IN THE kitchen, I watched as Noah flattened the chicken breasts and cut them up for the chicken picatta I was making.

Biting on my lip, I fought the urge to jump on top of him and demand he make love to me that very moment. Turning away from him, I started to heat the oil in the pan.

"Dip the chicken in the milk mixture and then the cornflake mixture, right?" Noah asked.

Feeling the throbbing increase between my legs, I said, "Yep." The sound of his sexy voice was killing me.

Quickly glancing over to the steamer, I smiled as my freshly-picked squash and zucchini steamed to perfection. Alex and I had built a small, raised flowerbed in the backyard and had tons of tomatoes and vegetables growing. I dare say, even Grams would be proud of our makeshift garden.

I added the butter and the garlic as I inhaled deeply through my nose to get the full effect of the smells.

"Are Alex and Will going to be joining us?" Noah asked as he handed me a plate full of coated chicken.

"No, I texted Alex when we were in HEB, and she said tonight was dinner and movie night for them."

Noah walked up next to me and leaned against the counter as I put the chicken into the skillet.

"Damn, that already smells good."

Smiling, I said, "It's the garlic. I love garlic."

Leaning closer to me, Noah whispered, "Will you still kiss me with garlic breath?"

Swallowing hard, I looked into Noah's eyes as my breathing increased tenfold. "Um . . . I sure will."

Oh Jesus. I sure will? What in the hell is wrong with me? I'm like a nervous girl waiting to have sex for the first time. Maybe I just needed Noah to bend me over the counter and fuck me.

Oh hell. I just turned myself on even more. Yes. Right here in the kitchen. A good hard—

"So, Alex is pregnant, huh? That's crazy. I bet Will is beyond happy to be a father."

Mention pregnancy and bam, the bubble I was just floating in instantly popped.

Nodding, I said, "Yes. They're both really happy. Alex is worried about us starting a new business and her having a newborn, but I think we can make it happen."

"I have no doubt you'll make it happen, Grace."

Looking back at the chicken, I moved it around in the pan. "Will you hand me a plate and turn on the oven warming drawer?"

Noah raised his eyebrows and smiled a smile so brilliant, I about dropped to the floor.

"Sure," he said as he pushed off the counter and stood in the middle of the kitchen. "Where are the plates?"

Turning the heat down, I walked over and reached up to open the cabinet door for a plate. Noah came up behind me and pinned me against the counter. My libido kicked into overdrive as I closed my eyes and took in a deep breath.

"Grace . . . I want you more than I want food right now."

Dropping my head back against his chest, Noah's lips moved across my neck.

"Noah," I whispered in a heavy breath.

Taking me by the arms, Noah spun me around and pressed his lips to mine. Wrapping my arms around his neck, he lifted me up and set me on the counter.

His hands moved over my legs as we kissed passionately. "Will it burn?" Noah asked against my lips.

With a breathy voice, I said, "Yes, and you worked so hard flattening the chicken."

Letting out a chuckle, Noah lifted me off the counter and set me on the floor as my knees shook.

"Let me do one thing," I said as I quickly took the cooked chicken out of the pan and placed it on the plate. Opening the warming drawer, I slid the plate in and stood. Turning to Noah, I couldn't help but notice the hungry look in his eyes.

"Grace," he said as he quickly rushed to me and pulled me to him. Our kisses were frantic as our hands explored each other.

"Are you sure Will and Alex won't be home soon?" Noah asked between pants.

"Positive. Noah, I need you to fuck me . . . now."

Turning me, Noah pushed me against the counter as I braced myself with my hands. Slipping my shorts off, Noah pushed my thong out of the way. Glancing over my shoulder I watched him open his jeans and push down to expose his long, hard dick.

Licking my lips, I moaned. My body was shaking with anticipation. I hadn't been with anyone since the last time

I was with Noah. Pushing my legs apart with his foot, I dropped my head and pulled in deep breath after deep breath. When his fingers touched my sensitive clit, I about let out a scream.

Slowly slipping his fingers inside of me, Noah let out what sounded like a growl. "You're so wet, Grace. God I want to make love to you, but I don't have a condom."

Feeling my heart slam in my chest, I looked back at him. "What? How in hell did you not think to bring a condom, Noah! I'm desperate here! Desperate!"

"Um . . . fuck I don't know. What if you didn't want to talk to me or something? I didn't want to get my hopes up."

Looking at his dick in his hand, I closed my eyes. "Have you been with anyone since . . . since our last time?"

Shaking his head, Noah said, "No! Grace, you're the only girl I've been with in almost two years."

My mouth dropped open. "W-what? Why?"

Smiling he said, "I haven't met anyone I wanted to be with."

My heartbeat picked up more and I fell a little bit more in love with Noah. I knew he had only been with one other girl before me, his high school sweetheart who he dated all through high school and his freshman year of college. I'd only been with Noah and Michael.

"I haven't been with anyone either."

"Grace, I've never had sex without a condom, and I won't risk the chance of getting you pregnant."

My body felt as if it was floating on a cloud. How I loved this man.

"I'm on birth control, Noah."

"Grace, the idea of being inside you without a condom makes me want to come now."

Letting out a giggle, I gave him a wink. "Then we better move quickly."

With that, Noah pushed himself into me as we both let

out a moan. My body needed to adjust to him as he stood there buried balls deep inside of me. More than a minute passed by and Noah was still perfectly still inside of me. I could feel his dick twitching and it was driving me insane.

"Noah . . . move! You have to move."

"Can't."

Looking back at him, he had his eyes closed. "What do you meant you can't?"

"I'm going to come the moment I move. It's been so long."

Biting on my lip, I let out a giggle. "Your dinner is going to get cold if you don't start moving."

Shaking his head, Noah said, "Lies! It's in the warming oven."

Dropping my head, I knew I had to take matters into my own hands. Slowly beginning to move so Noah's dick slid in and out of me in a painfully slow manner, I gripped harder onto the counter.

Holy hell. It was not going to take long before I exploded into an orgasm.

Noah grabbed onto my hips. "Too. Slow."

"Then fuck me, Noah! Now!"

Noah pulled out and pushed back into me relentlessly as my orgasm started to build. I could feel my body beginning to quiver as the orgasm rolled through me.

"Oh my God, yes!" I screamed. "Harder, Noah. Harder."

Letting out a groan, Noah moved faster and harder as I saw stars dancing behind my eyes.

"Grace, oh God."

Noah pulled out of me and I instantly felt his warm cum hitting my back. Closing my eyes, I tried to settle my breathing.

When Noah's breathing returned to normal, he softly said, "Hold on, baby, let me clean you up." I closed my eyes and smiled. This is what I had been missing. Not sex with Noah; okay that was a lie, because I missed sex with Noah like hell. What I had missed was just being with him. He made me feel safe. Like nothing in the world could happen to me as long as he was by my side.

Noah gently wiped his cum off my back. "Got it all," he said as he reached for my shorts and pulled them up. Turning around, I leaned against the counter as I fixed my shirt and smiled.

Frowning, Noah said, "That was not how I wanted our first time back with each other to go down."

Placing my hand on his chest, I let out a breath. "I'm certainly not going to complain. But, I'd like to take things a little slower later if you can stay all night."

Something quickly moved across Noah's face, but before I could read it, it was gone. "I'd love to stay with you tonight."

Smiling, I reached up and kissed his lips. "Good. Now let's get you fed.

Five

NOAH

LEANING BACK IN the chair, I let out a breath. "Man oh man was that good, Grace."

Grace sat across the table from me with a huge smile on her face. It was clear she loved being in the kitchen, and she was a wonderful cook. "I'm glad you liked it. I'm a woman of many . . . many talents."

Feeling my dick twitch in my pants, I raised my eyebrows and said, "When do I get to see them all?"

Letting out a laugh, Grace stood up and collected my plate along with hers. "Why, Mr. Bennet, if I showed you all my talents right up front, you'd get bored and move on."

Shaking my head, I said, "Never going to happen."

Watching Grace walk into the kitchen, I was overcome with emotion. This was what I wanted. I wanted to make a life with this woman.

Standing, I followed Grace into the kitchen. "What's for dessert?" I purred into Grace's ear as I wrapped my arms around her. Dropping her head back against my chest, Grace let out a contented sigh.

"Tell me I'm not dreaming. Because if I wake up and this all a dream, I'm going to be one horny, pissed off woman."

Letting out a chuckle, I turned Grace to face me. "I don't want to leave tomorrow."

Grace's eyes turned sad and I knew she was thinking the same thing I was. After tomorrow, I'd be back in Austin and she'd be here in College Station.

Grace opened her mouth to talk when the front door opened.

"Grace!" Alex called out before seeing us in the kitchen. "Oh hey, Noah!"

Smiling, I nodded and said, "Hey, Alex."

Will came walking in, talking on the phone to someone. "If you update the server, we're sure to be able to . . . um . . . we ah . . . hey, Luke, I'm gonna have to call you back."

Will swiped his phone and I knew by the way he was looking at me, he wasn't all that thrilled to see me standing in his kitchen. Alex must have kept it to herself that I was here.

"Will, how are you doing?" I asked.

Will looked at Grace and then back to me. "I'm doing good. What are you doing here, Noah?"

Feeling Grace begin to pull away, I dropped my arms and followed her out of the kitchen.

"Down, cowboy. Stow the daggers you're shooting Noah," Grace said as she made her way over to Alex and Will.

Will relaxed some as he looked at Grace. "Want to explain?"

Grace stopped and Alex whispered, "Oh hell."

Placing her hands on her hips, I fought to keep my smile back. Grace was spit and fire wrapped up in a sweet and beautiful package. I wasn't sure where this was going to lead.

"Do I care to explain what, Will?"

Will swallowed hard, but stood firm as he looked at me. "I thought he was married?"

Clearing my throat, I walked up next to Grace and placed my hands on her shoulders. "Misunderstanding. It was my sister Grace saw me with. The reason I left A&M is my mother is . . . um . . . well she has cancer and I needed to be back home in Austin."

Alex looked into my eyes with sympathy. I had told her about my mother, but asked her not to tell anyone. I wanted to be the one to tell Grace myself. I wasn't surprised to see she had kept that promise, so much so, she didn't even tell her husband.

"Shit, Noah, I'm sorry. I didn't . . . I didn't know," Will said.

Giving him a weak smile, I nodded slightly. "Don't worry about it, Will. I wouldn't have expected you to know. I came as soon as I could to talk to Grace and well . . . she was kind enough to make me a home-cooked meal."

"Uh-huh," Alex and Will said at once as Grace smacked Alex on the arm.

"Why are you both home so soon? I thought it was dinner and a movie?"

Alex chewed on her lip as Will lifted his eyebrows and pushed his hand through his hair. "Yeah, I don't think we're going to be allowed back into Joey's Pizza anytime soon," Will said as Alex glared at him.

"Why?" Grace asked as she leaned her body into me. God, I loved the feeling of being with her. It allowed me to forget everything else going on in my life.

"Do you want to tell them, Will? Or should I?" Alex asked, hands snapping to her hips as she narrowed her eyes at Will.

Will walked to the kitchen as he lifted his hand and

said, "You go right ahead, I'm getting a beer. Noah, want one?"

As much as I wanted one, I had given up drinking after I went on the drunken binge a few months back.

"No thanks, I don't drink anymore."

Grace looked up at me and gave me the sweetest smile.

Alex made her way over to the chair and sat as Grace took my hand in hers and led us to the sofa. Sitting, she motioned for Alex to begin with her story.

Alex cleared her throat and took a quick peek at Will. "Well, I've been having morning sickness, but it seems to come and go. It came tonight at Joey's Pizza. I was feeling nauseous. Will here, he decides it's funny seeing me gag when I see this guy . . . picking his—"

Alex covered her mouth and made a gagging sound as Will attempted to hold in a laugh as he walked up.

Dropping her hand, Alex yelled, "Stop it, Will!"

Holding up his hands, he shook his head. "I'm sorry! I can't help it."

Letting out a frustrated sigh, Alex continued on. "Anyway, Will here kept talking about it, even when I begged him to stop. We were standing in the buffet line and Will told me to look at the guy. I did."

"Oh holy hell," Grace whispered, "you didn't?"

Slowly nodding her head, Alex whispered back, "I did."

"Then Will gagged, because he looked at the guy who was . . . oh God . . . it's hitting me again."

Grace and I both leaned away from Alex.

Alex jumped up and ran into the half bath down the hall as Grace and I watched her and then turned back to Will. He was lifting his beer to his lips as he took a long drink and smiled.

"Long story short, she threw up all over the buffet. Twice."

"Gross," Grace and I said.

Letting out a chuckle, Will said, "That's not the worst

of it."

Shaking her head, Grace asked, "How could it be any worse?"

"Other people throwing up."

Grace quickly jumped up. "Okay well, we've had enough of that story. Noah and I are going for a drive."

"We are?" I asked as Grace turned and glared at me. "Yes, Noah. We are."

Will let out a laugh and shook his head. "No need to leave on our account. I'm going to get my beautiful, sweet pregnant wife to bed so she can rest up."

Reaching my hand out for Will's, I gave it a firm shake. "It's great seeing you again, Will."

Glancing at Grace and then back at me, Will smiled. "You too, Noah. Hope to see you around more often."

I gave Will a quick smile. "That's my goal." Taking a quick peek at Grace, I saw it on her face as well. I'd be spending a lot more time with Grace and her friends. When Grace and I started dating, I knew she was keeping our relationship on the down low with her friends. I didn't mind because I knew she had her reasons at the time. The closer we got, the more I started coming around, until Grace got spooked.

We were finally together again, but we weren't. Pushing it all from my mind, I wanted to enjoy tonight with her. I'd worry about our living arrangements later.

"So, midnight drive, my lady?" I asked as Grace gave me a naughty look.

Giving me a wink, she said, "*That* sounds amazing."

Six

GRACE

AFTER CHANGING INTO a skirt, we walked out to Noah's car. I couldn't shake the ill feeling I had. So far this day had been like a dream come true. A dream I knew wasn't going to last much longer.

Slipping into the front passenger seat, I worried on my lip. I didn't want to think about Noah leaving me and heading back to Austin to help his mother die . . . alone.

Noah backed out of the driveway and began driving. I could tell his mind was weighing heavy also. If I had learned anything this last year at all, it was talking was the number one thing Noah and I had to do.

"Noah, we need to talk about our situation."

Looking over at me quickly, Noah frowned. "What situation?"

"You in Austin. Me here. I only have three months left of school, but I feel like they are going to be the longest three months of my life and I don't know if . . . well . . . if—"

"My mother will pass away before then?"

Turning to look out the front window, I whispered, "Yes." Taking in a deep cleansing breath, I waited to get my emotions in check. The one thing Grams said to us girls that always stuck in my head was her advice on letting your emotions take over.

Take a deep breath. Count to five, then speak from your heart. Your heart never leads you astray.

Slowly blowing out the air, I closed my eyes before opening them and looking at Noah. "I don't want to be away from you. I know that much. After seeing one of my best friends almost die and what Colt went through . . . I know how precious life is. I don't want to waste another minute away from you."

Noah quickly pulled into the parking lot of Target. Putting his car in park, he dropped his head back against the headrest. Shaking his head, he opened the car door and quickly got out.

Following his lead, I walked over to him. "Talk to me, Noah."

Turning to face me, his eyes were filled with tears. "I won't let you give up what you've worked so hard for, Grace. It's only three months, baby. You'll graduate and then we can take it from there. You're not quitting school when you're this close."

Walking into his arms, I felt my tears slowly fall from my eyes. "I'm not quitting school, Noah. But I don't want you to leave, and I know that is so selfish of me."

Holding me close to his body, Noah kissed the top of my head. "Believe me, I don't want to leave, but we will make this work. I promise, baby."

Pulling my head back, I smiled and said, "I'm holding you to that promise."

Noah smiled the sweetest smile as he placed his hand on the side of my face. "I knew the moment you first looked into my eyes, you were it."

Grinning, I raised my eyebrows. "Oh yeah? What about on the beach? I saw you checking out my ass. You sure you weren't all about that booty?"

Laughing, Noah shook his head before his eyes turned serious. Searching my face, Noah's mouth turned up into a slight smile. "I was all about those eyes . . . those lips . . . that smile that makes my knees weak . . . your amazing laugh that rushes through my body and instantly makes me happier. It's even your smart-ass remarks you make when I least expect them. You're it for me, Grace. If I were to ever lose you again, I'd lose all control. I wouldn't be able to live and breathe without you."

Noah pressed his lips to mine as I let myself get lost in our kiss. Pulling back slightly, Noah spoke against my lips. "I love you, Grace Johnson."

Smiling, I replied back. "I love you the most, Noah Bennet."

Kissing me gently, Noah slowly pulled his lips back when we both needed air. "Impossible," he whispered.

NOAH AND I spent the next forty-five minutes sitting on the grass leaning up against a tree in the parking lot of Target, talking about our future. Noah had a degree in business management and I picked his brain about Alex and I opening Wild Flower, our nursery in Mason.

"When do you think y'all will open it?" Noah asked as he ran his fingers lightly across my hand.

"Dunno. Luke and Colt have been doing so much for us. We got a great piece of land that had an old house on it. My father paid next to nothing for it, and with the help of Gunner, Luke, and Colt, they've almost completed remodeling the inside. We have two offices and we're going to convert the third bedroom into a nursery playroom kind of thing. That way Alex can start working as soon as she wants and she can bring the baby. Originally, it was going to be a large storage room."

Noah smiled as he looked at me with pride. "I can't even begin to tell you how amazing I think it is that you know exactly what you want to do."

"You don't?" I asked as I studied his face.

Taking in a deep breath, Noah quickly pushed it out. "I thought I did at one time. I was going to take over my father's business."

"What did he do?"

"Private security. For some pretty big people. Mostly athletes, actors, and singers. He lived here in Austin and had another house right outside LA. That's where he's living now with some actress he's shacking up with."

My heart hurt for Noah. I couldn't believe his father up and left his family like he did. "That had to have been really hard on y'all when he left."

Noah looked away as he slowly nodded his head. "It was for my mother. She thought they were the real deal. Till death do us part and all that shit."

Swallowing hard, I chewed on my lower lip. I could tell Noah was getting lost in his thoughts. Time to take action. Moving, I crawled over and got on his lap as I faced him. Instantly smiling, Noah raised his brows. "So, about that ride, Mr. Bennet."

"Here? In the Target parking lot, Grace?"

Reaching down, I unbuttoned Noah's jeans. "Why not? It's always been one of my favorite stores."

Noah looked around. We were parked at the very back of the parking lot, sitting in a small area of grass that surrounded a few oak trees. "Grace," Noah chuckled. "There're people around."

Wiggling my eyebrows, I smiled, "Kind of makes it a little naughty, right?"

Noah pulled his head back, and giving me a shocked

look, said, "Kind of?"

I began grinding on his hardening dick as I moved my hands up to my breasts.

"Fuck," Noah hissed as he pulled my hips closer to him.

"If you say so," I purred as I unzipped his pants, releasing his hard length. Licking my lips, I pushed my panties out of the way as I lifted up and slowly sank down on Noah as my skirt covered what we were doing. I was silently thanking God I decided to change before we left for our drive. Dropping my head forward, I whispered, "Holy hell, that feels amazing."

"Grace," Noah panted as he quickly looked around. The sun was sinking in the sky and would set in about another hour.

Lifting up some, I slowly sank all the way onto Noah's dick. "I want to ride you so hard."

Noah dropped his head back against the tree. "What in the hell do you do to me, Grace?"

Smiling, I placed my hands on Noah's shoulders and peeked around the tree as I said, "We have a lot of time to make up for."

We were backed up to a heavily wooded area; no one was driving this way, so I went for it. Picking up my pace, I rode Noah hard and fast. The thrill of being out in the open and being with Noah overtook me.

"Noah, I'm going to come," I cried out as he pressed his lips to mine. I could feel myself squeezing his dick.

Noah moaned into my mouth as I moved like a crazed sex fiend. Grabbing onto my hips, Noah began moving. I knew he was close as I felt his dick grow bigger. The way we were moving had another orgasm quickly growing.

"Yes. Noah, I'm going to come again," I whispered against his lips.

Pulling back, Noah looked into my eyes as he spoke my name, "Grace."

Smiling, I pressed my lips to his as we came together.

Nothing else in the world mattered but the fact that Noah and I were one. Completely and utterly one.

We both stopped moving as I felt Noah's dick twitching inside of me as we leaned our foreheads together, searching for air.

"That was amazing," I mumbled with a smile.

"I've never done anything like that before."

"Me either. I'm pretty sure the security guards just got a show."

Laughing, Noah lifted me and his smile instantly faded. "Shit," he whispered as I moved my skirt out of the way and looked down.

Noah's dick was covered in cum. He'd cum inside of me and it was the most amazing moment ever.

Seven

NOAH

WHAT AN IDIOT. I cannot believe I forgot I wasn't wearing a condom. I got so caught up in what Grace and I were feeling, I let my damn guard down. Earlier I had the sense to at least pull out of Grace when I came. Regardless of if she was on birth control or not, I didn't want to risk her future.

Snapping my eyes back to Grace's, I tried to read her reaction. "Grace, I'm so sorry. I got so caught up, I didn't pull out."

Grace's face relaxed. "It's okay, Noah."

Shaking my head, I said, "I know you said you were on birth control, but the last thing I want is a baby."

Grace's face fell. "Right." Standing, Grace quickly got up and headed over to the car and got in.

My heart slammed in my chest and I was confused as hell. *Why is Grace angry with me?*

Making my way over to the car, I got in and started back for her place.

We drove in silence for a few minutes before I couldn't take it any longer. Pulling over to the side of the road, I put the car in park and dropped my head back.

"Grace, you've got to talk to me. I did or said something that pissed you off. I don't want this night to end with you angry with me and me leaving to go back to Austin."

Grace turned and looked at me. I could tell she was fighting hard to control her emotions. Reaching over to her, I placed my hand on the side of her face and gently rubbed my thumb over her beautiful skin. "Talk to me, baby."

"Your reaction," Grace whispered.

Narrowing my eyes, I asked, "My reaction?"

Slowly nodding her head, Grace looked at her hands. "I mean, I don't want a baby right now, but I do . . . I do . . . want one, and if the idea of something like that bothers you I should probably know now."

My eyes dropped to Grace's stomach. I could picture my child growing in her body. Looking back up, I placed my finger on her chin and made her look into my eyes.

"Grace, I'd be honored to be the father of your children. It's just, I've never had sex without a condom before today and it freaked me out. With my mother dying and us being a part, it's not the right timing is all I meant."

Grace's eyes lit up and she slowly smiled. "I feel like one of those overly-emotional women who get upset at the drop of a hat. I swear I'm not like that, and I totally read it all wrong. I'm sorry I got upset. It's just when I'm with you, my emotions are so raw and I'm not used to this."

Letting out a laugh, I tilted my head. "Grace, I love you. I knew the moment you looked into my eyes I was going to make you mine."

Grace's eyes burned with passion. "You sure took the long road in getting there."

Sliding my hand around her neck, I pulled her close to me as I leaned into her. "Yes, we both did. That was me being a stupid guy."

"Kind of like how you were a few minutes ago."

Laughing again, this time harder, I nodded my head. "Yes. I have a feeling I'm probably going to do a lot of stupid things, and I hope and pray we do what we just did, Grace. Talk to each other. Don't ever give up on me. Please."

Grace's smile faded as her eyes searched my face. "I promise I won't. And you don't know my father. He's probably fucked up more times with my mother than I can count on my hands. I had a good role model when it comes to that kind of stuff."

Leaning our foreheads together, I whispered, "Thank God."

"Noah?"

"Yeah, baby?"

Grace pulled her head back and smiled. "I'm sorry I jumped to conclusions and shut you out. I'm so sorry I pushed you away."

"Grace, my sweet, Grace."

Closing her eyes, she whispered, "Take me home. I want to be wrapped up in your arms."

OPENING MY EYES, I saw the daylight pooling in from the side of the blinds. Rolling over, I looked at my sleeping beauty. Her light-brown hair was spread across the pillow as she slept peacefully. Smiling, I lay there and watched her sleep. I didn't want to leave. I hated that I had to and I tried like hell not to be angry, but I was. Last night was the first night I'd slept more than four hours without the help of a pill.

Glancing to Grace's lips, I thought back to last night. Grace had taken me in the shower and worked her magic on my dick. I was almost positive I saw fucking stars when I came. Standing up, Grace had smiled and said something about cucumbers were her new favorite food. I had been too caught up in the moment to even ask where that had come from.

Hearing my phone buzz on the side table, I turned and saw I had two text messages from my sister.

Emily: Mom is doing good. She asked about you and I had to tell her.

Emily: Mom has been in an amazing mood today Noah! I think it's your news! She keeps asking about Grace.

Smiling, I hit reply.

Me: Really? Do you think I should talk to Grace about meeting mom? How would mom feel about that?

It didn't take my sister long to reply back.

Emily: Noah! Mom would LOVE that. She only wants you happy.

Me: Okay, I'll talk to Grace about it. I'll be leaving this afternoon to head back.

Emily: Maybe you should stay another day. Mom is doing fine. I swear.

Glancing back at Grace, I watched her sleep. She mentioned only having two classes then she was done for the week. Maybe we could spend the day together and then she could come back to Austin with me this weekend.

Me: I'll talk to Grace and let you know. Love you, sis.

Emily: Love you too boo bear.

Rolling my eyes at my sister's reference, I set my phone back on the side table. When I turned back over, Grace was smiling at me.

"Who were you texting?" Grace asked.

Leaning over, I kissed her on the nose. "My sister. She broke down and told my mother I was here, with you."

Grace's eyes worried. "Really?"

"Yeah, she said Mom was beyond thrilled and that she was having an amazing day. She's been in the hospital off and on so much the last month. It's nice knowing she is feeling happy about something."

Grace lifted her hand and placed it on the side of my face where I leaned into her touch. "I'm sure she wants to know you're happy, Noah. What mother wouldn't want that?"

Smiling, I nodded. "I know. Hey, I have something to ask you."

Grace rolled on her back and pushed the covers off of her, revealing her beautiful curvy body. My body instantly came to life.

"You never have to ask, Noah. I'm always ready for you."

My head began to spin, and I totally forgot what I was going to say as I climbed on top of her and slowly worked her with my fingers.

"Noah, please, I need to feel you inside of me," Grace begged. And Grace was not the type of girl to beg.

"I want to play, baby."

My lips found her tits as I sucked hard on her nipple, making sure to give her other nipple attention with my fingers. Her body trembled and I knew she was close.

"Noah," she panted between breaths. Moving my lips down, I planted them over her pussy and took what was mine. I sucked and licked Grace to one hell of an orgasm as she grabbed at the sheets and called out my name. I was praying like hell Alex and Will weren't home.

When her body finally stopped trembling, I positioned my dick at her entrance and slowly pushed in as I let out a moan. “You’re so warm.”

Looking into my eyes, Grace smiled. “I love you, Noah.”

Burying myself balls deep inside her, I let her words settle into my heart. “Mine. You’re forever mine,” I said as I pulled out and pushed back into her with force.

Grace’s eyes turned dark as she bit on her lip and said, “Yours. Now fuck me hard, Noah.”

And fuck her hard I did. Grace and I could make beautiful, slow, passionate love, or fuck like it was the last time we’d ever be together. All of it was amazing and felt like the first time.

Grace was my life.

From this day on, I would do whatever I had to do to keep her happy.

Eight

NOAH

THE DAY COULDN'T have been any more perfect. Grace went to her class while I took care of getting lunch ready. I planned on talking to her about coming back to Austin with me this weekend at lunch. I had a feeling she would, but I wasn't sure how she would feel about meeting my mother so soon. Time was of the essence though when it came to my mother.

Pulling up to the flower shop, I jumped out and headed in. The door chimed and a blonde girl came walking out from the back of the store.

"Good morning. How can I help you?"

I looked around the flower shop. "I need flowers."

Letting out a giggle, the clerk said, "Well, you've come to the right place. We sell flowers."

With a quick laugh, I nodded my head. "That you do. I'm setting up a surprise picnic for my girlfriend. I'd like to give her a bouquet of flowers. She is big into flowers and gardening."

"Okay, well do you know what her favorite flower is?" she asked.

Smiling, I said, "Sunflowers I know for sure. Really any flower. She plans on opening up a flower shop-nursery type place in a few months."

"Oh, how exciting! I've had my little shop here for a few years. Can't be depressed when you're surrounded by flowers every day."

Laughing, I said, "I guess not."

She tilted her head and narrowed her eyes. "Okay, well how about if I do a fall color bouquet. I'll pick some vibrant colors and make the bouquet. I'll be sure and put a few sunflowers in there as well."

"That sounds like the perfect plan. Thank you."

The girl nodded her head as she disappeared again.

Ten minutes later, she came walking out with a beautiful bouquet of flowers. It was huge.

"I got a little carried away," she said as she handed them to me.

Looking at the flowers, I said, "I'll say. How much do I owe you?"

Leaning back against the counter, she shook her head. "It's on the house. Once a day, I do a pay it forward for one of our customers. You're today's lucky winner. Just do me one favor?"

I couldn't believe my ears; was this girl for real? This bouquet would have cost me a fortune had I ordered it online. "Yes, of course I will."

"Never lose the chance to see something beautiful each day."

Smiling, I said, "I won't. And thank you very much. I truly appreciate your kindness."

Lifting her hand, she waved goodbye. "Have fun, and I hope she likes the flowers."

PULLING UP TO Grace's place, I jumped out and reached in for the flowers. Walking up the stairs, I went to ring the doorbell when the front door opened and Alex stood there with a stunned look on her face.

"She's on her way."

Staring at Alex like I had no clue what she was talking about, I said, "What? Who?"

Rolling her eyes, Alex grabbed my shirt and pulled me in. "Grace! She texted me to tell me she was going to surprise you and skip her last class. She'll be here any minute. But I have to tell you something else."

That's when it hit me. I wasn't done setting up. "Shit! I still need to finish getting everything ready." Rushing into the house, I made my way to the backyard, where I saw everything had already been set up. Looking to my left, I saw Will with two older guys. One looked familiar.

Very familiar.

Oh shit.

It's Grace's dad.

I'm so fucking dead right now.

The other guy walked up to me and smiled. "Hey, assmole. You want to date my Grace?"

Assmole? *His* Grace?

Looking back at Will, he stood there smiling.

Turning back to the guy standing in front of me, I asked, "Ah . . . I'm sorry. Your Grace?"

Nodding his head, he said again, "That's right, assmole. Grace is my niece. Jeff said you're not allowed to have my Grace."

Turning to Will, I asked in a hushed tone, "Assmole? Did he call me . . . assmole?"

"Daddy? Uncle Matt? What are you doing here?"

Spinning around, I saw Grace standing there with a smile on her face. She glanced to the picnic and then to the flowers in my hand as her face lit up bright, I couldn't help but smile back as she gazed into my eyes and whispered, "Noah, did you do this?"

"I wanted to surprise you."

Grace went to talk when her Uncle Matt tapped me on the shoulder. "You like Grace? You want to kiss Grace?"

Grace giggled and looked at Matt. "Oh, Uncle Matt. I missed you!"

Matt smiled. "Can I hug you, Grace?"

Nodding, Grace held open her arms as Matt quickly walked into them and gave her a hard but fast hug. Turning to me, he asked, "Assmole, can I hug you?"

"Um, sure?" I said as I looked around at everyone staring at me. Grace and Will wore smiles, but Jeff looked at me like he wanted to take my head off.

Matt walked up and hugged the hell out of me. He was fucking strong and I was not expecting him to squeeze me so tight. Stepping back, Matt laughed, then turned to Jeff. "Why do you want to hurt him, Jeff? He's nice."

My head snapped over to look at Jeff as Grace let out a nervous giggle. "Daddy. What are y'all doing here?"

Not taking his eyes off of me, Jeff said, "We decided to come and surprise you and bring you home for the weekend."

Grace's smile faded. Turning to look at me, I swallowed hard. Grace reached for my hand as I scouted the area for places to escape.

"Daddy, you should have called. I'm going to Austin this weekend with Noah. He came today to pick me up."

Oh God. She's lying to her father. He's old fashioned. What would he do if he knew I let his little girl fuck me in the parking lot of Target?

Shit. I'm so dead.

Dead.

I'm pretty sure if I had a head start, I could clear the back fence.

"Is that so? What's in Austin?" Jeff asked as I looked back at him. Clearly he was waiting for my response. Putting on a smile, I dug down deep inside and said a quick prayer.

Taking a few steps forward, I put my hand out and introduced myself. "Mr. Johnson, I'm Noah Bennet, Grace's boy—" My voice stopped.

Grace walked up next to me. "Boyfriend," she finished for me.

Jeff reluctantly took my hand and gave it two quick, but firm handshakes. "Are you unsure of your relationship status with my daughter, son?"

Shaking my head quickly, I said, "No. No, sir."

Lifting his eyebrow, Jeff asked again, "What's in Austin?"

Taking a quick look at Will, he gave me a head nod and winked. "My mother and sister. Um . . . you see, my mother is dying of cancer and we're not sure how much longer she has to live. She would like to meet Grace before . . . before um. Well, before she passes away."

My heart was pounding in my chest and I wasn't sure how Jeff would respond. His face relaxed a bit and he stole a look at Grace before looking back at me.

"I'm so sorry to hear that, Noah. That has to be very hard for your family. Your father especially."

Looking away, I cleared my throat. "My father didn't stick around when the going got tough, sir."

Shaking his head, Jeff gave me a polite sympathetic smile. "I'm sorry to hear that."

Turning to look at Grace, he asked, "Where are you staying Grace Hope?"

Oh hell. He used her middle name.

That can't be good.

Nine

GRACE

JESUS, MARY, AND Joseph. I was ready to kill my father. Why did he use my middle name? I'm twenty-one years old for Christ's sake. I don't have to answer to my father.

"With Noah of course."

Noah took a small step back as I squeezed his hand.

Daddy slowly nodded his head. "Grace, your family wasn't aware of you dating anyone. How long have y'all known each other?"

I already lied to him once when I said Noah came to pick me up today, I wasn't about to continue. "We met my freshman year when Alex and I made a trip to A&M. We've dated off and on since then."

Noah turned to look at me as I kept my eyes steady on my father. Matt was standing next to Daddy and kept repeating, "Oh no. Jeff is mad."

Daddy turned to Matt and in the same sweet and gentle voice he always used with Matt, he said, "Matt, I'm not mad. I'm . . . concerned."

Matt laughed. "You're mad." Pointing to poor Noah, Matt said, "He's mad at Noah. Noah, you're an assmole."

Noah swallowed hard and answered with what sounded more like a question. "Thank you?"

Will busted out laughing. "Noah, that's Matt's way of saying asshole."

Noah squeezed my hand. "Oh," he mumbled as my father fought to hold back a smile.

"Daddy, there is no reason to be concerned. Noah and I love each other and this is a big step for us. I would have rather have brought him home to the ranch to meet everyone, but I guess if he had to meet anyone first it should be you. On a surprise visit. Where you interrupted what clearly was going to be a romantic lunch."

My father balled his fists together as Matt started clapping. "Noah likes Grace and Grace likes Noah!"

"So it seems," my father spoke between gritted teeth, "how romantic."

Tilting my head, I glared at my father as I dropped Noah's hand and placed my hands on my hips.

"Oh shit. This is going to turn out bad . . . for me," Noah said under his breath.

"Oh I don't know, Dad. Maybe Noah might have proposed to me."

My father's jaw dropped open as he and Noah both asked, "What?"

Smiling, I continued. "Or, maybe some foreplay."

Noah reached for my arm and gently tugged on it. "Ah . . . Grace what are you doing?"

My father's face was turning red. "But, if I was *really* lucky, Alex and Will would have left and I would have gotten screw—"

Noah stepped in front of me and held up his hands. "Okay! Well, since the picnic is no longer, I don't think we need to talk about it in front of your dad."

"No. Let's talk about it. I'm curious to see where this would have led," Daddy said as he pushed Noah out of the way and stood in front of me.

Shaking my head, I spun on my heels and stormed into the house. I could feel my father following behind me. "Grace Hope Johnson, don't you walk away from me."

Stopping, I quickly turned around. "Daddy, I'm a grown woman and you can't come into my house and start questioning my life."

My father pulled his head back and laughed. "The hell I can't. I pay for this house. Therefore, I'm pretty damn sure I have a say."

Tears threatened to spill, I was so angry.

"Then I'll leave."

"Grace," Noah said from behind my father. Walking up, Noah stepped in between us. "Mr. Johnson, I won't be the reason for a fight between you and Grace. I love Grace; I'm not going to lie about that. If me being here or Grace coming home with me this weekend makes you uncomfortable, I'll gladly go ahead and take off."

My father looked at Noah and nodded. "Bye," he said as he waved his hand at Noah.

"Dad!" I shouted. "Jesus, Mary, and Joseph. I'm so angry with you right now. I . . . I have to take a time out!"

Spinning around, I ran upstairs to my room and slammed the door. Taking a quick look around, I saw Noah had a few things in my room. I quickly picked them up and threw them into my duffle bag. If I knew my father, he would be up to talk to me in less than five minutes.

Making up my bed, I turned and sat on the edge and waited.

Almost twenty minutes later, I made my way downstairs. I heard laughter coming from the back yard. Opening the back door, I stood there stunned. Everyone was sitting around the table, eating out of the picnic basket, listening to a story Noah was telling. Alex was sitting on Will's lap,

Matt was between my father and Noah, and my father was popping grapes into his mouth, laughing.

Letting the screen door slam, Noah stopped talking and everyone looked at me. Noah jumped up and made his way over to me. Stopping just in front of me, he placed both hands on my face and smiled that brilliant smile of his. Butterflies danced in my stomach and I wanted to throw myself into his arms.

"Are you okay, baby? I would have come upstairs, but I'm pretty sure your dad would have murdered me."

Nodding my head, I looked into his eyes. "Did you drug my father?"

Letting out a chuckle as he dropped his hands, Noah shook his head. "No, but we did have a heart to heart."

My finger came up to my mouth where I began chewing on my nail. Noah pulled it from my mouth. "Was it bad?" I asked.

Giving me another brilliant smile, Noah said, "No. It wasn't bad."

"What were you talking about?"

Noah took my hands in his as my heart rate increased. I'd never felt this way with anyone before but Noah. His touch, his smile . . . everything about him had my body reacting in some form. Even my father's presence hadn't lessened it any.

Letting out a chuckle, Noah answered. "I was telling them about a time I went on a fishing excursion with my father. It's pretty amusing."

My father appeared at Noah's side. "Hey, pumpkin. You feel like talking now?"

The anger came flooding back. "I guess."

My father reached his arm out for me to take it. That meant we were going on a walk alone together.

Slipping my hand through his arm, I felt calmed even though I wanted to be angry.

"Walk with me, Grace."

Nodding my head, I peeked at Noah who gave me a wink.

Daddy and I made our way to the front door. Opening it, I stepped outside and took in a deep breath as I made my way down the stairs. We walked a good block before he finally broke the silence.

"Why didn't you tell your mother and me about this Noah kid?"

I rolled my eyes and let out a frustrated sigh. "He's not a kid."

My father let out a deep laugh. "No, he certainly is not a kid. He's too good looking, and the way he looks at you pisses me off."

With a stunned look on my face, I turned to my father. "He's too good looking? What in the hell does that mean, Dad?"

His shoulders shrugged as he broke our stare and looked behind me. "Guys like that . . . I don't trust them."

I slowly shook my head as I placed my hands on my hips. "Guys like what?"

Piercing my eyes with his, I saw anger building. "I don't want you getting hurt, Grace. Guys like Noah, good looking and a built guy, he's going to have girls throwing themselves at him and well . . . well, he might be tempted by them."

Dropping my hands to my side, I balled them into fists. "Are you for real right now? You're standing here saying that I'm not good enough to keep a guy like Noah?"

My father jerked his head back in surprise. "I didn't say that."

"Yes you did, Dad. You did say that."

"I'm just saying that . . . that . . . oh God, I don't know what I'm saying, Grace. I'm a little out of my element here. You've only ever dated one guy that I've known of and he turned out to be a little prick, and I know there was more to that story that I never got. I show up to surprise you with a trip home and there is some guy setting up a picnic in the backyard and all I can think is—"

My father's voice cracked as he looked away. Placing my hand on his arm, I asked, "All you can think of is what?"

Slowly turning back to look at me, my father had tears building in his eyes. Sucking in a breath, I asked in a low voice, "Daddy, what's wrong?"

Swallowing hard, my father closed his eyes. "All I can think of is he's taking you away from me. The way he looks at you, I see it in his eyes—and yours. He's taking you from me."

Feeling my lower lip start quivering, I bit down on it and attempted to hold in my sob. When I felt like I could speak without crying, I gave him a smile. "Daddy, no one is ever going to take me from you. I haven't mentioned Noah because he and I haven't been dating for the last year. I was stupid and pushed him away when I realized I loved him, but he came for me. He loved me enough not to give up on me. Daddy, Noah makes me feel so happy and when I'm with him, I feel whole."

Closing his eyes, my father slowly nodded his head. "Grace, I don't want you to rush into something. You've got so much going for you."

Giving him a slight push, I said, "I'm not going to ruin my future, Daddy. I promise you."

"What about Wild Flower, your plans with Alex?" he asked as his eyes searched my face.

"That's still my plan. Noah is not going to stand in the way of my future. You have to trust me, Daddy. If anything, Noah will be a big part of my future."

Letting out a deep breath, my father ran his hand through his hair. "I do trust you, Grace. Why don't you come home this weekend, I'm sure Grams would love to see you."

I was standing at a crossroads, and I knew which road I wanted to take. I only hoped my father understood.

"Daddy, I love that you came all the way here to surprise me, but I do have a life and Noah is going to be a part of it. I really want to go to Austin with him this weekend, meet his family. It means a lot to him and I want to be by his side. He's going to lose his mom and I want him to know I'll be there for him."

The muscles in his jaw tightened. "Okay, well I guess this is a lesson for me to always call before I make a road trip."

Giving him a smirk, I nodded my head and said, "Yes. Yes it is."

"Will you be staying with Noah while you're in Austin?"

This was awkward.

"Yes."

Raising his eyebrow, my father asked, "Not in the same room though, right?"

"Daddy," I said as I narrowed my left eye.

"Fine, I won't ask any questions, but I swear to God if he gets you pregnant, I'll kill him with my bare hands. Or if he hurts you in any way."

Giving him a smile and a wink, I said, "Don't worry, Dad. I'm on birth control."

A look of horror moved across my father's face. "Ugh . . . really? Did you have to say that, Grace?"

"You took the conversation there, Dad, I didn't."

Turning, he started back toward the house as I let out a giggle. As we drew closer, I pulled on his arm to stop him. Glancing at me, he asked, "Did you change your mind? You picking your father over that little dickhead?"

Dropping my mouth open, I slapped him on the arm. "Dad! Don't call him that. I love him."

Rolling his eyes, my father looked away.

"So tell me something, Dad. You're very attractive and I've seen pictures of you when you and Mom started dating. Did you whore around on Mom?"

Choking on his own spit, my father asked, "Excuse

me?"

"You know, did women throw themselves at you? Was the temptation too much to handle?"

"Grace Hope Johnson. I would never cheat on your mother. Ever. I've never even looked twice at another woman."

Lifting my brows, I asked, "Never, Dad? Never a sideways glance?"

"No!"

Smiling from ear to ear, I patted his chest. "See! Goes to prove that just because a guy is good looking, it doesn't mean he is going to be a man-whore."

My father looked at me with a confused look as he shook his head. Walking around him, I headed back inside. For some reason, I felt the need to protect Noah. I just didn't know what from.

Ten

NOAH

I STOOD BY Grace and watched her say goodbye to her father and her Uncle Matt. It didn't take me long to figure out why Grace loved Matt so much. He was Grace's mother's brother and he had Fragile X. Grace had mentioned it before, but I had forgotten. I made a mental note to look it up and read about it. Matt was funny as hell, repeated things he probably shouldn't be repeating and was probably the most talented painter I'd ever seen. Grace had showed me some pictures on her phone that she took of Matt's paintings.

Matt walked up to me and smiled. "I like you, Noah. But you are still an assmole. Jeff says so."

Peeking over to Jeff, I saw him look away. Will let out a laugh as Alex said, "Matt! It's not nice to call people assmole."

"Unless they are," Jeff said with a smirk.

Shit. I could see it was going to take a lot to win Grace's

father over. I was willing to do whatever it took, though. It wasn't starting off too well. It was obvious he was pissed Grace wasn't going home this weekend. The fact that Grace told him she was coming back to Austin with me had me wanting to scream from the mountaintops how much I loved her. We'd only been back together for two days, but it felt like we had been together for the last year. We picked up pretty much where we left off, except this time our relationship was coming out to more people in our families.

Matt walked a few steps closer to me. "I'm going to hug you now, Noah."

"O-okay, Matt," I said as I held my arms out and Matt slammed his body into mine, causing me to stumble backward. Jesus, this guy was huge!

After a quick hug, Matt turned and looked at Grace. "Bye, Grace." Turning, he walked over to Jeff's truck and got inside. Grace stood there with her jaw to the ground.

"I didn't get a hug. I've always gotten a hug," Grace said as she turned to me.

"I got one!" Alex said.

"Screw you, Alex," Grace said as she leaned into me while I slipped my arm around her waist.

The moment Jeff turned and looked at me with a look like he was ready to kill me, I pulled my hand back and took a step away from Grace.

Jeff walked up to Grace and took her in his arms as he whispered something into her ear. Grace smiled at her father and gave him a wink.

Jeff took a step back and turned to me as he held out his hand. Reaching my hand out, I said, "It was a pleasure meeting you, Mr. Johnson."

Nodding his head, Jeff said, "Same here, and it's Jeff. Maybe you can come to Mason soon, meet the rest of the family. I'm sure Ari would love to meet the man my daughter says she's in love with."

Holy shit.

I was stunned by Jeff's words and my heart felt like it was about burst from my chest. Knowing Grace told her father she loved me did weird things to my body. Good weird things. I couldn't help but smile at Jeff.

Flashing me a quick smile, it was as if Jeff knew exactly how I was feeling because he had felt it before himself. His smile was gone as quick as it came.

After saying goodbye to Alex and Will, Jeff got in the truck and pulled out of the driveway.

Grace and I stood there and watched them until he turned the corner and was out of sight. I quickly leaned over and placed my hands on my knees and dragged in breath after breath as Will laughed his ass off.

Will walked up to me and gave me a push. "Holy shit! Dude if you could have seen your face the moment you realized it was Grace's dad in the backyard. Priceless!"

Alex walked up and took Will by the arm and pulled him away before I could tackle him to the ground and start beating on him. "Dick," I murmured as Will laughed harder.

Grace ran her hand up and down my back. "It wasn't that bad. I think he likes you."

Turning my head and looking up at Grace, I snarled my lip. "Likes me? He looked like he wanted to kill me every time he looked at me."

Grace giggled and said, "Let me run upstairs and pack a bag for this weekend. I won't be long."

Before Grace headed back into the house, I took her by the arm. "Thank you, Grace. I'm sure you miss your mom and brother. Thank you for coming home with me this weekend."

Grace placed her hands on my chest as she flashed the most breathtaking smile I'd ever seen. "Noah, I just got you back. There is no way in hell I'm going to let you go that easy. The more time I can spend with you, the better. We have a lot of time to make up for."

I laced my fingers through Grace's hair and pulled her lips to mine as I said, "Yes we do."

As Grace pressed her lips to mine, she smiled and I felt a fire quickly race through my veins. I couldn't wait to have Grace in my arms for the next few nights.

GRACE LET OUT a chuckle as I pulled down the street that led to my house. "Are you kidding me? You live on this street?"

I looked at Grace and said, "Yeah. Why?"

"How long have you lived here?"

"We moved to this house when I was four."

Shaking her head, Grace placed her hands over her mouth and started laughing. "What's so funny?" I asked.

Looking over at me, Grace said, "Noah! My grandparents live on this street!"

My stomach dropped at the idea of Grace being so close to me for all those years. "What?"

Putting my signal on, I turned into the driveway that led to the house my mother and father had raised my sister and I in.

"Holy hell. They live one block away, Noah! One. Block."
Putting my car in park, I looked at Grace. "I wonder if we've ever seen each other? Like when we were little."

Just then a memory flooded my mind. "Hey, you didn't happen to be the little girl who pushed me off the swing and I got up and pulled her pigtails, were you?"

Laughing, I shook my head as Grace's smile faded.

"That. Was. You?"

"Huh?" I asked as I saw the pissed off look move across Grace's face. "Wait. Are you serious, Grace? Because I totally had a crush on that little girl." Letting out a chuckle, I kept talking as I thought back. "She used to come to the park with her older brother and grand—"

Pressing her lips together, Grace gave me a look while she slowly tilted her head. "That was me, Noah. That was me! You pulled my pigtails, you asshole. How could you pull my pigtails? I went back to my grandparents' house and cried for hours!"

My heart started feeling funny as I took all this in. I used to go to the park every Saturday and look for the little girl in pigtails. "You cried? You punched the hell out of my chest, Grace. I couldn't breathe right for days!"

Smirking, Grace said, "Good. You deserved it. Why would you pull my pigtails?"

Shaking my head, I quickly looked around, as if I needed someone to save me. "I don't know. That's what little boys do when they like a girl."

"And do they also push you into the sandbox?"

Closing my eyes, I let out a laugh as I took in the memory. "Holy shit . . . I remember that day." Opening my eyes, I couldn't help but start laughing. "I can't believe that was you. I loved you then, Grace."

Grace's face turned from hard to soft. "What?" she whispered.

Reaching over, I placed my hand on the side of Grace's face. "I had the biggest crush on you. I compared every girl in elementary school to you. I'm pretty sure middle school and high school too."

Leaning her head into my hand, Grace licked her lips before talking. "I liked that stupid little boy too. I hated him for pulling my pigtails, but I use to get butterflies in my stomach every single time my grandparents took us to the park. I would pray so hard to see you." Closing her eyes, Grace smiled softly. "I can't believe that was you."

Grace opened her eyes as I leaned over and gently kissed her lips. "Fate, Grace. It was fate that led you to bumping into me again at A&M, and then the coast."

"Fate," Grace whispered as she pressed her lips to

mine.

A loud knock on the window had both of us jumping. Turning, I looked to see my cousin Grayson standing there with a smirk on his face.

"Son-of-a-bitch," I said with a smile. "It's my cousin. He told me he was coming in from Colorado, but I didn't expect him until next week."

Grace smiled as I quickly got out of the car and reached for Grayson's hand. "What the hell, dude! I wasn't expecting you until next week."

Grayson reached for my hand and shook it. He looked great, but then Grayson always looked great. I was sure he had to work out constantly to maintain the shape he was in. Especially since he worked his way through college as a male stripper.

"Holy hell, it's you!" Grace said as she walked up to me.

Grayson turned and looked at Grace and smiled. "Wow, small world."

Looking between Grayson and Grace, I tried to connect how they knew each other.

Grace nodded her head and laughed. "Sure is."

"How did y'all meet?"

"We all went to Durango for a girls' trip last summer. We kind of had a bet going on between us girls and Lauren found herself Grayson here. He did a little show for the bar."

Turning back to Grayson, I raised my eyebrow as I got a sinking feeling in my stomach. If Grace saw my cousin naked, I wasn't sure how I was going to feel. "Not that kind of show, I hope. Not sure I like the idea of the woman I love seeing my cousin's junk."

Grayson threw his head back and laughed. "No, bro. Not that kind of show." Turning to Grace he said, "I'm sorry, I never did get all of the girls' names. I certainly remember you and your red-haired friend. Seems to me y'all were a bit . . . eager to see more."

Laughing, I knew what Grayson was doing. He always did have my back.

"Cool your stripper chaps there ,big boy. I wasn't with Noah then, so I wasn't stepping out on anyone. The name is Grace by the way."

Grayson visibly relaxed. "I like you already, Grace."

Smiling, I pulled Grace next to me. "You staying here?"

Grayson shook his head as he looked between Grace and me. "Nah, I'm staying with a buddy of mine. He flew down here with me this weekend. His parents have a place on Lake Travis."

"Awesome, you haven't been here long have you?" I asked as I reached into the backseat of my car and grabbed Grace's bag and mine.

"No, Emily sent me a text and said you were almost home. I just pulled up," Grayson said as he reached for Grace's bag and threw it over his shoulder. "What would y'all think about hitting dinner before heading up to see Aunt Lisa?"

My heart felt as if someone was squeezing it as soon as Grayson mentioned my mother. Swallowing hard, I nodded my head as I looked at Grace. Giving me a sweet smile, she winked and grabbed my hand as we followed Grayson up to the front door.

"Tell me Flores is still open. I'm dying for some good Mexican food," Grayson said as I unlocked the door and pushed it open. Turning off the alarm, we walked through the giant foyer.

"Jesus, Mary, and Joseph. This house doesn't look this big from the outside," Grace said.

Grayson let out a rumbled laugh as he made his way into the main living room. "That's one thing about Uncle Pete, he loved his money and his precious name."

I nodded in agreement at Grayson's comment. Grayson hated my father, especially since he cut his sister out of his life after she got pregnant with Grayson. My father left his sister to live a life of struggle. She was too proud to take anything from anyone, including my mother who attempted to help her out more than once.

"Uncle Pete?" Grace asked with a confused look on her face.

Letting out a sigh, I said, "My father. I'll tell you about it later."

Concern washed over Grace's face. Kissing her gently on the forehead, I said, "Grayson has issues with my father disowning his mom. It's a long story I'd rather save for later."

Grace nodded her head as she softly spoke. "Okay. Later."

Taking a step away from me, Grace looked around the house, taking everything in. "Wow. This house is amazing. It reminds me of my grandparents' house."

Tossing my bag onto the sofa, I cursed under my breath. Grace turned and looked at me. "What's wrong, Noah?"

Grayson set Grace's bag down and gave me a small punch in the arm. "He's just pissed at his old man, Grace. The dirty bastard is selling the house."

Hearing Grace suck in a breath, I pushed away the idea that bringing her home might have been a bad idea. I didn't want her to find out what a rotten bastard my father really was.

Turning around quickly, I couldn't help but see the look of pity on Grace's face. Clapping my hands, I said, "Let's go eat. I'm starved."

Grayson jumped up and said, "Hell to the yes. Let's go!"

Grace gave me a funny look and I knew she had a million questions.

Questions I wasn't ready to answer yet.

Answering questions meant accepting the truth.

Eleven

GRACE

STILL TRYING TO process the fact that Noah's father was selling their family house while Noah's mother was dying, I attempted to pay attention to the conversation going on around me.

"How long are you staying, Gray?" Noah asked his cousin.

"I have to fly out Monday. I've got a class that afternoon."

Turning to look behind me, I asked Grayson a question. "What's your major?"

"Criminal Justice. I'm actually getting my master's degree this year."

Raising my eyebrows, I looked at Grayson. I knew it was wrong of me to stereotype him. I asked, "Masters in criminal justice, huh? How old are you?"

Laughing as he threw his head back, Grayson said, "Don't look so shocked, Grace. There is more to me than just being a stripper. And I'll be twenty-three in a couple of months."

"He's a Christmas baby," Noah said.

The three of us stepped out of Noah's car and headed toward the restaurant.

Something about Grayson intrigued me. "Seriously though, how is it you're getting a master's degree so quickly?"

Grayson smiled at me as he looked straight ahead. "I took a lot of classes in high school to start toward my degree. Then I applied for an advanced course toward my masters. My grades were there, so I was easily accepted."

Nodding my head, I smiled. "One of my best friends is getting her degree in social work; she's also talking about a master's degree. Up at Baylor."

Grayson turned to me with a surprised look. "Really? That's awesome. Was she with you in Colorado?"

"Yep," I said as I popped my p. "The red head."

Grayson laughed. "Ah yes. If my memory is correct, she was the other one yelling for me to take it off."

Letting out a chuckle, I said, "You are correct."

Noah held the door open for me as Grayson said, "I'll have to meet this friend of yours."

I glanced back over my shoulder and gave Grayson a smile. "Oh, I have no doubt in my mind, Meg would be very eager to meet you, Grayson."

"Gray, call me Gray."

I made a mental note to send Meg a text message about Grayson. Noah leaned in and spoke softly in my ear. "You have a look of pure evil on your face, Grace Johnson. What are you up to?"

Giving Noah a look of innocence, I smiled and said, "I have no idea what you're talking about."

"Uh-huh. Sure you don't," Noah said as he took my hand and led me to a booth.

Grayson and Noah talked about everything from sports, to Grayson's volunteer work at a kick-start program for boys from troubled homes. After a few questions, I quickly found out Grayson grew up very differently from Noah. His mother struggled to make ends meet. In order for Grayson to afford to go to school, he took up working at a strip club. Apparently, stripping paid really well. Really, *really* well.

"Are y'all ready to head up to the hospital and see Aunt Lisa?" Grayson asked.

My heart dropped and I was overcome with anxiety. Peeking over to Noah, he was smiling from ear to ear as he stood. Clearly he was not worried about me meeting his mother, so maybe I shouldn't be either.

Lifting my index finger to my mouth, I chewed on my fingernail as I walked toward the exit. Grayson reached over and pulled it from my mouth. "Breathe in, Grace, breathe out. I promise she is going to love you."

Worrying my bottom lip, I whispered, "How do you know?"

Grayson looked over to Noah and smiled as he shook his head. "One look at him and it's written all over his face."

Glancing over to Noah, he was walking slightly ahead of us while texting someone. Most likely his sister to let her know we were on our way.

"What is?" I asked.

Grayson looked at me and winked. "Noah is clearly in love with you, Grace. I've never seen him so happy."

Feeling my face turn hot, I looked back at Noah as a calmness swept through my body. "The feeling is mutual."

"And Aunt Lisa is going to see it the moment the two of you walk in to the room. Trust me."

I would have been nervous as hell meeting Noah's mother just under normal circumstances. Meeting her knowing she was dying heightened my nerves. Giving Grayson a weak smile, I nodded slightly and said under my breath, "I hope you're right."

NOAH AND I walked hand in hand as we approached his mother's hospital room. My feet felt as if I were walking through thick mud the closer I got. Stopping right before her room, I stood frozen.

What if I she hated me?

Oh God, please don't let her hate me.

Grayson and Noah stopped and looked at me. Grayson hit Noah on the back and said, "I'll go in first and say hi. Y'all take your time."

Noah continued to look at me as he nodded in acknowledgment to his cousin. "Sounds good," he said with a smile. Slowly walking up to me, Noah placed his hands on my arms and gave me the most breathtaking smile. I couldn't help but smile back.

"Talk to me, Grace."

Looking down the hallway, I swallowed hard. "What if I'm not what your mother wants for you?" Looking into Noah's eyes, I waited to see what he said. "What if she doesn't like me, Noah?"

Noah's eyes lit up with something I'd never seen before. I was instantly calmed, and somehow in that moment I knew no matter what, Noah loved me and I loved him. I was a strong person; I knew I would never let my fears push him away again. I was going to fight for our love.

I smiled as I leaned up and kissed him gently on the lips. Pulling slightly back, I spoke against his lips, "I love you, Noah."

"It's you and me, Grace."

Feeling tears threaten, I nodded my head and said, "You and me."

Noah kissed the back of my hand before he slowly pushed the door open. I took in a deep breath as I said a quick prayer.

Stepping into the room, I quickly looked around. Grayson was sitting next to the bed holding Noah's mothers hand as Noah's sister stood behind him leaning against the windowsill. Looking into her eyes, I could see how tired she looked. No, stressed was more like it.

Glancing to Lisa, our eyes met. They were a beautiful green and they were filled with tears.

"Mom, how are you feeling?" Noah asked as he dropped my hand and moved toward his mother. Taking a quick look at Grayson, he winked at me and nodded. Giving him a quick nod, I glanced back over to Emily. She pushed off the windowsill and moved toward me with a huge smile on her face. Pulling me into an embrace, she whispered in my ear, "Thank you so much for coming. You'll never know what this means to my mother and Noah."

Pulling back, I smiled and said, "Of course."

Emily squeezed my hand slightly and stepped out of the way as Noah motioned for me to walk up next to him.

My pulse raced as my heartbeat thrashed in my ears. Stopping next to Noah, I looked at the woman who Noah resembled so much. Her beautiful emerald eyes stood out and I could tell at one point she must have had dark hair like Noah's.

Noah cleared his throat before he spoke. "Mom, this is Grace Johnson. Grace, this is my mother, Lisa Bennet."

Smiling, I dug deep to find my voice. "Hello, Mrs. Bennet. It's such a pleasure meeting you."

And there is where Noah got his amazing smile. From his mother. She smiled so big I couldn't help but smile bigger myself. "Grace, such a beautiful name. What's your middle name, sweetheart?"

Noah ran his thumb quickly over my hand. "Hope. It's Grace Hope. My mother always told me it was by the grace of God that I was born. That I gave my parents hope."

Nodding her head, Lisa smiled. "I prayed my Noah

would find a beautiful, strong, independent woman. It seems God answered my prayers. He gave me hope."

A single tear rolled down my cheek as I quickly wiped it away.

Lisa turned and looked at Noah. "May I have a few minutes alone with Grace?"

Oh shit.

Pressing my lips together, I dug deep and pulled out something my mother used to always tell me.

Your strength lies within you. It's always there, Grace Hope. You just need to use it.

Turning to Noah, I smiled as I gave him a kiss. "You and me." Noah's eyes filled with tears as he nodded. Grayson and Emily walked out of the room as Noah took a few steps backward before turning and walking out the door.

Slowly taking in a deep breath, I walked over to the chair where Grayson had been sitting. Smiling at Lisa, I sat and waited for her to begin talking.

Closing her eyes, she began to talk. "I think I remember the moment I realized my son had fallen in love."

My eyes stayed on her face as I watched her closely and whispered, "When?"

"It was his sophomore year of college. He had come home and told me he had finally felt it."

Leaning closer, I asked, "Felt what?"

Lisa opened her eyes and turned to me. "Love. He had run into a beautiful girl with hazel eyes and light-brown hair. Said he knocked her down while walking out a door. The moment he touched her hand to help her up, he felt it."

My heart slammed against my chest as I listened to Noah's mother talk about the first time I'd ever met Noah.

Smiling, I took myself back to the first time I met Noah. "I felt it too when we touched. I'll never forget the first time I saw his smile or I heard his voice. I never believed in love at first sight until I saw Noah's eyes staring into mine."

A tear rolled down her cheek as her eyes searched my face. "I don't know what happened between you both Grace, but I knew my son was unhappy not only because of me, but because he thought he lost you."

Looking away, I mumbled, "That was my fault. I . . . I let my own fears push him away." Closing my eyes, I turned back to Lisa. "Noah came for me and something inside me has changed. I don't really know how to explain it, but I know it's so very real. There isn't anything I wouldn't do for him."

"Good. Because he's going to need you, Grace. When he found out my cancer was back and his father left, Noah snapped. He turned to alcohol and prescription drugs to numb the pain."

Reaching for Lisa's hand, I held it gently. "Lisa, Noah doesn't drink anymore. You don't have to worry about that."

Closing her eyes, she slowly shook her head. "Grace, some day when you become a mother, you're going to know things. Things you can't really explain. A sixth sense maybe?"

Pulling back, I looked Lisa in the eyes. "Do you think something's wrong?"

Her eyes pierced mine. "Yes. I've seen him take pills. He says they are for his anxiety, and sometimes he takes them to help him sleep."

My mind quickly thought back to the last two days I'd been with Noah. I hadn't seen him take any pills. "I've been with him the last few days, Lisa. I haven't seen him take any pills."

Lisa smiled weakly. "Grace, I know you're meeting me for the first time and the circumstances are not as neither of us would have wanted. I also know I'm asking a lot of you, but I need you to promise me you won't give up on him. No matter how hard it might get. Love isn't always pretty."

A shiver raced through my body as I stared at Lisa. It was almost as if she knew something no one else knew.

Swallowing hard, I whispered, "I promise you, I'll never give up on him." Wiping a tear from my face, I repeated my promise. "I'll never give up on him, or us."

Nodding her head, Lisa turned and stared straight up at the ceiling. "I've laid here countless hours and tried to picture what my children's lives would be like once I've passed away." My heart ached for Lisa as I watched her pained expression while she talked about her children's future.

"Which one of them would have a child first? Would it be a boy or a girl? What will they do for a living? I worry about Noah. He was always a momma's boy. So sensitive to everything." A sob escaped Lisa's lips as she looked away. Reaching my hand out, I gently gave her hand a squeeze.

"I'm so sorry, Grace. Here you are meeting me for the first time and I'm behaving in such a way."

Your strength lies within you. It's always there, Grace Hope. You just need to use it.

"Lisa, I wish like hell we had met under different circumstances. I wish we were all sitting in your beautiful home at your dining room table eating an amazing meal. I'd help you clean up the dishes, and we'd stand in the kitchen and talk about Noah and what he was like as a young boy. Then we'd move to the living room where Emily would pull out old pictures of Noah in middle school. There would be lots of stories being told and Noah would probably get mad at his sister at least two or three times for some silly story she shared."

Lisa let out a soft chuckle. I knew the love I felt for Noah was clear in my words to his mother. I could see it in her eyes she knew how much I loved her son. Noah was our instant tie to each other. The common ground between us. I also knew if Lisa wasn't dying, we would have most likely become very close.

"I love him. I'll love him forever. I promise you."

Nodding her head, Lisa wiped another tear away. "Thank you, Grace. Thank you."

"Thank you for raising such an amazing man."

Lisa's eyes sparkled as she nodded her head in agreement. There was a light knock on the door as I said, "Come in."

Noah and Emily walked in with Grayson following behind them. Noah glanced between his mother and me. I could tell he was nervous, unsure of what was said. "Everything okay in here?"

Letting out a soft laugh, Lisa held her hand out for Noah. "I wanted to get to know Grace a little better, and it's hard with everyone standing around listening to us talk."

Noah's eyes drifted over to me. They were filled with uncertainty as he looked back at his mother and to me again. Smiling, I attempted to seem normal, but my mind was all over the place. *Why did Lisa think Noah was taking pills? Was Noah taking pills? Would he lose it when his mother died? What if I was in College Station and he was here . . . alone?*

Trying to push my fears away, I stood and stepped away from Lisa's bed as she visited with her children and her nephew. Feeling my phone go off in my pocket, I excused myself and headed out to the small waiting room by the elevators.

Closing my eyes, I leaned against the wall as I pulled my phone out and read the text. It was a message from Alex asking how everything was going.

Slipping the phone back into my pocket, I fought to hold my tears back. Just when it felt like I had gotten Noah back, a nagging feeling told me I was going to be in for one hell of a fight to keep him.

Twelve

NOAH

MY EYES NEVER left Grace as she walked out of my mother's room. What had they talked about? Was it good? Surely my mother liked Grace. Emily had told me to settle down as I paced back and forth the entire time Grace was alone with my mother.

Not knowing where Grace had gone off to, I excused myself and went to find her.

Seeing a nurse walking toward me, I smiled as I asked, "Excuse me, ma'am. Have you seen the girl I came in with earlier?"

Giving me a polite smile in return, she nodded and said, "She headed toward the elevators."

Feeling my heart drop, I thanked the nurse and quickly made my way to the elevators.

Shit. What did my mother say that would make Grace leave?

As I rounded the corner, I searched frantically for

Grace. Pushing the button for down, I pulled my phone out and sent Grace a text.

> *Me: Hey. Is everything okay? You disappeared on me.*

Staring at my phone, I jumped when the elevator doors opened and Grace spoke.

"Hey, I'm sorry I disappeared like that."

My eyes met hers as I searched them to see if she was okay. "Grace, whatever my mother said to upset you, I'm so sorry."

Grace pulled her head back in confusion as she narrowed her eyebrows at me. "Your mother didn't say anything to upset me. I got a text from Alex, and I needed some air to think."

"To think?" I asked.

Grace stepped off the elevator as I took a step back. It didn't take long for her to give me that smile that melted my insides. "Yes, to think."

Grace's smile faded as she looked intently in my eyes. "Noah, I'm not really sure how to ask this, but, I have to ask."

Not knowing where Grace was going with this, I swallowed hard and motioned for her to sit in the chair. Grace sat and chewed on her bottom lip.

"Grace, you're kind of freaking me out here. What's going through your head?"

Grace took my hands in hers and kissed the back of each one. "Nothing is wrong, I'm sorry I worried you. It's just, after talking to your mother, I got to thinking. Noah, how long have the doctors given your mother to live?"

Feeling tears threaten to build, I closed my eyes and counted to ten. Opening my eyes, I said, "About a month. Maybe two."

Grace slowly nodded her head. "Why isn't your mom at home?"

Standing quickly, I walked away from Grace. *Did she really honestly think I wanted to see my mother die in a fucking hospital and not in her own home where she wanted to be?* I could feel her following me as I made my way to the elevator and hit the button for down. The doors opened as I stepped in and Grace followed.

Neither one of us said a word as we rode to the first floor. The moment the fresh air hit my face, I sucked in a deep breath.

"Noah, talk to me, please," Grace said as she placed her hand on my arm.

Pushing both hands through my hair, I turned to Grace. "You don't think my sister and I want our mother home? That we'd rather her die with a bit of peace and in her own home instead of in a small room?"

Grace took a step back as she shook her head. "I wasn't trying to . . . I mean . . . I just thought. I didn't mean to upset you."

"Yeah, well you fucking did."

The hurt look on Grace's face pierced my heart like someone driving a knife through it. The moment the words left my mouth, I regretted them. Grace's eyes turned dark as she stared at me. "When you're ready to talk without being an asshole, call me. Until then, I'm going to go check in to a hotel."

Grace pushed past me as all the air left my lungs and I fought to keep standing. "Wait, Grace, please. I didn't mean to say that."

Grace stopped walking and slowly turned around. "Listen, I can't even imagine what you and Emily are going through right now, but that doesn't give you a free pass to walk all over me or talk to me like that. If I overstepped my place, fine, just tell me."

"It's not that, Grace. I'd give anything to have my mother home. We can't though. My father is selling the house. He had my mother sign the house over to him before he left. Told her it was paperwork that needed to be signed, and she had no idea what she was doing. If we brought her home and the house sold, we'd just have to put her in hospice and that would for sure kill her before the cancer did."

Grace placed her hand over her mouth as she stared at me with a stunned expression. "He's selling your childhood home? Why would he do that, Noah? Why wouldn't he at least let your mother . . . let her . . . why wouldn't he—"

"Why wouldn't he let her die there? Because he's an asshole, Grace. He's a selfish son-of-a-bitch who doesn't give a fuck about anyone but himself and the young blonde on his arm."

Grace dropped her hand and was about say something when Grayson came running over to us calling out my name.

"Noah! It's Aunt Lisa, she's having trouble breathing. Come quick."

STARING AT MY mother as she slept, I tried to push all the fear away. I ended up spending the night at the hospital while Emily and Grace headed back to the house. I felt like shit for leaving Grace alone, but I couldn't leave my mother.

Dropping my head, I rested my forehead on the back of my hands as I listened to my mother's breathing. It was shallow, but still strong. She had been having problems breathing and twice her heart had stopped. When the doctor told Emily and I hospice needed to be brought in, I felt like I'd lost a small part of my mother. Emily and I had to decide what to do. Risk bringing her home and having to end up moving her to the Christopher House, or just going straight there. Either option sucked. But it would be worse having her home, only to take her away again.

The door to the room slowly opened as I lifted my head and saw Grace. The energy in the room changed as she gave me a sweet smile. Standing up, I quickly made my way over to her and wrapped her in my arms.

"I'm so sorry, Grace. I'm so sorry I brought you here and then left you all alone last night."

Grace wrapped her arms around me tightly as she spoke softly in my ear. "Noah, please don't apologize. It's really okay. Besides, I have an idea of how you can make it up to me."

I pulled back and looked into her eyes as I smiled. "Really?"

Nodding, she wiggled her eyebrows. I knew Grace was trying her best to keep my mind focused on something other than my mother, and I loved her so much for that. "Yep. And it involves hot fudge."

Smirking, I asked, "Hot fudge?"

Grace let out a soft laugh as she placed her hand on the side of my face. Looking over my shoulder at my mother who was still sleeping, Grace cleared her throat. Pinning her with her eyes, she said, "I need to talk to you, in private."

"Sure," I said as I motioned for Grace to head back out of the room. Grace walked a little ways from my mother's room and before she stopped. Turning to me, she handed me an envelope.

"What is this?"

Grace looked into my eyes and whispered, "It's the deed to your house."

Narrowing my eyes, I looked at the envelope and then back at Grace. "What do you mean, it's the deed to my house?"

Grace stood a bit taller as she cleared her throat. "I talked to my grandfather yesterday afternoon. He put a cash offer on your home that your father couldn't refuse. With my grandfather's connections, he was able to purchase the house and get the deed transferred over to your name and get it all done this morning. The house is yours, Noah."

Feeling my legs give out, I leaned against the wall to hold myself up. A sinking feeling came over me as I thought about what Grace had just done. "Grace . . . I don't have that kind of money. I'd never be able to pay him back and I can't accept this. I won't accept it. Tell your grandfather, while I certainly appreciate the offer, it's too much for me to take."

Grace looked down at the floor as she said, "It's a wedding present."

"What? A wedding present for who?"

Grace's eyes met mine. "Us."

My eyes widened as my stomach clenched. "Us?"

Before I could ask any more questions, Emily came walking up with a huge smile on her face. "Noah! Isn't it amazing? Dad took the house off the market and gave it to you. I can't believe it! When the lawyers delivered the documents this morning, I broke down in tears. I've already started making the plans to have Mom transferred home instead of the Christopher House. She's going to be over the moon to know she'll be home, Noah. She's going to be home!"

Emily threw herself into my arms as she sobbed. "She's going to be able to die at home in her own bed with us surrounding her, Noah. Our prayers were answered."

Closing my eyes, I counted to ten before I opened them and looked directly at Grace. "By the Grace of God, Emily, our prayers were answered."

Grace smiled as tears built up in her eyes. I didn't know when I would get the chance to talk to her about this whole marriage thing. All I knew was she made my dying mother's wishes come true and she managed to make my sister believe my father had a shred of decency.

"I PROMISE, GRACE. I'm doing fine."

Grace had been back in College Station for two weeks. She wasn't able to come to Austin last weekend due to a paper she had to write. The weekend before that, she had a cold and didn't dare come near my mother or me for fear of getting either one of us sick.

"Noah, I can hear it in your voice. You're tired. Have you slept at all?" Grace asked.

Pushing my hand through my hair, I let out a sigh and said, "It's hard to sleep, Grace. I keep checking on her and as soon as I do fall asleep, Emily calls and wakes me up."

"Noah, I'm telling you right now, you need to rest in order to take care of your mother."

Glancing over at the bottle of Ativan, I nodded my head. "I'm going to check on Mom now and then head to bed. The hospice nurse is coming for the night. I think she saw how tired I was and she offered to come back and stay the whole night."

Hearing Grace let out a sigh of relief, I smiled. "Please don't worry about me, baby. I'm fine. You know, Grace, we still need to talk about what you told your grandfather. You know I can't accept that."

A few moments of silence filled the line. "I know. We'll talk when I come this weekend."

Closing my eyes, I let out a breath. "I wish you were here."

Clearing her throat, I knew Grace was attempting to keep herself from crying before she spoke.

"I should be there with you."

Opening my eyes, I cursed to myself. Just when Grace and I were finally back together . . . we were being kept apart by life. "I miss you."

"Noah, I miss you too."

"You and me, together forever."

Grace let a small sob out as she barely said, "Forever."

Feeling like I was about to lose it and beg her to come to me, I took in a deep breath. "I'm going to try and get some sleep. I'll call you tomorrow."

Grace cleared her throat. "Okay. Give Lisa a hug and kiss for me, and tell her I'll see her in a few days."

Closing my eyes, I said, "Will do. Bye, Grace. I love you."

"Bye, Noah. I love you the most."

Smiling, I pulled the phone away and hit End. Dropping my phone onto the chair, I quickly walked over to the bottle of pills and took one. I needed sleep desperately.

Hearing a light knock on the door, I grabbed the pills, opened the side drawer on the side table and tossed them into the drawer.

Turning, I said, "Come on in."

Angela, the young hospice nurse, gave me a polite smile and said, "I gave your mom some pain medicine and I'm pretty sure she is out for the night. I'm going to put a movie on, would you like to join me?"

The way she was looking at me had me giving her an awkward smile. "You know, I'm exhausted. I think I'm going to hop in the shower and get some sleep while mom is sleeping."

Angela smiled bigger and nodded her head. "I'll let you know if anything happens, but I'm confident she'll sleep all night."

Nodding, I said, "Great. Thanks so much. You'll never know how much I appreciate you staying tonight."

Giving me a wink, Angela said, "Oh it's my pleasure. This is what I'm here for, Noah."

The moment the door shut, I let out the breath I had been holding. Waiting a few minutes, I headed downstairs to the kitchen. I could hear the television on in the guest room. Opening the refrigerator, I looked at the beer Grayson had left behind two weeks ago. Reaching out for them, I saw Grace's face flash before my eyes. My hand stopped and I grabbed a bottle of water instead.

By the time I made it back up to my room, I could hardly keep my eyes open. I sat on the bed and fell backward as I closed my eyes.

Slowly I felt relief coming. My mind cleared and I drifted off to sleep.

Thirteen

GRACE

OPENING THE FRONT door, I stepped out and ran right into someone. Looking up, I let out a small squeal as my father looked at me.

“Daddy! Another surprise visit?” I asked as I saw my mother standing slightly behind him.

“Mom!” Moving toward her, she opened her arms and held me tightly. “What have you done, Grace?” she whispered into my ear.

Pulling back, I looked at her cautiously. “What?” I asked as I glanced between the two of them.

“Are you headed to class?” my father asked in a stern voice. I was instantly transported back to the night I got busted for sneaking out of the house and heading to a party Jimmy Clay was throwing before he left for the Army.

“Um . . . I was going to grab lunch.”

Glaring at me, my father stepped forward and opened the door as he said, “Lunch can wait. We need to talk.”

Swallowing hard, I knew what it was about. My grandfather must have told them about Noah's house.

Deciding now was not the time to stand up to my father; I turned and headed back into the house. "Alex and Will are both in class so it's just us," I said as I walked in to the kitchen.

"Something to drink?" I asked as I pulled out a water for myself.

"No thank you," my father said as he sat on the sofa.

Smiling weakly, my mother said, "No, Grace. Why don't you come on in here so we can talk."

Dragging in a deep breath, I walked confidently into the living room. If there was ever a time I listened to Luke's advice, it was when he told me how to act around my parents when we were in trouble. Never show weakness. My father would go in for the attack.

Sitting, I smiled at them both. "So, what's so important that you had to drive all the way here to talk to me in person?"

Knowing the answer, I looked at each of them and gave them a fake-ass smile.

"So, you're getting married?" my father busted out as my smile quickly faded.

Fuck a duck.

I totally forgot I told my grandfather Noah had asked me to marry him.

"Um, well . . . ah . . . um . . . I . . . well Noah and I, we um—"

Shit. I was not expecting this. How stupid of me to have forgotten.

My father cracked his neck and slowly let out a breath. "When were you planning on telling us this new plan, Grace? Does Alex know? Does she know you're walking away from the dream you both shared? Did you even have the decency to tell her?"

Anger quickly raced through my body as my mouth

dropped open.

Looking at my father, my mother shook her head and said, "Jeff, what did I say on the way here?"

Standing, my father pushed his hand through his hair and cursed under his breath.

"Bullshit, Ari. We worked our asses off to put this girl through school. She's less than two months away from having everything, and she's throwing it away for some asshole who we don't even know."

Heat flushed through my entire body as my heart rate increased.

"Jeff!" my mother called out.

"How dare you!" I said as I slowly stood up and balled my fists to the side. "How dare you start throwing out accusations? You know nothing, Dad. Nothing at all of what my plans are."

Turning to face me, he pointed at me as he spoke. "You went to your grandfather and asked him to buy a house, Grace! A fucking house that belongs to this boyfriend of yours that no one even knew about."

I tried to calm myself before I spoke. "I was desperate and I knew I couldn't ask you."

Jerking his head back, my father's eyes grew bigger. "Holy shit. You're pregnant, aren't you? That's why you couldn't come to us."

My mother quickly stood up as I laughed. "Really, Dad? The first thing that comes to your mind when I say I couldn't come to you is that I'm pregnant. Well, I'm sorry to disappoint you, but no, I'm not pregnant. I'm a little bit more responsible than that. But hey, thanks for the vote of confidence there, Dad."

"Grace Hope, don't use that tone with your father. We have every right to question you after my father just put down over four hundred thousand dollars on a house that belonged to Noah's parents. Then we find out you're getting married. What else do you think we're going to deduce out of that?"

Chewing on my lower lip, I knew my mother was right. "I certainly didn't think y'all would drive all the way here and treat me like a child," I said as I glared back over to my father.

Throwing his head back, he laughed before looking back at me. "If you don't want to be treated like a child, don't act like one, Grace."

My heart felt as if someone had stabbed a knife through it. Feeling tears slowly build up, I turned away from my father.

"Noah's mother is dying of cancer. Her husband walked out on her when she found out the cancer was back. He also decided to sell the house that Noah and his sister, Emily, grew up in. Their mother wanted nothing more than to be in her own home as she . . . as she . . . as she died. I didn't know any other way. They were getting ready to put her in a hospice facility. I did what I thought was the right thing to do at the time."

Slowly turning around, I looked at my mother, who quickly wiped a tear away. Looking at the ground I said, "I know you don't want to hear this, Daddy, but I love Noah and I'll do whatever I can for him and his mother." I caught my father's stare as I glanced up. "I knew you didn't like him. I also knew if I came to you and asked you for the money, you would tell me it wasn't my concern. Granddad was my only hope. I told him everything, and I also told him Noah had asked me to marry him." Shaking my head, I wiped a tear away.

I shrugged my shoulders as I looked away. "I guess I thought if Granddad thought I was marrying Noah, he might be more willing to help. He told me once that he and Gram had set money aside for both Luke and I. When I presented him with the offer, I asked if they would change things up and just use the money they set aside for me to buy the house. They could consider it a wedding gift.

Noah hasn't asked me to marry him, and I keep putting off talking to him about this. He was upset I had asked Granddad, and at first he said he wouldn't take it. Then his sister came to him crying because their mother was going to get to go home. Noah didn't have the heart to tell her the truth. He's already begun selling off some things, like jewelry, that has been in their family for some time. His mother had stocks that he has also begun selling off. He plans on paying Granddad back every penny."

My mother put her hand over her mouth as she slowly sat. My father looked over at her and then turned away from both of us.

Dropping her hands to her lap, my mother asked, "Noah's father was selling the house out from under his family? Why couldn't he let his wife have her dying wish?"

Pressing my lips together, I said, "No one knows. Noah said his dad is a selfish son-of-a-bitch who only cares about himself."

"Are Noah and his sister both living in the house right now?" my mother asked.

Clearing my throat, I sat across from my mother. "No. Emily recently got married and her husband took a job in Virginia. She moved a few weeks ago and it about killed her. She's trying to come back down, but they aren't sure how long their mother will . . . um . . . well they don't know when it will happen. It could be tomorrow, or in two months."

Turning back to us, my father finally spoke. "Who is taking care of their mother?"

Not bothering to look at him, I said, "Noah. Hospice comes in once a day. One of the hospice nurses has stayed a few nights so Noah can get a good night's sleep. It's hard for him, though. He hasn't been sleeping well and he's all alone and—"

Looking away, I choked back my tears.

Shaking her head, my mother gasped. "That poor

family."

Sitting next to my mother, my father took in a deep breath and slowly blew it out. "You still shouldn't have gone to your grandfather, Grace. I don't want to see you getting lost in this Noah guy. Focus on finishing up your degree, moving back to Mason and getting your business started with Alex."

I couldn't believe my ears. Who was this man sitting in front of me?

"Do you really think so little of me, Dad?"

Snapping his eyes over to me, my father narrowed an eye and asked, "Excuse me?"

"You really think I'm going to give up everything, walk away from it all, because I'm in love with one of the most amazing men I've ever known." Holding up my finger, I tilted my head and said, "Oh wait. You wouldn't know what an amazing person he is because you're too busy judging him."

My father's eyes grew dark. "My job as your father is to protect you."

"From what? Please, Dad, tell me from what?"

Standing, he pointed at me as he raised his voice. "From borrowing money from your grandfather, quitting school, running off with someone we know nothing about. From ruining your life, Grace."

Standing, my mother put her hand on my father's arm and pulled him back some. "Jeff, I think you need to step outside and get some fresh air."

Standing up, I felt my whole body shaking. "Ruining my life? How in the hell am I ruining my life? By being in love? You raised me, Dad, to always try and help those you love. Well I did. I did what I thought was the right thing to do at the time. Noah is paying Granddad back. I'm guessing you chose not to hear that part. He is selling off *everything* he can. He will not take the money as a handout, because that is the type of man he is."

My father stood there staring at me. His body tense, his chest heaved as I spoke.

"As far as me quitting school, I don't even know how to respond to that. I've given you no indication I'm quitting school. I'm not stupid, Dad. As much as I want to be with Noah, I'm here." Pointing down, I repeated myself. "Here, Dad. Not where I really want to be."

"What about after school, Grace, when you are supposed to be starting up your career? Will you be there for Alex or for Noah?"

My mother sucked in a breath as she stood in front of my father. "Stop. You're angry and you need to stop before you say something you'll regret."

Feeling the tears roll down my face, I looked away. Seeing my purse, I knew exactly what I needed to do. Everything in that moment became clear to me. Walking over to it, I picked it up and headed for the front door.

"Grace? Sweetheart, where are you going?" my mother asked as I reached for the door and opened it.

Looking back over my shoulder, I caught my father's eyes. "If you ever ask me to choose between Noah and my family, I'm going to pick Noah."

Opening the door, I walked through and shut it as I heard my father call out for me. The moment I hit the bottom stair, I took off running. The further away I got, the better.

Fourteen

GRACE

STANDING ON THE front porch, I sucked in a deep breath and held it for a few seconds before blowing it out. Knocking lightly, I stepped back and waited.

Noah opened the door and stared at me as if he was dreaming.

"Please tell me you're standing on my porch and I'm not dreaming."

Letting out a chuckle, I set my duffle bag down and nodded my head. "I'm standing on your porch, and you are certainly not dreaming."

Noah smiled and I slammed my body into his as he held me. Somehow I managed to keep my tears at bay. I swore to myself I wasn't going to be weak any longer. I needed to be strong for Noah. For us.

Pulling back, Noah looked into my eyes as he searched for answers.

"It's only an hour and a half drive. I'm going to commute

for the rest of the year. Besides, Alex is so damn horny all the time, I can't stomach to see her and Will all over each other. It's enough to make me want to rip my eyes out."

Noah smiled a brilliant smile as he shook his head. "Grace, that's a lot of driving."

Placing my hand on the side of his face, I gave him a gentle smile. "You're worth it. We've been apart for far too long. I want to be here for you as much as I can. Besides, school is almost over."

Taking me into his arms again, Noah held me close to him as he spoke softly. "I love you so much. Somehow you show up when I need you the most."

Dropping his embrace, I grinned and gave him a wink. "I could say the same thing about you."

Noah gave me a quick kiss on the lips and then grabbed my bag. "Mom will be so happy to see you."

My stomach dropped slightly and I wasn't really sure why. Nerves maybe? Seeing his mother again and fearing she'd gotten worse? I wasn't sure. All I was really sure of was that I was where I needed to be.

After my mother and father had left College Station and headed back to Mason, I packed a small bag and headed for Austin. My heart was telling me where I needed to be. For once in my life, I was listening to it loud and clear.

"Do your parents know you're staying here?" Noah asked.

Glancing over to him, I wanted to ask if my parents had stopped by here. I wouldn't have put it past my father at this point to check up on my story.

Giving Noah a nod, I said, "Yes. I sent my mother a text to let her know."

Noah raised an eyebrow and said, "A text? Really?"

"Yep," I said as I let out a quick breath. "Is Lisa sleeping?"

Noah stared at me for a few moments before snapping out of it and shaking his head. "No, I was just reading to her."

My heart melted. The love Noah had for his mother was amazing. The way he had given everything up to care for her had me wanting to throw myself at him again and beg him to make love to me.

"What were you reading?" I asked as I followed Noah upstairs to his room.

"Emma," Noah said barely above a whisper.

Grinning like a fool, I said, "Ah, Jane Austen. A true classic."

Noah let out a chuckle. "Jane Austen is one of my mother's favorite authors."

"Mine too," I said as I made my way into Noah's room. Taking in a deep breath, I let the smell of the man I love invade my senses. My body quickly came to life as I took everything in. It wasn't the first time I'd been in this room. I'd stayed in here one night alone, two nights with Noah. Two glorious romantic nights.

"I'm sure she'd love to have you read it to her. I'm afraid I don't put much emotion into it. Or at least that's what she told me earlier."

Setting my purse on the bed, my eyes moved to the side table. Three bottles of pills where sitting there. Noah had walked into the bathroom that was attached to his room. Looking over my shoulder back at him, I walked toward the side table as I said, "I'd love to read to her."

Picking up the first bottle, I read the name of the prescription. Ativan. Noah started to tell me how Emily thought she'd be back down for Thanksgiving, but her new job wasn't going to let her off.

Setting the sleeping pills down, I picked up the next bottle. Valium. My heart began beating slightly faster. The third bottle was Klonopin. Setting the two other bottles down, I quickly walked away and headed toward the bathroom as I attempted not to over react. Noah had every reason to have each of those. I knew Ativan was a sleeping pill and the Klonopin was for panic attacks. The Valium must have also been for anxiety. *Was he taking all three of them? How often did he take them?*

Noah had started a bath and was filling it up with lavender. "You looked like you needed to relax."

My stomach fluttered. This man was incredible. Here had been attending his mother non-stop and yet he was drawing me a bath. Smiling, I wrapped my arms around him and looked into his eyes. "Why don't you soak in the tub and I'll go say hi to your mom. Maybe even read a few chapters of *Emma.*"

Noah pinched his eyebrows and went to protest. Lifting my finger, I placed it on his lips. "Nope, no arguing. You soak; I'll go let your mother know I'm here."

Noah closed his eyes. It looked like he was attempting to control his emotions. He did it often and I was pretty sure he counted to ten or something. Opening his eyes, he gave me a sexy grin. "A hot bath does sound pretty relaxing."

"Then strip yourself out of those clothes and climb your sexy ass into the bathtub. I'll be back in a little bit and we will have a small reunion celebration."

Wiggling my eyebrows, Noah laughed and quickly undressed. Watching him strip out of his clothes had my lower stomach tugging. Deciding I needed to leave before I changed my mind, I spun on my heels and called over my shoulder, "See you in a few."

As I made my way down the stairs, I pulled out my phone and texted Meagan. I wasn't going to be able to put the thoughts to rest until I talked to someone.

Me: Hey, I have a question.

It didn't take Meagan long before she texted back.

Meg: Shoot!

Stopping outside the master bedroom, I asked the one question I was scared to death to know the answer to.

Me: Is it safe to take Ativan, Klonopin and Valium all together?

Meg: I think if you're following your doctor's advice. Valium though can become additive. Same with the Ativan and shouldn't be taken for long periods of time. It is highly addictive.

Dropping my head back against the wall, I said a quick prayer Noah wasn't taking either of them on a daily basis.

Me: Thanks, Meg. Are you still coming home for Thanksgiving?

Meg: Considering my father lectured the hell out of me the last time I was home. No.

My heart broke for Meagan. Her father was so tough on her and we had begged her to talk to her parents about the stress she had been facing. Not only with the high expectations from her dad, Brad, but also with the bullying she'd faced at Baylor. I admired Meagan. She pushed through and didn't let it defeat her. It inspired her to pursue a career in helping people.

Me: Well I just moved in with Noah. In Austin. My father is going to blow a gasket. You could always come here and stay with us. There is plenty of room and I'm sure Noah won't mind.

Meg: That might actually be a great idea. Talk to Noah and let me know. Got to run. Late for a study group! Just a few more weeks and this shit will be over!

Letting out a soft giggle, I smiled as I typed my response back.

Me: Hell yes! Then we are getting trashed!

Meg: And I'm having hot sex with a guy I don't know!

Laughing, I shook my head. Lisa coughed and called out for Noah. Quickly pushing the phone into my back pocket, I made my way into her room. Glancing up, Lisa's smile spread across her face as she covered her mouth and coughed again.

"Grace, what a wonderful surprise. Are you here visiting?"

Pushing a loose curl behind my ear, I walked over to Lisa. Sitting on the chair next to the bed, I saw the book Noah had been reading. "Actually, with just a few weeks of school left, I decided to come and stay with you and Noah."

Relief washed over Lisa's face as she closed her eyes and whispered something.

"What was that? I didn't hear you, Lisa?" I said as I leaned in closer.

Shaking her head slowly, she said, "Nothing. I'm just very happy to know you'll be here."

Reaching her hand out for mine, I took it. She'd lost so much weight since the last time I'd seen her. She was much weaker. It was as if it took all her might to hold her hand out for me.

Sitting, I smiled sweetly. "I have a few more weeks of school before I graduate, but I'm not that far from College Station."

Lisa's smile vanished. "You're driving back and forth?"

Giving her a look of reassurance, I said, "I've only got a few classes and I don't have to drive back and forth each day. Just a few. Besides, Thanksgiving will be coming up in a few weeks. I plan on whipping up a huge meal for us. You'll have to be sure to tell me what some of your favorites are as well as Noah's."

Lisa let out a soft chuckle before her smile faded and

sadness filled her eyes. "Noah told me Em can't make it for Thanksgiving. I'm trying not to let him know how sad that makes me feel. I can only imagine how it's tearing Em up inside."

Taking my other hand and softly placing it over Lisa's hand, I nodded in agreement. "I'm sure it is, but Noah did mention Christmas."

A spark came back to Lisa's eyes as she nodded her head. "Yes. Em would never miss Christmas."

Pulling her eyes from me, Lisa stared up at the ceiling. Not really knowing what to do, I peeked over at the book. "Would you like me to read to you, Lisa?"

Turning to look at me, Lisa grinned and said, "Oh yes, please. Noah tries, but that boy puts zero emotion into reading."

Laughing, I let go of Lisa's hand, picked up the book, and settled into the chair as I opened it to the last page that Noah was reading from.

Before I knew it, Lisa had fallen asleep and there was a light tap on the door. Looking up, I saw a woman standing in the doorway.

Smiling, I placed the bookmark in the book and stood up as she walked in. Glancing at Lisa, she nodded and then turned back to me. "She looks comfortable." Picking up a chart, she glanced over it. "Noah gave her some pain med's about an hour ago. Good." Her eyes looked up and met mine. "The idea is to keep her comfortable. If she requests more, give it to her."

Swallowing hard, I nodded my head. "Of course." Glancing at her name tag, it read Angela and her scrubs said hospice.

It was then I wondered how the nurse got in. "Um, do you mind if I ask how you got in?"

She went about her business and didn't answer me. I studied her as she moved about the room, never taking my eyes off of her.

After checking on a few things, Angela motioned for me to leave the room with her. Following her, I peeked back at Lisa. She looked peaceful. If I hadn't known any better, I'd have thought she was simply taking a nap.

Angela made her way into the kitchen and turned back to face me. Coming to a stop, I smiled and looked around awkwardly. I wasn't sure why this woman made me feel so nervous. All I knew was is I didn't like the way she made me feel and I took note of it.

"I'm the hospice nurse assigned to Mrs. Bennet. I have a house key that Noah had made for me. Sometimes Noah is sleeping and doesn't hear the doorbell."

Narrowing my eye, I tilted my head and said, "If he can't hear the doorbell, how does he hear his mother?"

She gave me a displeased look. "He's usually in the master bedroom, sleeping on the sofa."

Giving her a slight nod, I asked, "Do you stop by every day?"

Turning away from me, Angela grabbed the coffee pot and filled it up with water. "Now I do. Mrs. Bennet's condition is starting to worsen. She has requested no life-saving intervention. So, now all we do is keep her heavily medicated to ease the pain."

Placing my hand on my stomach, I fought to hold the bile down.

"I see," I softly said as I sat.

Leaning against the counter, Angela narrowed her eye at me. "May I ask who you are?"

Sucking in a deep breath, I let it out as I gave her a weak smile. "I'm so sorry. Grace Johnson. I'm Noah's girlfriend."

Lifting her eyebrows ever so slightly, she said, "Noah never mentioned you."

The feeling of someone slapping me across the face caused me to sit up a bit straighter. My eyes moved across Angela's body, and for the first time since she walked into this house, I noticed how beautiful she was. "Why would he?"

Angela gave me a smirk and shrugged her shoulders before turning and reaching into the cabinet for a coffee mug. She sure as shit has made herself at home here. "Want a cup?" she asked.

I watched as she moved about the kitchen, almost as if she had been coming here for years and was a part of the family. Jealousy raced through my veins and I tried to like hell to push it away.

For Christ's sakes Grace. It's the hospice nurse. Calm your ass down.

I wasn't sure what came over me, but I quickly stood up and gave Angela a smile. "Well, I've moved in and will be staying here. Considering how the situation has changed, I think it would be awkward with you having a key to the house."

Taking a sip of her coffee, Angela asked, "How so?"

My eyes widened as I let out a chuckle. Okay sister. You want to play, let's play.

Tilting my head, I gave her a warning look before I continued to speak. "Well imagine if you had a key and walked in here to the kitchen and Noah was fucking me from behind. I'm thinking that would be pretty awkward."

Angela's mouth dropped open as she stood there stunned.

Going to say something again, I thought about Noah.

Shit! Noah was in the bathtub. Turning, I quickly ran into the living room and up the stairs.

Oh my God. What if he took a sleeping pill and fell asleep in the tub. Rushing into the master bedroom, I stopped dead in my tracks.

Letting out a sigh of relief, I dropped my head and took in a few deep breaths as Noah lay across his bed in nothing but a towel wrapped around his waist. Lifting my head, I glanced over to the side table. I couldn't help but wonder if he took anything.

Pushing my fears away, I walked over to Noah. Smiling, I reached down and kissed him gently on the lips. Moaning out my name, I felt my heart squeeze in my chest.

Reaching for the blanket that was on the chair in the corner, I covered Noah up and kissed him again, as I brushed my lips gently over his, "I love you."

Taking a step back, I turned and let out a gasp. Angela was standing in the doorway. "Did he take an Ativan?"

Not really sure what to say or do, I stood there. What in the hell was she doing up in his room, and more importantly, how does she know about his prescription pills?

"I-I don't know. He took a hot bath, so I'm hoping that relaxed him."

Angela quickly glanced at Noah and then back to me. Pressing her lips together, she shook her head. "I doubt it."

Turning, she quickly headed back downstairs, leaving me standing in the middle of Noah's room a confused mess.

Fifteen

NOAH

STRETCHING MY ARMS over my head, I let out a soft moan. My eyes sprung open and I quickly looked around. I was in my bedroom. In my bed. And I felt like I'd slept for a week. Sitting up, I looked around before a moment of panic set in.

My mother. Fuck!

Jumping up, I looked down to see I had no clothes on. I raced over to my dresser as I felt my heart pounding practically out of my chest. I opened a drawer and pulled on a pair of sweats and an old T-shirt.

Son-of-a-bitch I can't believe I left her alone. Quickly making my way downstairs, I headed to my mother's room. The closer I got, I heard her voice.

Grace.

Everything came flooding back. Grace was here. My heart felt light as a feeling of happiness swept over my body.

Grace was here.

Stopping right outside the door, I heard Grace talking. It sounded as if she was reading something. I knew for a fact it wasn't the book I had been reading.

Pushing the door open, I peeked in. Grace's back was faced toward the door. My mother was looking out the window as Grace read.

"To be sure you have a successful winter garden, you need to prepare it ahead of time. This means work."

Smiling, I shook my head. Grace was reading something to my mother about gardening.

Clearing my voice, the two loves of my life both turned and looked at me. My mother gave me a huge smile, as Grace jumped up and headed over to me. "Hey, sleepyhead. You must have needed the sleep."

My smile faded some. "How long was I sleeping for?"

Grace looked back over her shoulder and then back to me. Glancing down to her ever-present watch on her wrist, she said, "Two days."

Taking a step back, I said, "Impossible."

Giving me a slight grin, Grace said, "Like I said, you must have needed the rest."

Narrowing my eyes at her, I asked, "What day is it?"

Grace's smile faded some as the look in her eyes changed. "It's Sunday."

Pushing my hands through my hair, I walked past Grace and up to my mother. "Mom, I'm so sorry. I had no idea I'd sleep like that."

My mother's face constricted as she looked at me. "Noah, sweetheart, you needed the sleep. I'm glad you got it. Everything was fine. Grace was here for me if I needed anything."

"I'm supposed to be here for you, Mom. Not Grace."

Hearing Grace's intake of air caused a pain in my chest.

"Excuse me," Grace whispered as she quickly left the room.

Closing my eyes, I shook the guilt away and looked back at my mother. "I'm sorry, Mom. I swear to you I won't leave you alone like that again."

Hurt washed over my mother's face. "Noah Pete Bennet. I wasn't alone. Grace was here and I might add, she was a breath of fresh air. Besides, Angela was here as well."

"What if . . . what if something had happened to you and I was passed out upstairs?"

"You were sleeping, Noah. If anything had happened, Grace would have woken you up."

Knowing I had taken the Ativan and the Valium, guilt washed over my body. I was desperate for sleep and the hot bath had only relaxed me some. I'd never taken both before but the feeling of almost instant relaxation was too good to pass up.

Looking away from my mother, I pressed my lips together. "I know. I'm sorry."

Taking my hand, my mother attempted to squeeze it. She was growing weaker by the day. "You go say you're sorry to Grace."

Capturing her eyes with mine, I smiled as I nodded my head. "Yes ma'am."

Leaning over, I kissed her gently on the cheek before making my way through the house to find Grace.

Hearing her in the kitchen, I made my way there. Instantly, I could tell she was distant.

"Hey," I whispered. Grace had been whipping eggs together in a bowl when I walked into the kitchen. Stopping, she turned and looked at me.

"There is one thing you better learn about me now, Noah. I will not be treated like a doormat."

"I didn't mean to treat you that way. I'm sorry if I made you feel like that, Grace."

Worrying her bottom lip, Grace glanced down. "How many pills did you take?"

"What?" I asked, even though I heard her question.

Grace looked at me as we stared into each other's eyes. "Pills, Noah. How many of them did you take? You were knocked out for two days."

"I'm not a child, Grace, and I don't need looking after. I know how many prescription pills to take."

Walking by her, I reached for the coffee pot, only to have Grace grab my arm. Narrowing her eyes, Grace stared at me. "I will not stand by and watch you become dependent on those pills."

Letting out a nervous chuckle, I said, "I'm not dependent on them, Grace."

"Then tell me how many you took, Noah," Grace said as her eyes turned glassy.

"I took one Ativan. I hadn't been sleeping but a few hours a night. It must have all caught up to me. I guess knowing you were here, I felt relaxed knowing my mother was okay."

Grace continued to stare at me and I knew I wouldn't be able to hold back the truth from her. "And one Valium. I also took a Valium."

Closing her eyes, Grace slowly shook her head. "Noah, you can't do that ever again. Promise me you won't do that again."

Seeing the love in her eyes, and hearing the concern in her voice, I did just what she asked. "I promise, Grace. I won't ever take them both together again."

Grace smiled as she reached up and kissed me. "We're going to do this together. You and me. You're not alone. You don't need the pills."

Placing my hand behind her neck, I pulled her lips to mine as I kissed her. Grace's kisses were always my weakness. She tasted of pure honey. It wasn't long before Grace was turning off the stove and I was picking her up to carry her upstairs.

"Make love to me, Noah," Grace spoke against my lips.

Before we made it to the stairs, the front door opened

and Angela walked in. Stopping in my tracks, I quickly set Grace down. Angela's face turned red as she nodded at us and quickly walked by. "I'll just be heading on back to check on, Mrs. Bennet."

Peeking over to Grace, I watched as she shot daggers at Angela the entire time she walked through the house. Turning back to me, her hands went to her hips and she let out a huff. "I told her to give me her key, but she wouldn't. She said you told her you needed her to have it in case you didn't hear her at the door."

"It's hard, Grace. When I do finally fall asleep, I'm out and I'm only tuned in to my mother's voice. There have been plenty of times Angela has had to bang on the door and call the house for me to let her in."

Something moved across Grace's face and I wasn't able to read it. Before I was able to say anything to her, she walked by me and back into the kitchen. Frowning, I turned and followed her. "Are you mad?" I asked as she turned the stove back on.

Without looking at me, Grace shook her head. "This is your house, Noah. You need to do what you feel is right and safe for your mother. I'm not mad; I'm upset that we were interrupted. I was looking forward to being with you."

Smiling, I walked up behind Grace and pulled her against my body. She needed to feel how much I was disappointed myself.

"I promise I'll make it up to you later, Grace."

Turning around, Grace smiled as she wrapped her arms around my neck. "You bet your ass you're going to make it up to me."

Lifting an eyebrow, I asked, "What did you have in mind?"

Angela cleared her throat and Grace dropped her arms and spun back toward the stove.

"Excuse me, Noah. Your mom is asking for more morphine. When I was talking to her, she seemed to be getting confused very easily."

My heart felt as if it stopped beating.

"I noticed that earlier as well," Grace said in almost a whisper.

Angela looked down and cleared her throat again before glancing back up at me. "Noah, I think we're now looking at a matter of days. Her pain is growing worse and the more morphine we give her . . . well . . . you know this because we've talked about it."

Nodding my head, I swallowed hard as Grace took my hand in her hand. "Do I need to call Emily?"

Angela took in a deep breath and pushed it back out quickly. "I can't be sure. It could be another two weeks, or it could be another two hours."

Sucking in a breath of air, I closed my eyes and counted to ten. My whole body felt as if it was slowly beginning to shut down.

"At the very least, I think you need to let her know. I'm going to go sit in there for awhile. I'd like to watch her breathing for a bit more."

Nodding my head, I fought to find the words to speak. It felt as if my world seemed to slow down. I wasn't sure what to do.

How would I be able to go on without my mother?

"Noah, why don't you go on in with your mom and Angela and I'll finish making breakfast."

Looking directly at Grace, it felt as if I was seeing through her and staring out into a vast land of nothing.

Grace took a step closer to me and cupped my face with her hands. "Noah, look into my eyes."

Doing as she asked, I was immediately taken with her soft hazel eyes. "Reach deep down inside of you, Noah. You have the strength . . . you just need to find it. Your mother needs to know you're going to be okay."

Closing my eyes, I asked, "Will I be okay?"

My body came to life as I felt Grace's lips softly touch

mine. "Yes, because I'm going to be right here with you. I'll be your strength, Noah."

Grace's words penetrated my mind and my heart. I knew she was right. My mother wouldn't want me falling apart. I needed to be strong for her. To show her it was okay to leave the pain behind.

Placing my hand over Grace's, I leaned my head into her hand. "Thank you, Grace."

Giving me a wink, Grace quickly kissed me and then dropped her hands and went back to cooking.

Walking out of the kitchen, I slowly made my way back to my mother. Stopping right outside the door, Angela looked at me. "If she falls into a coma, she'll still be able to hear you. Don't be afraid to talk to her. We find with most patients they wait until their loved ones say goodbye. Once she knows you're going to be okay, she'll move on."

Move on.

Balling up my fists, I closed my eyes. I didn't want my mother to move on. She needed to be here watching as my relationship with Grace grew to something more. Marriage. A family.

She needed to be here.

"Noah? Are you hearing what I'm saying to you?"

Nodding, I pulled out my phone and found Emily's number. "I'll be right in. I'm calling my sister."

Angela nodded and opened the door. I peeked into the room and saw my mother sleeping. She looked like an angel. You'd never be able to tell that the cancer was destroying her a little bit more each day.

Hitting Emily's number, I held my breath and waited for her to answer.

"H-hello. Noah, is everything okay?" I knew every time the phone rang Emily was on edge. Each time I'd delivered a normal update. This time I had to tell my baby sister that our mother was going to die soon.

And only God knew when.

Sixteen

GRACE

SITTING ON THE sofa in the living room, I rubbed the palms of my hands down my jeans again. Noah and Emily were in with their mother. Lisa had held on for another few weeks, but had taken a drastic turn for the worse. Every time I left for school, I prayed that Noah wouldn't be here alone if it happened. Each night I came home, Noah took an Ativan and slept for a few hours. I was scared to death at the little amount of sleep he was living on. Plus the fact that I wasn't sure how long he had been taking the Ativan. The longer he stayed on it, the worse it would be to stop taking it.

Glancing over to my right, I looked at all the boxes I'd brought with me from College Station. I'd gone back to College Station this past weekend to help Alex and Will pack up the house. It was Thanksgiving break and after that, it was two more weeks of school and then finals. Commencement was December eighteenth. After that, I had no idea what I was going to do. Did I stay here with Noah and wait? Or did I go to Mason and start helping Alex with our new flower nursery?

Standing up, I let out a long drawn-out sigh. My phone went off as I looked to see it was text from Alex.

Alex: Everyone wishes you were here, but we understand.

Feeling tears build up in my eyes, I squeezed them shut. "Please don't let her die on Thanksgiving. Please." I prayed as I hit reply.

Me: I'm scared, Alex. I don't know what this is going to do to Noah.

Alex replied almost within seconds.

Alex: He's going to fall apart, Grace. Just be there to catch him.

Smiling, I ran my finger over the text message. If anyone knew what it was like to lose a part of them, it was Alex.

Me: Alex, I love you. Have Will kiss your tummy!

Alex: I love you too. I certainly will. Your mom would love a call I'm sure.

Sighing, I dropped my phone down to my side. I hadn't talked to either of my parents since I moved in with Noah. I wanted desperately to call her. My father was furious with me because I moved out of the house in College Station and in with Noah. My mother was more understanding. She didn't like that I was adding more stress to my life, but she got why I was doing it.

My finger hovered above the number as I tried to decide what to do. Pulling my hand back, I looked for another number.

Only ringing twice, Meagan promptly answered.

"Hey, is everything okay? I'm driving back to Austin right now."

Grinning, I sat back on the sofa and pulled my knees into my chest. "Hey. No, Meg. It's not okay. Hospice said she only has a few hours left to live. Noah and his sister have been in with her for the last two hours. I don't know if I should stay out here or go inside."

"Is she in a coma?" Meg asked.

My eyes burned as I fought to control my tears. "Y-yes."

"Grace, you need to go in. You need to be a part of this. To say goodbye and let Noah's mother know you're going to be there for him. I'm about forty minutes away. I have Noah's address plugged into my GPS. I'll text before I get there."

Nodding my head, even though I knew she could see me. I mumbled, "O-okay. Be careful."

There was a slight sniffle on the other end of the phone. I knew Meagan wasn't used to hearing me sound so defeated. I wasn't used to hearing it myself.

"I will be, sweets. See you soon."

"Okay."

Hitting End, I stood up and took in a few deep-cleansing breaths. Closing my eyes, I dug deep down inside to find the strength I knew I needed.

Opening my eyes, I made my way to the room. I knocked softly on the door as I opened it. My eyes looked between Noah and Emily and I couldn't help but notice how defeated Emily looked. Noah stood next to his mother as he spoke softly into his mother's ear.

Quickly glancing to my left, I saw Angela. She wiped a tear away and gave me a sweet smile. I'd come to really like her in the last few weeks. Her heart was beyond amazing and I felt foolish for the jealousy that raced through my body when I first met her.

Giving her a questioning look, she nodded and

mouthed, "Almost time."

Swallowing hard, I turned back to Lisa. I'd never experienced something like this before. Everyone I had loved and was close to was still alive. I had no way of knowing what Noah and Emily were experiencing as they watched their mother slowly begin her journey home.

Noah must have seen me from the corner of his eye. Lifting his head, he smiled so big, I had to place my hands on my stomach. His face lit up and he motioned for me to come to him. Knowing that just merely me being here for him caused such a reaction did insane things to my heart and stomach.

Walking up to the side of the bed he was on, I held my breath. "Grace, I'm so glad you came in. I was saying goodbye to, Mom." Turning, Noah leaned down a little bit further. "Mom, Grace is here. Grace is here with me, Mom."

Emily covered her mouth in an attempt not to cry. My eyes caught hers and I was overtaken with how sad she looked. My heart broke even more.

Looking back at Noah, he motioned for me to talk to his mother as he backed away from the bed. "I'll be right back. Em, let's go grab a drink of water."

Panic set in as I realized Noah was leaving me alone with his mother. Frozen in place, I tried to open my mouth in protest to beg him not to leave me alone with Lisa. Nothing came out. Not even the breath of air I was still holding in.

Angela walked up to me and whispered, "It's important to Noah, therefore it's important to Lisa for you to say your goodbyes."

Nodding my head, I turned and stepped into the spot Noah had been. My eyes searched Lisa's face. She seemed to be sleeping peacefully. Her breathing had settled and now it was as if she was perfectly fine. I watched as her chest rose up slowly, then slowly released. My heart raced when it didn't rise back up as fast as I thought it should.

I knew her body was slowly shutting down. Bit by bit, she was letting go.

Reaching for her hand, I couldn't help but suck in a gasp as I felt how cold it was. "Hi Lisa, it's me, Grace. I totally forgot to bring the latest gardening book with me. I'm sure you are wondering about how we are going to get that spring garden ready."

My body slumped and I rolled my eyes. *Jesus H. Christ. Did I really just say that?* The poor woman is dying and I cracked a joke. A stupid one at that. Looking over my shoulder at Angela, I couldn't help but notice she was chuckling. Motioning for me to keep talking, I turned back to Lisa.

"I might as well go ahead and confess this. I've never been known for telling a good joke."

Lisa's hand jerked under mine. *She can hear me. She knows what I'm saying to her.*

"There will always be a part of me that will wish we could have gotten to know each other better. After all, we both love the same man. I think we would have been wonderful friends. Lisa, I need you to know that I'm going to be Noah's strength. I promise you. He's going to be lost for a bit . . . I know this. But I won't leave his side. I'll fight for him when he has no fight left. Did Noah tell you he asked me to marry him? I will say this though, he isn't terribly romantic. He asked me in the backyard, while I was digging up a hole to plant some lettuce."

Lisa's hand moved slightly again as I gently squeezed it back. "He claimed it was his practice run, and that he had something more grand planned. Here's to hoping."

Angela giggled behind me as I bit hard on my lower lip to gain control of my shaking voice. Dragging in a deep breath, I fought to try and figure out how to say goodbye to Lisa. I wanted more than anything for her to stay with us. For Noah and I to tell her we were engaged. To tell her she was going to be a grandmother and see her hold our child for the first time.

This isn't fair.

Closing my eyes, I let my tears fall. Angela's hand rested softly on my shoulder as it squeezed ever so slightly. Giving me just the strength I needed to keep talking.

Opening my eyes, I smiled as I continued to talk to Lisa. "I know you'll always be here for Noah and Em, I strongly believe that. There won't be a day that goes by that they won't miss you or think about you, Lisa. But they also don't want to see you in pain anymore. It's okay to let go. They're both ready, and they will be okay. They're hurting more now watching you suffer." Lifting Lisa's hand, I gently kissed the back of it.

"I swear to you, I'll take care of them both. I swear."

The door to the bedroom opened as I glanced over and saw Noah, Emily, and Grayson walk in. Grayson gave me a weak smile. Noah had called him yesterday and Grayson said he would be on the next plane out. Even though Noah had only been in Grayson's life off and on growing up, they had grown close these last four years.

"Hey, your favorite nephew, Gray, is here," I said as I stood up and stepped back so Noah, Emily, and Grayson could stand around Lisa.

Grayson wiped away a single tear that had managed to escape and make its way down his face. Leaning over, Grayson kissed her forehead and gently spoke, "Aunt Lisa, I love you. I'll miss you but I swear, I won't let Noah become a male stripper."

The room erupted in laughter. It was a magical thing to hear. When everyone finally settled down and the room became quiet, Lisa opened her eyes. My breath caught in my throat as I stood back and watched. Lisa looked at Grayson first, then Emily, and finally Noah. Angela grabbed my hand and squeezed it.

This must be it.

Lisa stared at Noah for a few moments before turning

her head and looking straight up at the ceiling.

After a few moments, Lisa's eyes closed . . . and she took her last breath.

GRAYSON AND I stood in the living room while Noah and Emily spent a few moments with their mother. Angela had made all the necessary phone calls that needed to be made.

When my phone went off with a text, I knew it was Meagan. Rushing to the front door, I threw it open and ran outside. Meg was getting out of her Honda Accord and rushing around the front of it. Slamming into her body, I lost it. I'd never in my life cried like I cried when I saw her.

"She's gone, Meg. She's gone."

Meagan held onto me tightly as she whispered, "Shh, it's okay, Grace. She's in a better place. There's no more pain."

Feeling my legs wanting to give out, I fought with all my might to stay standing. "I'm scared for, Noah. I'm so scared for him."

Meagan continued to talk me down from the ledge I was walking on. When I finally pulled back, I didn't have any tears left to cry.

"Better?" she asked.

Nodding my head, I wiped my face clear of tears. "Damn, you always did have good timing."

Meagan shrugged. "What can I say? It's a gift some of us have. Remember the time I busted into the bathroom right before Drake the mistake almost gave you your first hickey?"

Laughing, I nodded my head. "Yes. I do remember that."

Meagan looked over my shoulder. Dropping her mouth open, she said, "Holy strip me out of my clothes and take me now."

Looking back over my shoulder, I saw Grayson standing on the porch. Lifting his hand, he gave a weak smile. "You okay, Grace?"

Barely lifting my hand, I nodded. "Yeah. Sorry, I'll be right in."

Grayson nodded and then looked at Meagan. Something passed over his face, but he turned before I could read it. Glancing back at Meagan, I watched as she stared after Grayson.

"Fuck. Me."

"You wish he would," I said with a snicker.

Meagan snapped her head back at me and said, "That's the stripper! The guy who Lauren had wrapped around her finger in Durango."

Widening my eyes, I said, "Have I not told you about Grayson?"

Meagan's mouth dropped open as her hands moved to her hips. "Um, no. But considering the circumstances, I'll let it slide and you can tell me later. There are more important things to deal with rather than the fact that I just found my next mistake."

Laughing, I wrapped my arm around Meagan's waist. "Your luggage?"

Meagan motioned for me to walk toward the house. "It can wait. Noah's going to need you; here come the folks to take his mother's body."

Looking down the street, I saw the black hearse pulling up and my stomach instantly recoiled and felt sick.

Meagan guided me back into the house as I softly spoke, "Noah."

Seventeen

NOAH

NUMB.

My body felt numb.

But I was relaxed beyond belief as I searched for my seat. Grayson had flown in and was planning on staying with us over the Christmas holidays. He walked beside me as we headed toward the front door of the house Grace grew up in.

The Valium I popped on the way here would help me get through today. It would be the first time I was seeing Grace's parents, Jeff and Ari again. They had made it known they were not happy about Grace moving in with me.

The front door opened and Alex walked out. I could see the pity etched on her face and I hated it.

"Holy shit. She's prego," Grayson said with a chuckle.

Alex walked up to me and gave me a hug. "Hey, Noah. I'm so glad you're here."

Smiling, I glanced down to her stomach and shook my head. "March is getting closer, Alex."

Laughing, she nodded her head. "Tell me about it. Thank goodness I'm graduated and back home now."

Nodding my head, I looked over her shoulder and saw the love of my life standing there. And behind her, was her father.

"Noah," Grace said as she made her way down to me. I prayed like hell she wouldn't be able to tell I had drugged myself up to make it through this day. Grace had been splitting her time between Mason and Austin. I'd gotten pretty good at hiding the fact that I took pills to keep me calm and pills to help me sleep.

Smiling, I got ready for her to jump into my arms. Catching her when she did, I spun her around as I whispered in her ear, "I fucking missed you."

"It's been two days." She giggled in my ear.

It had been the longest two days of my life. Grayson was staying with me for the whole month of December and the fucker watched me like a hawk. At least he let me get drunk with him last night.

Grace pulled her head back and stared at me.

Fuck.

Smiling, I tilted my head and said, "You forget what I looked like?"

Her smile faded some as she peeked over to Grayson. "What did y'all do last night?" Grace asked as she stared at Grayson.

Leaning forward, Grayson said, "We got drunk and I got laid."

"Uh-huh. Sounds like that was a fun time."

"Not really," Grayson said with a shrug. "My hand doesn't really count."

Grace's face coiled up as she said, "Ugh, you sick bastard. I didn't need that visual."

A smirk quickly grew across Grace's face. "Guess who

is here?"

Grayson yawned like he was bored already. "The whole gang from Durango?"

"Yep. Even Meg. Seems like she perked up a little when she found out you were in town. Want to explain?" Grace asked as she crossed her arms in front of her and raised her eyebrow.

Grayson tossed his head back and laughed with a roar.

Grace and I both stared at Grayson. The way he couldn't keep his eyes off of Meagan last month didn't slip by anyone. Even me, and I was consumed by my mother's death.

Thinking about my mother was slowly bringing the pain back to the surface. I needed to push it back down and fast. Pulling my eyes from Grayson, I focused on Jeff.

Smiling at him, I made my way up the stairs and held out my hand. "Good afternoon, Jeff. Thank you for inviting us to stay with y'all."

Jeff looked me over before he let his eyes settle into mine. I wasn't sure how long we stood there and stared at each other before Ari cleared her throat.

Looking over at her, I smiled and said, "It's a pleasure seeing you again, Ari."

Walking up to me, Ari gave me a soft kiss on my cheek. "The pleasure is all mine, Noah. Come on in, I want to introduce you to everyone."

Taking in a deep breath, I glanced back to Jeff who smiled and motioned for me to follow Ari. Grace was next to me as we walked into the house. Alex was walking behind us talking to Grayson. It seems she was filling him in on Lauren and Colt.

As we made our way through the house, Ari pointed out the guest bathroom and where to get water, soda or beer if I needed one.

The moment the back screen door opened and we all stepped outside; everyone turned and looked at me. I felt like the new kid in class as all eyes fell upon me. *Holy shit, there are a lot of fucking people here.* My heart began to race, and I prayed like hell I wouldn't have a panic attack.

It didn't take long for Ari to start with the introductions.

"Noah, this is my father and mother, Mark and Susan."

Smiling the moment I saw Mark, I said, "Mark, it's great seeing you again so soon."

Everyone froze. Including Grace.

"W-what? When did you meet my grandfather?"

Risking a chance to look over at Jeff, I quickly turned back to Grace. "We met a few weeks ago over dinner."

Mark smiled and said, "You've got a good catch here, Grace Hope. This young man called me up and told me he wanted to talk to me about the house. Imagine my surprise when he handed me a check for the cost of the house, plus interest."

Grace's mouth dropped open as she looked at me. "Noah. How?"

I didn't really want to tell Grace I had used my mother's life insurance policy to pay her grandfather back, so I winked and said, "I'll tell you later. By the way, your grandfather told me how you used the money they had set aside for you."

The feel of Jeff's eyes on me caused me to glance over in his direction again. Taking a sip of his beer, he smiled and gave me a head nod. I was hoping like hell I had gained some respect from him by paying back Grace's grandfather.

The rest of the afternoon was spent meeting and talking to everyone. I sat and talked to Gramps a lot. We talked mostly about the cattle business that his grandson, Gunner, and Jeff, now ran. It didn't take long for Gunner, Jeff, Will and Luke to start asking me questions about business plans, marketing tools and other things to make a business run smooth. Surely they didn't need my opinions, after all, they were running a multi-million dollar cattle business, on top of a breeding business.

Jeff sat back and took all of it in, while Gunner hit me with question after question. Especially when he found out I had a minor in finance. "So you don't agree with paying off the equipment ahead of time? Explain why you think like that?" Gunner asked.

Shrugging my shoulders, I said, "Well, look at it like this. You hold a very low interest rate on those two loans. Why would you want to take your cash and pay them off, when you could invest it in a CD? Carrying some debt is not bad."

Jeff nodded and looked at Gunner. Grace walked up to me and smiled as she sat down next to me. "Are you talking numbers and all that shit?"

"Grace Hope," Jeff said as he furrowed his brows at her.

Laughing, Grace shook head and said, "Daddy, please. Don't act like you have virgin ears. For goodness' sake, look at your damn T-shirt."

Glancing down, it was then I noticed what it said. The bright-yellow arrow pointed down and the shirt read:

You know you're curious.

Jeff looked at his shirt and said, "What? There is nothing wrong with this shirt."

Letting out a chuckle, I looked at Grace who made a face at her father. "Really, Dad?"

Jeff smiled and winked at me as he finished off his beer. Standing up, he motioned for me to follow. "Walk with me, son. It's time to bond and all that shit."

TWENTY MINUTES LATER, I was on horseback following Jeff down a trail. I quickly came up with scenarios of how I could escape if he turned a gun on me. Thank God my parents put me on a horse when I was young and I learned to ride.

"So, you're in love with my daughter?" Jeff asked as we rode side by side in an open field.

Seeing Grace's face pop into my head, I smiled. "Yes, sir. I think I was in love with her the first time I ever saw her."

Letting out a gruff laugh, Jeff looked over at me. "She looks like her mother . . . thank God."

Nodding in agreement, I agreed. "Yes, she very much does."

Shaking his head, Jeff expelled a quick breath. "Damn, the first time I met Ari I wasn't sure if I wanted to kiss her or knock her silly."

Pulling my head back in surprise, I asked, "Really?"

"Oh yeah. She's hard headed, opinionated like you wouldn't believe, a mouth that would make a sailor blush, and a smile that made my knees feel like they could no longer hold up my body."

Laughing, I looked straight ahead. "Sort of sounds like your daughter."

"Oh hell, son, you don't need to tell me. Try living with both of them in the same house. Poor Luke and I went on our fair share of fishing and hunting trips. Just to catch a break from the two of them."

"Sounds brutal," I said as I looked straight ahead. A memory of my mother and Emily standing in the kitchen bitching at me for drinking from the milk carton flooded my mind.

Jeff and I rode along for a few minutes in silence. I could hear the river in the distance and I knew we were getting closer.

Jeff walked his horse up to a tree and jumped off. Following his lead, I did the same.

"Don't worry about them. They'll just graze on the grass. Follow me; I want to show you something, Noah."

Doing as he asked, I draped the reins over the horses

shoulder and followed Jeff toward the water. There was a giant rock that was set back about fifteen feet from the water. Jeff walked over to it and jumped up on it. It was large enough for at least four men to stand up there.

Figuring he wanted me to follow, I climbed up and stood next to him. The view was amazing.

"Wow," I whispered as I watched the river meander along its path.

"When I was about your age, I lost my mother, but not like how you lost your mother. Actually, I lost my mother a number of years before that."

Turning to look at him, I asked, "How did you lose her?"

Jeff continued to look out over the water as it rushed over rocks. "Alcohol. My father left my mother when my sister, Ellie, and I were young. My mother couldn't handle it and turned to drinking to hide the pain. The problem was, no amount of drinking . . . or drugs . . . could numb the pain."

My head snapped over to Jeff as our eyes met. "No sir, it cannot. I turned to alcohol when my mother's cancer came back. Spent a number of nights drowning my sorrow in it."

Not taking his eyes off of me, Jeff asked, "And what made you stop?"

"Grace. Even though we weren't together at the time, I knew she would have been disappointed in me."

Letting a small smile play across his lips, Jeff nodded and looked back over the river. "Love will do that. Save you from the deepest depths of sorrow and pain."

Nodding in agreement, I felt my heart squeeze in my stomach. I was not going to hurt Grace. No matter how much I wanted the pills, I wouldn't put Grace through that.

"What if, you find yourself slipping back down the hole? Even with love there to pull you back?" I asked.

Jeff turned and faced me. "You fight."

"And if you don't feel like you have the strength?"

Slowly shaking his head, Jeff's eyes turned sad. "You always have the strength, Noah. You just need to know where to look for it. That's the first step."

"The second step?" I asked.

Not taking his eyes from mine, Jeff said, "Stop depending on the pills. It's a weakness. Not a strength."

My entire world stopped as a shiver ran across my entire body. The only thing I could hear was my own breathing and the sound of the water rushing along. In that moment I felt like the river, flowing downstream into the unknown. There was only one question I needed to find the answer to.

Was there a place I was running to . . . or running from? I either ran to Grace . . . or the pills. My pain was pulling me under—she was my only saving grace. It was time to make a decision and I knew exactly where it would lead me.

To Grace.

Eighteen

GRACE

WHEN DADDY AND Noah took off for a ride, I couldn't stop thinking about what they were talking about. Was Daddy being mean? Were they maybe bonding? Was Noah going to be okay alone with my father?

Alex walked up to me and handed me my old worn out gardening gloves as she gave me a wink. As we walked through the garden with our arms laced through Gram's, I couldn't help but feel a sense of calm come over me. I loved getting my hands in the dirt. Emma motioned for us to get to work as she took a seat.

Laughing, I said, "There's nothing to do, Emma. Nothing needs picking and my mother has this garden so well taken care of there isn't a weed to be found."

Tilting her head, she stared into my eyes. "Dig."

Pinching my eyebrows together, I repeated what she said, "Dig?"

Alex giggled and slowly dropped down and did exactly

what her great-grandmother told her to do.

"So you want me to just dig?"

Nodding her head, she said, "Yes, Grace. I want you to just dig."

There was something about digging in the dirt that relaxed me. It always had and I knew Grams felt the same way.

Shrugging my shoulders, I did what she told me to do. Turning, I found a spot and dropped to my knees. Sticking the garden shovel into the dirt, I scoped out some dirt. Then I scoped more out. My mind quickly got lost in thought as I thought about how Noah had been acting the last couple of weeks since his mother passed away. I'd readied myself for him to break down, but he never did.

He was relaxed.

Too relaxed.

All the time he seemed relaxed.

The shovel dug in deeper as I closed my eyes and remembered seeing Noah taking a sleeping pill. I didn't think much of it as I walked into the room and saw him put it in his mouth and down it with a Coke. He'd hardly been sleeping. One to two hours a night. Maybe in my mind I justified it, thinking he needed it.

"Grams, did you dig often in your garden for no reason?" Alex asked with a chuckle.

"Oh yes, Alexandra. There were times I was in my garden in the middle of the night. Something about being with the dirt cleared my head. Allowed me to focus on the things that were right in front of me that I couldn't see."

Grams words slammed into my head as my heart felt like someone was gripping it and squeezing as hard as they could.

Dig faster, Grace. Deeper.

Noah. Oh God. Noah's been taking pills to deal with his mother's death and he's been doing it right in front of me.

I've been allowing it to happen.

Dropping the shovel, I dug with my hands. I promised her. I promised Lisa I would be his strength.

I failed her.

I failed Noah.

Using both of my hands, I frantically began digging out more dirt as Alex called out my name.

"Grace?"

Anger built up in my body as I realized how stupid and naïve I had allowed myself to me. Using my left hand to hold up my body, I rested it on the ground as I used my right hand to dig harder.

"Stupid!" I cried out as I worked harder.

"Grace! Stop!" Alex called out to me.

"I can't believe I was so blind!"

Alex placed her hand on my shoulder and gave me a pull. "Grace Johnson! What are you doing?"

Jumping up, I spun around and faced Alex. "The one thing I promised Lisa and Noah I would do . . . I didn't do."

Alex gave me a confused look. "What in the hell are you talking about?"

Looking past Alex, I caught Gram's stare. Her blue eyes pierced mine. "How did you know?"

Smiling, she slowly shook her head. "As we grow older, we see things. We learn things. Some of it is from experience, some from just listening to our gut feelings."

Alex reached out and took my hand. "Grace, please tell me what's going on."

"It's Noah. He's been using drugs to deal with his mother's death. He's been doing it right in front of me and I've put blinders on."

Alex's mouth dropped open. "Grace, are you sure?"

The sound of a horse walking up caused me to turn. My father and Noah were walking back toward the barn.

Swallowing hard, I stood up taller and nodded my head. "I'm positive. If y'all will excuse me, I need to find Gray and Meg."

I wasn't sure how this was all going to work or how Noah would handle it. But I knew I had four people I could count on to help me get Noah through this.

SITTING IN THE formal dining room, I sat next to Noah, who sat across from Brad, Meagan and Taylor's father. Brad had gone through a rough patch earlier on in his marriage to Amanda. I knew he had been in rehab and had worked for many years with outreach programs. He also volunteered a lot at the rehab clinic he had been in.

"What do I need to do?" Noah asked.

Brad slowly took in a deep breath and just as slow, blew it out. "Noah, I don't think you've become dangerously addicted to the pills. But you are very dependent on them. You have two options. Check into a rehab clinic or go cold turkey and suffer through the withdrawals. In the rehab clinic, they will slowly bring you down. That's probably how you should go with the Ativan."

I quickly glanced at my mother and father as I moved about in my seat, before turning back to Brad. "How bad will they be? The withdrawals?"

Shaking his head, Brad said, "I don't know. It really depends on how long and how much Noah has been taking. I will tell you this though. The fact that Noah was the one to recognize the problem is the biggest hurdle. It's the first step and most people need an intervention just to get started."

I took Noah's hand in mine. After I had set out to find Meagan and Grayson, Noah and my father had found Brad. My father had told Noah about Brad's addictions and how he spent time fighting them.

Noah asked me, Grayson, and my parents to sit and talk to Brad with him. Meagan joined us at my request.

"The only thing in this life that matters to me is sitting right here next to me. I swore I would never do anything to hurt her or her future." Noah turned and looked into my eyes. "You have beautiful dreams, Grace. Dreams I want to be a part of. I'll do anything to be a part of them. I'll do anything," Noah whispered.

"You and me. Together forever," I said as I placed my hand on the side of his face.

Noah gave me a breathtaking smile that slowly faded. "Um . . . I want to do this at home. I *need* to do it at home. It's where my demons started, I need to win my battle against them there."

Nodding my head, I looked past Noah at Grayson. Giving me a wink, I knew we would be able to help Noah. I still wasn't sure how often and how much Noah had been taking the pills. A part of me didn't want to know and that filled me with guilt.

Looking back into Noah's eyes, I gave him a weak smile. "I'll be by your side the entire time, Noah. We'll fight this battle together."

SITTING AT THE kitchen island, Meagan let out a sigh as she sat next to me.

Glancing up from my book, I asked, "What's wrong?"

Making a face of frustration, Meagan rolled her eyes. "I need to get laid so bad."

Making a gruff laugh, I looked back at my book. "What's it been, Meg? A week?"

"Fuck you, Grace. You're riding the dick. I haven't in months. Years to be exact."

Dropping my book, I narrowed my eye at her as I studied her face. "I'm riding the dick? Really? So classy, Meg."

Shrugging her shoulders, she let out a breath. "I dare

you to deny it. Have you not noticed me being a complete bitch the last two and a half years?"

"First off, I won't deny it, but I went for a good while not riding it and I was perfectly fine. And no, I haven't noticed you being a complete bitch because that's just who you are."

Shooting me a dirty look, Meagan got up and walked to the refrigerator. "Please, you were miserable without Noah."

I couldn't argue with her on that one. "Meg, did the bullying ever stop? I mean, is that why you never got involved with anyone from school?"

Meagan's head was buried in the refrigerator as she looked around for something. She popped back out, and turned to face me as she held a bottle of orange juice. "For the longest time I let a small group of people dictate how I lived my life. It was miserable, Grace." Leaning against the door of the refrigerator, Meagan gave me a weak smile.

My heart broke for Meagan. Closing my book, I slide it off to the side. "Did you ever talk to your dad about all of it? The intense pressure he put on you and what was happening at school?"

Lifting her eyebrows, Meagan pushed out a fast deep breath. "When I told them I was looking at moving to Durango my father about flipped out and said I couldn't run from my problems, I needed to face them head on. He wasn't too pleased when I mentioned he was part of the reason I was running. My mom, well, she understood. She's always been the one who seemed to relate a bit more with me though."

"Did you tell them about what happened in school?"

Sitting, Meagan's eyes briefly filled with tears. "Yes. They were both devastated and I think a bit angry with themselves that I didn't feel like I could talk to them about it. When I changed my degree plan though, my father really seemed to lighten up on the whole 'You have to be greater than everyone' bit. One thing's for sure though," Meagan said as she reached for an apple and took a bite. "They no longer compare me to Taylor."

Laughing, I said, "Well, you had to go through a shit storm for that to happen."

Meagan giggled and said, "But it's over. I'm ready to move on with my life and help others."

Tilting my head, I asked Meagan, "Whatever happened to the group of girls who used to spread all that shit about you?"

An evil smile spread across Meagan's face. "You know, some crazy shit happened to each of them. The mastermind ended up having all her beautiful blonde locks fall out. Seems someone put something in her shampoo."

Holding back my laughter, I shook my head and said, "You don't say."

Taking another bite of her apple, Meagan smiled bigger. "The other little bitch that fabricated the blowjob stories, someone spiked her toothpaste with black dye."

Covering my mouth, I let out a laugh. "Holy hell. You didn't?"

Letting out a laugh, Meagan nodded her head. "Oh, that was just the beginning. There was a reason we grew up with Will, Luke, and Colt and all the stupid ass pranks they pulled on us. I must say though, Luke driving in and being my accomplice was probably the nicest thing that bastard as ever done for me."

My mouth dropped open as my eyes grew wider. "He didn't? Did Libby know?"

"Yep. He did and yep, she supplied the dye," Meagan said as she popped her p loudly.

Meagan and I busted out laughing as Grayson walked into the kitchen. I couldn't help but notice how he stared at Meagan.

Turning to look at him, Meagan attempted not to be affected by the fact that Grayson was shirtless and just coming back from a run.

Meagan covered her eyes and looked away. "Jesus, dude put a T-shirt on. No one wants to look at your baby smooth skin. Ugh."

Grayson leaned over and smiled at Meagan. "You're just jealous my skin is smoother than yours."

Meagan dropped her hands and looked at Grayson. "Puh-lease. Go practice your dance moves, you damn gigolo."

Shaking my head, I reached back for my book and asked, "Seriously though, Gray, do you shave every day?"

Grayson grabbed a bottle of water and leaned against the counter. "Why look at this. Y'all are jealous of my silky smooth skin."

Rolling my eyes, I said, "Please. You've had more skanks up on you than I care to know about. I'll take my healthy clean skin over yours any day."

Letting out a roar of laughter, Grayson sat next to Meagan as she moved away a little bit from him.

"I don't have cooties, Meg," Grayson said with a smile that surely would melt the panties off of any willing girl.

Raising my eyebrow, I asked, "You sure about that, Gray? When was the last time you got your little boy parts checked?"

Grayson's eyes widened as his mouth fell open. "Little? Did you really just call my sergeant little?"

Meagan choked on her orange juice as I jumped up and hit her back as I died laughing.

As Meagan tried to control her cough, I looked at Grayson and shook my head. "Did you really name your dick, Gray?"

Pulling his head back like he was in shock I'd even questioned him, he nodded his head. "Fuck yeah, I did. Noah has a name for his too."

Standing up, I said, "What? How do you know?"

Shrugging, Grayson smiled as the bottle of water hit

the edge of his lips. "He told me."

"What, do guys just sit around and talk about naming their dicks? Does this make you feel powerful?" I asked as I looked back at Meagan who was still trying to recover from the name of Grayson's dick.

"No different than women sitting around talking."

Pinching my eyebrows together, I said, "We don't name our vajayjay's, Gray."

"If I named mine, it would be Wonder Woman," Meagan said as Grayson and I both looked at her with stunned expressions.

Swallowing hard, Grayson asked, "Why?"

Meagan stood up and said, "Because she wonders why she can't find a dick who knows what in the hell it's doing."

Grayson stood up and took a few steps closer to Meagan, causing her to take a step back and hit the counter.

"Seems like she hasn't met the right dick for the job."

Smiling, I waited with bated breath for Meagan's reply. "Oh trust me, stripper boy. She's met plenty of dicks. Lots of dicks, to be exact. For now she's sticking with cucumbers."

Grayson stared at Meagan with a look of disbelief as I let out a chuckle. "I'm going to check on Noah. You two behave."

Grayson took in a deep breath through his nose as he leaned closer to Meagan. "Headed to the shower. Would you like the sergeant to show Wonder Woman how it's done?"

Meagan let out a nervous laugh, "Please. That dick will never see my Wonder Woman. Ever."

Grayson leaned in and whispered against Meagan's ear as he pushed away and walked past me.

I couldn't help but notice Meagan's chest heaving up and down. Before I turned away, I gave Meagan a wink. "You just woke up a sleeping beast."

Licking her lips and running her hand across the side of her neck, Meagan barely said, "I know."

Nineteen

GRACE

WALKING INTO NOAH'S room, I stopped and stared at him. He was sitting on the window seat staring straight out the window. I knew this was going to be a tough road. I'd read up on the withdrawals that Noah would most likely go through. Panic attacks, body tremors, hallucinations, confusion, throwing up, mood swings . . . the list went on. Since Noah had been taking three different pills. Each one had their own set of withdrawal demons.

Putting on a smile the best I could, I cleared my throat and said, "Hey. How's it going?"

Noah didn't look at me as he focused on something outside.

"Sounds like you're having fun with Gray."

Making my way over toward him, I let out a small laugh. "Nah, Meg was just giving him a hard time."

Turning to me, Noah glared at me as sweat poured down his face. Sucking in a breath, I quickly made my way over to him.

"Oh my God. Noah, are you running a fever?" Going to touch his forehead, he jerked away.

"Don't touch me. Matter of fact, just get out of here. I don't need you, Grace."

My stomach dropped, I stood firm as I thought back to what Brad had told us before we started this. Noah was going to change. Do and say things he didn't mean.

Sitting next to him, I pulled my knees up to my chest as I watched him turn and look back out the window.

"I'm not leaving, Noah. You can be pissed and angry as much as you want. I'm not leaving."

Closing his eyes, Noah barely spoke above a whisper. "Please, let me just take one Ativan, Grace. I'm so tired."

It felt as if a vice was wrapped around my chest and was slowly squeezing down on me.

Resting my chin on my knee, I watched for his reaction, as I said, "No. It's not time to take one." The doctor had advised for Noah not to go cold turkey on the Ativan but to come down from it slowly. We were tapering his dose back over the next two weeks.

Noah slammed his head against the wall and yelled out, "Fuck!" Jumping a little, I didn't move.

Noah rolled his head back and forth against the wall. "Just give me one fucking pill, Grace. Jesus, I just want to sleep."

"I love you, Noah. But there are no pills in this house."

Noah snapped his head forward and glared at me. "What?"

Dropping my knees, I turned my body to face him. "Noah, think about what you're asking me. Gray has the Ativan somewhere else and will bring the pill when it's time to take it."

Leaning forward, Noah grabbed my hands as tears filled his eyes. "Baby, please. Just this once. *Please*, Grace."

Noah's body trembled as he pleaded with me.

I was lost in his eyes.

Lost in his tears.

My goal was to pull him out of the darkness—even if it dragged me in as well.

Slowly shaking my head, I said, "No."

Dropping my hands, Noah stood up and pointed to me. "Fuck you, Grace! You have no fucking idea what I'm going through."

Feeling the anger build, I stood up and pushed his hand away. "Really? Because I'm standing here looking at the man I love falling apart right before my eyes. The man I want to spend the rest of my life building a future with is standing here telling me to fuck off. Well you know what? Fuck you, Noah. Fuck you and those fucking pills you depended on. You have me now, and if I'm not good enough for you to lean on, then we have a serious problem. But for right now, my focus is on you getting through this. So you can call me every name in the book and tell me to leave but I'm not going anywhere, you stupid asshole! Do you hear me, Noah? I'm not going anywhere. If finding you means losing a part of me—then I'll do it."

Noah stood before me wearing a downcast expression. "I feel sick," he murmured. Turning quickly, Noah rushed into his bathroom and began throwing up.

Dropping my head back, I looked up. "Why puke, God? I can handle anything but puke."

Meagan came rushing into the bedroom. "I heard yelling. Is everything okay?"

Noah started throwing up again as Meagan rushed into the bathroom and called out, "It's puke, Grace! I've got this one."

Clearly Meagan remembered I couldn't handle someone throwing up. Letting out the breath I hadn't even realized I was holding in, I sat back down on the window seat and placed my face in my hands as I sobbed.

That was the first confrontation with Noah. How much

worse would it get? What if he ended up hating me because of this? Dropping my hands, I pulled my phone out of my back pocket. Pulling up his number, I typed out my message.

Me: He told me to leave.

Daddy: He didn't mean it.

Me: He was so angry, Daddy.

Daddy: Are Grayson and Meagan there?

Me: Yes. Noah's throwing up right now. Meg is helping him.

Daddy: Do you want me there?

Swallowing hard, I closed my eyes and prayed silently for my answer. Opening my eyes, I typed out my reply.

Me: No. I just got him back, Daddy. I won't lose him again. I just had a moment of weakness.

Daddy: That's what causes us to be stronger. I'm here for you.

Pressing my lips together, I nodded my head and stood up. Typing one last reply, I knew what I had to do.

Me: I know. I love you. Will call later. Bye Daddy.

Pushing my phone into my back pocket, I made my way to the bathroom. Noah was sitting on the floor shivering. Meagan looked up at me and frowned. "He has a fever. He's also starting to hallucinate. It has to be the Ativan."

Nodding my head, I said, "I'll get some cold washcloths. We can put them on his wrists. I think if we try to give him something for the fever he'll just throw it up."

"Mom? Mom, you're back? Mom, I need you to help me," Noah called out.

Feeling the air leave my lungs, I took a step back to steady myself. I wasn't expecting that. My eyes landed back on Meagan's as she gave me a sympathetic smile.

"Gray can put him in bed. Let me go get him." Spinning around on my heels, I practically ran to Grayson's room. Each of the bedrooms had their own bathrooms. I was praying he was out of the shower and dressed now.

Knocking on the door, Grayson opened it and looked at me. His eyes widened and he glanced down the hall. "Noah?"

"It's started. He's moody, yelling, hallucinating and throwing up. I need to get him into bed. He's running a fever."

Nodding his head, Grayson reached for a T-shirt and slipped it over his head as we made our way back to Noah.

Walking into the room, Meagan was slowly trying to walk Noah to his bed. Grayson walked up and took over as he led Noah to the bed.

"Get the fuck off of me, you fucking asshole. You're sleeping with her, aren't you?" Noah yelled out as Grayson ignored him.

"You're a dick, do you know that? You could have anyone you want, but you take my girlfriend. Get the hell out of my house!" Noah screamed.

Grayson pushed Noah as he fell back onto the bed. Leaning over Noah, Grayson said, "Say that one more time, Noah, and I'm going to grab your balls and twist them until you scream for mercy."

Meagan and I both looked at each other and then back at Noah and Grayson.

"You wouldn't," Noah whispered.

"I'm going to get a bucket for the next time you puke. Can you behave while I'm gone?"

Noah rolled his eyes and looked away. "Fuck you."

Grayson laughed as he headed to the door. "I love you too, bro. Come on Meg, let's go find a bucket together."

Grayson grabbed Meagan's hand and pulled her out the door as I watched them disappear.

Breathing in through my nose, I calmly blew it out as I walked over to Noah's bed. His body was trembling, so I pulled the covers up and over him. Sitting on the bed, I reached for his hand.

Noah turned to me as our eyes met. His once beautiful caramel-colored eyes looked dark and empty. His brown hair was a mess from where he had been running his hands through it and pulling on it. "I want to be alone."

Shrugging my shoulders, I whispered, "Too bad. I'm not leaving."

Trying desperately to find a spark of life in his eyes, I continued to stare into them. "Grace, don't you get it. I don't want you here. You need to leave. *Now.*"

Slowly shaking my head, I let a single tear fall from my eye. Noah watched as it made its way down my cheek. "I'm not leaving you, Noah. You can say whatever you want, but I'm not leaving."

Reaching his hand up, Noah wiped the tear away as our eyes met and something moved across Noah's face. "Please don't give up on us."

Giving him a weak smile, I said, "Never."

"What if you lose me, Grace? What if I can't come back to you?"

Leaning down, I kissed Noah gently on the cheek as I moved my lips to his ears. "I'll find you, Noah. I swear to you. I'll find you."

Noah wrapped his arms around me and pulled me to him as he finally let go. Sobs shook his body as he held me like it was the last time he would ever have me in his arms again.

THE COOL EVENING breeze blew through the trees as it gently whipped my hair about. Bringing the coffee cup up to my lips, I took a sip. Closing my eyes, I let the sound of silence penetrate my mind and soul.

Two weeks had passed since Noah stopped taking Ativan, Valium, and Klonopin. Christmas had come and gone as I spent every moment either with Noah or on this porch. Hearing Grayson drive up, I opened my eyes and watched him pull in to the driveway.

"Hey," I said with a whisper. Grayson had decided to stay another few weeks until Noah was feeling back to a hundred percent.

"Hey back at ya." Grayson said with a smile. "Where's Meg?"

Smiling softly, I said, "Why? Is the sergeant looking for his new soldier?"

Pushing my shoulder softly, Grayson sat next to me. "Very funny. That girl is hard to read. One minute I think she is into me and the next, she tells me what a whore I am."

Laughing, I shook my head. "You are a stripper, Gray. You don't seriously want a girlfriend, do you?"

Holding up his hands, Grayson gave me a fake laugh. "Whoa, turn it down, Johnson. No one mentioned the G word. I'm looking for a little P action and that's it."

Lifting my eyebrows, I did the one thing I knew I shouldn't do. I asked what he meant. "What is P action?"

"Seriously, Grace? Sometimes I'm so disappointed in you. Pussy action."

Rolling my eyes, I let out a disgusted sigh. "Ugh. Men are pigs. No, I take that back. You're a pig."

Standing up, Grayson rubbed his hand on the top of

my head before heading into the house and calling over his shoulder, "I may be a pig, but I can dance better than you."

"Bullshit!" I shouted. Taking the last drink of my coffee, I stood and looked down the street for Meagan. She'd gone for a run about an hour ago. She had left right after Grayson left. Something was off, but I couldn't put my finger on it. There was something different about Meagan this morning.

"Grace?"

Spinning around, I smiled when I saw Noah standing there. "Hey there. Did you get some good sleep?"

Giving me a smile so bright I had to catch my breath, Noah nodded. "Yeah. I did actually."

"Good. Are you hungry?" I asked as I walked up to him.

"Um, not really. But I was wondering if we could take a walk? I wanted to talk to you."

A feeling of uneasiness bubbled up as I attempted to smile. "Sure. Right now?"

"Yeah, if that's okay?"

Swallowing hard, I nodded and said, "Let me put this coffee mug in the kitchen."

Noah glanced away and stared down the street. "I'll wait right here."

My voice abandoned me as I made my way past him and into the kitchen.

Setting the mug into the sink, I leaned against the counter and dragged in a few deep breaths.

Whatever was about to happen, I knew it wasn't going to be good. The look in Noah's eyes scared me shitless.

Noah had grown distant the last two weeks. The better he seemed to get, the more withdrawn he became.

I was losing him and no matter how hard I tried to fight, I wasn't winning this battle.

Twenty

NOAH

GRACE AND I walked along the street in silence as I fought for a way to tell her how I was feeling. These last two weeks had opened up my eyes to so many things. I wasn't the man I wanted to be for Grace. I wanted to be so much more for her. I needed to be the strength . . . not her. If I kept going down this path, Grace wouldn't be able to follow her dreams.

Finally breaking the silence, Grace spoke. "How are you feeling today?"

Nodding my head, I said, "Good. Today I think my mind has been the most clear."

"Good," Grace said just above a whisper.

"Have you talked to Alex about the nursery? How are things moving along?"

Grace worried on her bottom lip. "Um, we've hit a couple of snags, but I don't think it's going to be anything that puts us too far behind. I told Alex I'd be there this weekend. I was hoping you and I could go stay a couple days at my parents' house."

The dull ache in my chest grew stronger; I knew I was the cause of the snags. "Grace, maybe you should head to Mason. I've kept you away for so long and it has to be stressful for Alex to tend to this all herself."

Grace stopped walking and took my hand. "A few weeks ago you told me to get the fuck out of your house. Do you remember that?"

Making a grimace, I shook my head. "No. I don't remember that and you have to know I didn't mean it."

Smiling a smile so brilliant, I quickly found myself smiling back. "I knew then you didn't mean it, just like I know now you don't mean what you're saying."

It felt as if the entire world was resting on my shoulders and I wasn't sure how to push it off. "Grace, maybe I should take some time and go travel, or visit Em. Your parents probably want their daughter back and I don't feel like I'm . . . like I'm–"

Placing her fingers up to my lips, Grace's eyes burned with a fire I was used to seeing. Some days it burned brighter than other days. "Stop talking, Noah. You are my everything. It's you and me. Remember?"

"Grace," I whispered as I took her hand and kissed her wrist. "I feel like I've failed you and your family. I'm not the man I want to be for you."

Walking closer to me, Grace placed both hands on my chest and looked deep into my eyes. There were so many moments I'd found myself lost in those emerald eyes. "You are the man I want you to be. Flaws and all. You can't be who you think I want you to be if you're not with me, Noah. I won't . . . no . . . I can't lose you again."

My knees felt weak as my eyes searched Grace's face. "How did I get so lucky with you?"

Giving me a sexy smile and a wink, Grace replied, "I could say the same thing. There is something though that we do need to talk about, now that you are feeling better."

Pulling her closer to me, I kissed the tip of her nose. "What's that?"

"Sex. If I have to stick my hand into my panties one more time, I'm going to have to start paying myself."

My dick instantly came to life. A feeling I had not been feeling since my mother passed away rushed through my body. "I believe I owe you a few Christmas presents as well."

Licking her lips, Grace slid her hand down and grabbed my dick as we both let out a moan. "Noah, take me home. I've missed you."

Grabbing Grace's hand, I quickly started back toward the house. We had some serious love making to make up for.

Practically pulling Grace back to the house, I felt a surge of energy I hadn't felt in weeks.

Running up the stairs of the front porch, I pushed open the front door, grabbed Grace and pinned her against the wall as I attacked her lips. Her hands pushed through my hair as she took a handful and pulled. God I wanted to be buried deep inside of her.

Pushing my hand up and under her shirt, I pushed her bra out of the way and played with her nipple. Grace moaned into my mouth as she pushed her hips into me.

"Now, Noah. I need you now."

Grace and I quickly made our way up to my room when we heard noises coming from Grayson's room. Stopping, we both leaned closer to his door.

That's when we heard it.

"Oh God. Harder!"

Dropping her mouth open, Grace jumped back and hit me on the arm as she pointed to the door and covered her mouth. "Oh my God! He brought a whore home!"

Shaking my head, I pulled back and stared at her. "What? Why do you assume it's a whore?"

Giving me a look like I had just grown to heads, Grace tilted her head and said, "Hello? Stripper?"

"Stop labeling him, Grace. Besides, he quit his stripper job."

Grace was about to say something when everything got quite. The strange female voice grew louder as she moved toward the door. Grace and I pushed each other as we ran down the hall and into my bedroom. Pushing Grace in, we shut the door but not all the way.

Barely opening the door, Grace and I put our ear to the opening. "Grace and Noah should be getting back any moment."

Grace sucked in a breath of air and looked at me with a stunned look on her face. "Holy shit, Gray and Meg?" I asked.

Grace made a funny face and said, "Well, I wasn't too far off with my whore comment."

Giving her a nudge, I attempted to keep my laughter in. Grace and I used to talk on the phone for hours and I learned a lot about her friends during those conversations. From what I gathered from Grace, Meagan was the more sexual friend in the bunch. But she'd also had a very rough time at college with being bullied.

"That's not even funny, Grace."

The loud knock on my bedroom door caused both Grace and I to let out a scream. The door pushed open and Grayson came charging in.

"Shh! What in the hell is wrong with you two?" Grayson said as he looked between us. "Y'all are not supposed to be here. You said you were going for a walk."

Grace smiled and said, "I'm kind of feeling a little bad for Meg if you only need that short of a time span to get it on, Gray."

Hiding my smile, I looked away as Grayson gave Grace the finger. "Go to hell, Grace."

"Hey! That's my girlfriend, asshole. And we were

coming back home to spend some time together."

Grayson's face busted out with a huge smile. "Ah, so I wasn't the only one hoping to get lucky."

Grace pushed Grayson on the chest. "Wait. You and Meg? How long? When did this happen? You better have worn a condom." Grace's faces turned white as a ghost. "Oh my God. That's twice I've heard Meg calling out to God while being—"

"Shut up, Grace. I don't need to hear about Meg's past sex life," Grayson said as he pushed his hand through his hair.

Grace sucked in a breath and pointed to Grayson. "You like her. Holy hell, you like Meg."

Grayson shook his head. "No I don't. She came on to me, said she wanted to have a good time, so we did. Listen, she doesn't want you to know we hooked up."

"Why?" Grace asked.

Shrugging his shoulders, Grayson said, "I don't know. She just said if I told either one of y'all she'd cut my balls off and something about hanging me from a rafter first."

Grace giggled and then put her finger up to her mouth. Grayson spun around. "Shit, she's coming back upstairs. You weren't here!"

Grabbing Grayson's arm, I pulled him to a stop. "But we are on our way back! No more screwing around. I'm never going to be able to erase what I heard. Ever!"

Rolling his eyes, Grayson pushed my hand away and headed out of my room and into the hall, but not before he slammed the bedroom door shut.

Grace and I took one look at each other and busted out laughing as quietly as we could.

"Should we sneak back out and then come back in?" Grace asked.

Nodding, I said, "Yeah, let's hurry before she leaves his room again."

Tiptoeing back down the hall and to the stairs, Grace

and I pretended to walk back into the house. As I shut the front door, Grace started laughing, loudly. Too loudly.

"Jesus, you were never in the drama club, were you?" I asked as Grace gave me the finger.

Tilting her head, she playfully ran her hand up and down her body. "If I remember correctly, Mr. Bennet. You were about to take me up to your room."

Walking up, I slid my hand behind Grace's neck as I pulled her lips to mine. Slamming my lips to hers, I slid my tongue in and moaned, as I tasted her.

"Ugh, do the two of you mind? I mean I'm happy you've got your mojo back and all, Noah, but seriously. We all don't need to hear you moaning." Meagan said as she walked past us.

Pulling my lips from Grace's we both laughed. If Meagan only knew.

"Take me upstairs, Noah."

Reaching down, I lifted Grace and walked up the stairs. "My pleasure, baby."

It didn't take long for either of us to strip out of our clothes. Grace sat on the bed and slid back as I crawled on after her.

"You're so fucking beautiful," I said as I moved my hand up her leg. Slipping my fingers inside her, Grace hissed as she threw her head back against the headboard.

"Oh God," she gasped as I worked my fingers in and out of her.

Kissing the inside of her thigh, I whispered against her soft skin, "I've missed you so much, baby."

Grace's hand went to my head as she grabbed and pulled at my hair. Smiling, I knew what she wanted and I was more than willing to give it to her.

Moving my lips closer to her, I pushed my thumb against her clit as she gasped and began to shake. It wouldn't take long for her to come.

Pulling my fingers away, I buried my face between her

legs and went to town on her pussy. I loved the way Grace's body responded to me. From the first touch, I knew we had something amazing together.

"Fucking hell!" Grace called out as she grabbed a pillow and screamed into it as her orgasm rolled through her body. Her hand pushed my head into her as she grinded her pussy into my face.

I had to fight like hell not to come. My dick was so hard and my balls pulled up so far I knew the moment I pushed into her I would come harder than I ever have before.

When her body finally settled down, I got up and pulled her down further on the bed. Before she could even respond, I pushed my dick into her and fucked her. I'd never been this rough with Grace before, but I could tell we both needed this right now. It had been far to long since the last time we made love.

"Yes!" Grace said as she dug her nails into my ass.

Pulling out and pushing back into her, I fought to hold off. "You like that baby?" I asked as I moved in and out of her body like I couldn't get enough of her.

Closing her eyes, Grace arched her back. "Harder. Noah, give it to me harder!"

Pulling out, I flipped Grace's body around as I fucked her from behind. I could go deeper this way and I knew Grace liked it from behind.

Burying her face into the bed, she called out my name as she squeezed around my dick, pulling out the most intense orgasm I'd ever had. It felt like I was going to come forever.

Pulling out of her, I collapsed next to her as I dragged in air. "Holy fucking shit."

Grace rolled over and placed her chin on my chest as she took in one deep breath after another. "We . . . forgot . . . again," she said as she lifted her lift eyebrow.

"Oh fuck. Condom."

"Honestly, Noah. I don't want to use them anymore. It

feels too good without them."

Looking into her eyes, I ran my finger along her cheek. "Are you sure? It's just more added protection."

Nodding her head, Grace blew me away with her smile as my heart began to beat harder in my chest. Her expression was beaming and there was a glow about her cheeks. One I wanted to see every single day.

"I've never been so sure of anything in my entire life, Noah."

Euphoria surrounded both of us in that moment. I walked back into this woman's life and turned it upside down, yet she stood by me through all it. It was my turn to do something for her.

It was time to do the one thing I've wanted to do since the first time I laid eyes on Grace.

Now all I needed to do was set the plan in motion.

Twenty-One

GRACE

THE LAST MONTH flew by as Alex and I finished up the details for the grand opening of Wild Flower. As I walked amongst the flowers, herbs, and garden decorations, I wanted to pinch myself. Our dream was about to come true.

"Is it crazy we're opening a nursery in the winter?" Alex asked from behind me. Turning around, my eyes landed on her eight-month pregnant belly.

"When have you ever known us to not do something crazy and out of the normal, Alex? Besides, spring isn't to far off and everyone is getting their spring gardens ready."

Laughing, she rested her hand on her stomach. "Are you nervous?" Alex asked as she bit down on her lower lip and wore a worried expression.

"Did Jesus walk on water?"

Alex rolled her eyes as she giggled. "Oh my gosh, Grace. It's February and the baby will be here next month.

Everyone is going to be getting their spring gardens going and I'll be dealing with a newborn baby. How are you going to do it?"

Walking up to Alex, I put my hands on the top of her arms and smiled. "Alex. Stop worrying. We've got Noah."

Shaking her head, Alex said, "He doesn't know shit about plants!"

Pressing my lips together, I held back my laugh. "But he knows about business, and he is handling all the back office shit that neither one of us was wanting to do. All we have to focus on is helping people dig in the dirt and have fun while Noah runs the business side of things."

Alex looked down and I couldn't help but notice the tears building in her eyes. Placing my finger on her chin, I pulled her eyes up to mine. "What's really going on, Alex?"

Seeing her chin tremble and tears roll down her face had my heart breaking for her. "I'm scared, Grace. What if I'm not a good mother? What if I can't manage to be a mom and work? What if I can't even birth this child?"

Narrowing my eyes, I said, "Well that last one certainly threw me for a loop. Alex, women have been pushing out babies for years. I don't think God is going to decide that you're going to be the first woman to not be able to deliver a child."

Letting out a nervous chuckle, Alex shook her head. "That's not what I meant. Oh gosh, I have no clue what I'm even saying. I'm just so afraid."

Taking Alex's hand, I led her over to a small wooden bench Will's father, Josh, made for the nursery. "Alex, have you talked to your mom? Or Heather, about how you're feeling?"

"God no, Grace! They are like super moms. If I tell them I'm scared, what will they think?"

Cocking my head, I lifted a single brow and said, "Jesus, Mary, and Joseph. Did you really just say that? Alex, I would bet this whole place that both your mother and Heather, and hell my mother too, freaked the hell out before they had us. Do you remember Amanda telling us that when she was pregnant with Meagan she ate this really spicy food and she started having what she thought were contractions? She said she was so afraid to tell Brad because she thought she had thrown herself into early labor!"

Alex laughed and nodded her head. "Yeah, turns out they were just Braxton Hicks contractions."

Taking Alex's hand in mine, I giggled. "Yes! I would imagine every mother is nervous no matter if this is their first or the fifth time giving birth."

Alex worried her lip. "I know. It's just I have this really weird feeling and I can't shake it."

"Listen, why don't you head on home and take it easy. I can take care of the little things that need to be done. Besides, I've got Noah and Luke here helping. Just go home, take a nice bath and relax, Alex."

Alex's eyes lit up. "Oh a nice warm bath to soak in would feel so good about right now."

Standing up, I helped my very pregnant best friend up into a standing position. "Then go take one."

"Promise you're okay with this?"

Tilting my head and sighing, I gave her a stern look. "Alex, you were here handling everything when I was helping Noah. Please. I've got this."

"Okay, I think I'm going to do what you say. I'm feeling so tired for some reason."

Leading Alex out back through the building, I glanced over to see Noah sitting behind the computer. He was setting up all the financial stuff for the nursery. Smiling, I couldn't help but notice how happy he looked.

Alex grabbed her purse from the countertop and gave me the sweetest smile ever. "Thanks, Grace. I love you."

Giving Alex a hug, I whispered in her ear, "By the way, you look beautiful."

Alex pulled back and blushed has she brushed me off

with her hand. "Oh stop!"

Letting out a chortle, I said, "Want me to walk you to your car?"

Alex shook her head, "Nah, I'll call you later to see how everything went today."

"Sounds good. Love you."

Alex called out over her shoulder, "Love you back. Bye, Noah!"

Turning to Noah, he looked up as he lifted his hand, "Later, Alex!"

Letting out a deep sigh, I walked over to Noah as he pushed his chair back. "What's going on? Is Alex okay?"

Sitting on his lap, I wrapped my arms around Noah's neck. I was so proud of Noah and how well he was doing with his recovery. I knew he missed his sister but knowing Emily was happy made Noah happy. "I think so. She's started to get nervous about things, but I think she'll be okay."

Noah's hand rubbed on the inside of my thigh and my lower stomach instantly craved for more.

"Is she nervous about the opening?" Noah asked as his lips moved ever so softly across my neck.

"Um . . . I don't . . . think . . . that's . . . it," I said as I exposed more of my neck to him.

My body was on fire as Noah's hand moved up and under my shirt. "What is she nervous about then?"

My mind was spinning and I was silently begging Noah to take me right then and there. Never mind the fact that my father and Luke would be showing up any minute to help with the last bit of things to check off our list before we opened.

"W-what are we talking about?" I panted out.

Noah's lips moved over to my ear where he gently bit down on my earlobe and then sucked on it before whispering, "Alex, you said she was nervous."

Can't take much more.

Moving quickly, I straddled Noah and grinded against his hard dick. The friction of his jeans against mine was adding fuel to the fire.

"Noah," I begged as I pushed harder against him. "Take me now, please."

Noah's hands grabbed my ass as his mouth took mine in a frenzied kiss. "Your dad is on his way, baby. We can't."

Pressing my hands against his chest, I pushed back and looked into his eyes. Those dreamy light-brown eyes of his. "Yes! Yes we can. Just be quick about it."

Noah threw his head back and laughed.

"Noah, I'm being serious."

Looking back at me, Noah lifted me off the chair and stood up as he adjusted his dick. "I know you are. That's what's so funny, Grace. The last thing I'd ever want to happen is for your dad to walk in here while we were—"

The front door to the nursery opened and my father and Luke walked in. "While you were what?" Daddy asked as he made his way over to us. I knew my face was still flushed from our little make-out session and I quickly tried to appear normal. Glancing over to Luke, he wore a huge smile and shook his head slightly as he spoke under his breath, "Been there done that."

Giving him an evil eye, I turned to my father. "Hey, there is so much to do. Let me grab the list and we can get to it."

My father looked at me and then turned to Noah. "Why are you breathing like that?"

Noah's eyes widened as he said, "Um . . . w-what? I mean, excuse me sir? Ah, breathing heavy?"

Narrowing his eyes at Noah, Luke walked up and hit Noah on the back and said, "Dude, you just fucked up."

Taking a step closer to Noah, my father got his face so close to Noah's I was almost positive I heard Noah whimper. "I didn't say you were breathing hard. Why would you pick that word to describe your breathing?"

Noah swallowed hard. "I um, I was just you know." Noah looked at me and I shook my head.

What was he doing? What. In. The. Hell. Was. He. Doing?

"No, I don't know. Enlighten me, Noah."

Pointing to me, Noah yelled out, "It was Grace's fault. She started kissing me and then sat on my lap and started doing this thing . . . but I stopped her! I said you were um . . . on your way and we couldn't!"

Dropping my mouth open, I gave Noah an incredulous stare. Turning to look at Luke, I noticed he was sitting in the chair laughing his ass off.

Jerking my head back toward Noah and my father, I walked up to them and pushed Daddy away as I turned to Noah. "My fault? Did you seriously just say it was my fault?"

Leaning over and looking past me to my father, Noah said, "See. Sir, she can be demanding."

"Jesus H. Christ. You're selling me out to my own father, you pansy ass!"

Leaning closer to me, Noah said, "Baby, you don't understand, I need him on my side. He knows people who know people."

Sucking in a breath, I stepped back and placed my hands on my hips as I glared at Noah. "Is that so?"

Noah nodded his head and gave me a weak smile. Turning around, I gave my father a once over. He had a satisfied smirk on his face. "Oh, you . . . you just wipe that smile off your face, dear old Dad. Yes. I asked Noah for sex."

My father's smile dropped as his eyes widened. "But don't worry, Dad. That little stunt Noah just pulled guarantees no sex from me for a very long time."

"What?" my father and Noah both asked in stunned voices as Luke let out another round of roaring laughter. "Shit, this is the best thing I've seen in months!" Luke said as he crossed his arms over his chest.

Looking between Noah and my father, I rolled my eyes and stomped off to the back office where I slammed the door and made my way over to my desk. Plopping on my desk chair, I let out a scream loud enough for the whole county of Mason to hear.

Ugh. Men.

Twenty-Two

NOAH

LEANING BACK IN the rocking chair, I took a drink from my bottle of water. I loved being out here in Mason. The fresh air cleared my head and the peacefulness calmed my nerves. There were still days I wanted to take a pill, but they were less and less. With Grace by my side each night, I was sleeping the best I had in years. The anxiety was still there, especially when I thought of my mother. Or the future I was planning with Grace. I never wanted to let her down.

Glancing over to Jeff, I watched as he stared out over the countryside. "It's beautiful here. I swear I could sit here for hours and be happy."

Jeff nodded his head and smiled. "There is not a place on Earth like the view off this back porch."

Nodding my head in agreement, we sat in silence another five minutes or so. "Are you going to ask me Noah, or not?"

My throat constricted as I fought to find the words to speak. I rubbed the palms of my hands on my pant legs and pulled up the speech I'd been practicing in my mind.

"Um . . . yes, sir." Turning my body toward Grace's father more, I gave him a weak smile as he stared blankly at me. Holy shit. He looked like he was ready to chew me up and spit me out.

"The reason I asked to speak with you alone sir is because I'd like to ask for Grace's hand in marriage. I love her very much and I'll spend the rest of my life doing whatever I have to do to make sure she is happy."

Lifting his eyebrows, he stared into my eyes. I'd never been so unsure of myself in my entire life. *Would he think I was good enough for her? Did he believe me when I said I would do anything to make her happy?*

"Marriage huh?"

My eyes widened as I felt a panic attack starting to build. "Shit. I wasn't planning on you saying that. It wasn't part of my planned speech."

Narrowing his left eye at me, I closed my eyes. *I can't believe I just said that.*

"Noah, open your eyes for Christ's sake."

Snapping my eyes open, I attempted to get spit into my bone-dry mouth. "I didn't mean to say that out loud and well this is not how this is supposed to go." Shaking my head, I let out a frustrated sigh.

Jeff let out a laugh as he stood up. "Walk with me, Noah."

Doing as he said, I quickly jumped up and followed him toward the barn. Once we walked inside, I smiled as all the horses popped their heads out one by one to see who had walked in.

"Tell me why you want to marry my daughter."

Oh this was easy.

Grinning like a fool, I walked up to a bay horse and ran my hand along his neck. "Why do I want to marry Grace?"

Letting out a small chuckle, I pictured all the crazy things Grace has done and said since I've met her. The time she tied me up to the bedpost at my apartment in College Station and left me there after she got pissed when I accidentally called her another girls name when I asked her what kind of pizza she wanted.

Then there was the time she called me a cocksucking, dirty rotten, pussyfaced, bastard when I tickled her so much she peed her pants. I'd never known anyone to string curse words together like Grace.

"I want to marry, Grace because I love her like I've never loved anyone in my life. She makes me laugh and sometimes she gets me so frustrated. Her smile—" Closing my eyes, I grinned from ear to ear before opening my eyes and looking at the beautiful horse in front of me. "Grace was there for me during the darkest time of my life. The love she has for me pulled me out and saved me." Shaking my head, I let out another soft chuckle. "God her smile makes my stomach flip and my knees weak just as much as they did the first time she looked at me. If I was lucky enough to wake up every morning to her beautiful face, I'd count myself the luckiest bastard in the world. If I had to live without her, it would be like living with no air.

Glancing away from the horse, I looked over to Jeff. He was sitting on a hay bale with a stunned look on his face. Finally, he frowned and said, "Did you fucking talk to Gunner before you talked to me?"

Letting out a nervous chuckle, I said, "Um, no, sir, I didn't speak with Gunner first."

Shaking his head, Jeff appeared to be deep in thought. Letting out a quick breath, he slapped his hands on his legs and stood up. "Damn boy, I gotta tell ya, that hit me right here." Placing his hand over his heart, Jeff nodded. "Where in the hell were you when I asked Ari's dad if I could marry her."

Tilting my head, I gave Jeff an amused look. "Not even

thought of yet, sir."

"No, I guess you weren't." Jeff walked into the feed room and grabbed some oats and walked back out to give them to the horse I had been giving attention to.

"This is Jack. Jack is probably the meanest mother-fucking horse we have on the ranch and son you walked right up to him and started touching him. Now, I let you do it because two things could have happened. One, he'd have bitten the shit out of you, or two, he'd let you touch him. He's only let two other people touch him that I know of."

Looking back at Jack, I smiled as he bopped his head up and down. "Who's that?"

Jeff gave Jack the oats and then gave him a good hard pat on the neck before he turned around and said, "Me and Grace."

Offering up a bemused smile, I said, "No kidding."

Jeff smiled and said, "No kidding. You can thank Jack for the answer you're about to get."

My smile faded and was replaced by a look of confusion? "O-okay."

Placing his hand on my shoulder, Jeff gave it a slight squeeze. "Yes, you have mine and Ari's blessings to ask Grace to marry you."

A feeling of relief washed over my body as I let out a sigh of relief. Reaching my hand out for Jeff's, I said, "Thank you so much sir. I promise you, I'll love her till the day I die."

Jeff's eyes appeared to glass over as he looked away and said, "You'll never love her like I love her. Never."

With that, Jeff started walking out of the barn. Jack started nickering as he bopped his head like he was also pleased with Jeff's permission.

Wait. Did he really base his decision on if the damn horse liked me or not? Quickly turning, I jogged out of the barn and up to Jeff.

"Um, Mr. Johnson?"

"Call me Jeff, Noah. You're going to be my son-in-law. We can be on first names."

Agreeing with a quick nod, I asked, "Sir, did you really base your answer to me on whether or not Jack liked me?"

Jeff stopped walking and looked me straight in the eye. Then he busted out laughing and headed into the house as I stood there not really knowing what to do.

Looking all around, I glanced back and watched as Jeff disappeared into the house. "What in the fuck just happened?"

GRACE WAS STANDING at the kitchen sink helping her mother wash dishes while Jeff and I played a card game with Matt. It threw me every time Matt called me an assmole.

"Noah, it's your turn to go fish," Matt said with a smile.

Returning the smile, I said, "Wow! My turn already?"

Matt rolled his eyes and laughed. "Noah, you're an assmole."

Ari called over her shoulder and said, "Matt, you know that's not a nice word."

Jeff cleared his throat and said, "Yeah, you also know that only Josh gets called assmole 'cause he is one."

Matt chuckled and agreed with Jeff. "Yes. Josh is an assmole. But he made me a cabinet for my paintings. I love, Josh."

Oh gosh. Either I was truly turning into a pansy ass or I was falling hard for Matt. He may have been in his late thirties, but he still acted so young at heart. I knew it was from the Fragile X. His heart was so pure and good. He loved making people laugh too and he knew he did it by using the word assmole.

"Matt, do you think you could paint me a picture?" I

asked.

Matt's eyes lit up and he jumped up. "Yes, Noah. I can paint you a picture. What of?"

Giving him a wink, I asked, "Can it be a secret?"

From the corner of my eye, I saw Grace turn and look at me. I could feel the love pouring off her body and I knew if I turned to look at her she would be smiling.

"A secret? I'm good at keeping secrets. Ask Jeff. I keep lots of his secrets. Like the one of him backing Ari's car into the fence post."

Ari spun around and said, "I knew it! I knew that wasn't me who put that dent in the back of my car."

Jeff held up his hands as he laughed. Ari walked up to Jeff and snapped his leg with the dishtowel. "You dirty rotten, son-of-a-bitch, bastard, asshole!"

"Assmole, Jeff!" Matt called out.

"Yes! He is an assmole, Matt. The biggest one of them all. How could you make me think I did that, Jeff?"

Tears were running down Jeff's face as he held onto his stomach. I couldn't help but laugh, especially with Matt now repeating what Ari had called him.

"Jeff is a dirty rotten, son-of-a-bitch, bastard assmole!"

Grace covered her mouth in a poor attempt at hiding her laughter.

Jeff finally stood and pulled Ari into his arms as she wrapped her legs around him. "You are so lucky I love you as much as I do," she said before she kissed him hard.

Jeff walked over and set Ari on the counter and placed his hands on the sides of her face. "I am lucky. And I love you too, Ari."

Ari leaned over and kissed Jeff. You couldn't help but feel the love from both of them.

Finally breaking their kiss, Ari peeked over at me and winked as I gave her a smile. Jeff helped her off the counter and hit her ass as she walked back to the kitchen sink. Grace's cheeks were red, but she didn't say a word to her parents. How could you say anything negative when you just witnessed two people so madly in love? I never saw my parents act like that with each other. Not one single time. My father was never intimate toward my mother, at least not around Emily and me.

My eyes landed on Grace's as they sparkled and I knew she was thinking the same thing I was. What just happened in this kitchen between her parents is what I wanted our future to be like. To be able to show her how much I loved her at any given moment was something I longed for.

It was something I dreamed of.

My plan was to ask Grace to marry me after the grand opening of her and Alex's nursery. But the moment was now. I wanted her parents to witness the love that Grace and I shared together. I reached into my pocket and pulled the blue velvet pouch out I'd been carrying with me since we got to Mason.

Grace's mom said something to Grace that caused her to laugh. Her laughter rushed through my veins like fire rushing through an opened pasture. Walking up to Grace, I put my hand on her arm and turned her to me. Her smile was beyond anything I'd ever seen. Maybe it was the moment, or maybe it was just her smile. I didn't know and I didn't care. All I knew was that she was smiling at me exactly how Ari was smiling at Jeff less than two minutes ago.

"Grace," I whispered as I dropped to one knee. Slamming her hands over her mouth, Ari quickly turned around and let out a gasp.

"Grace Hope Johnson, I love you so very much. Would you do me the honor of becoming my wife and letting me love you every day . . . for the rest of our days?"

Tears fell freely from Grace's eyes as she dropped to the floor in front of me and pressed her lips together as she nodded and then finally whispered, "Yes. Yes, yes, yes!"

Throwing her body into mine, our lips crashed together. This was probably one of the most amazing moments of my life.

Finally pulling our lips apart, Grace looked into my eyes and said, "You totally just won so many points from my father. You do know that right?"

The room erupted in laughter as I pulled the emerald cut diamond that once belonged to my mother, from the pouch. I'd had the main diamond that was in my mother's engagement ring, which was originally my great-grandmothers ring, pulled out of her setting and made a new setting for Grace. Two rose-colored diamonds sat on either side of the main diamond followed by smaller diamonds that ran down each side of the platinum band.

Grace sucked in a breath as I slipped the ring on her finger. "This engagement diamond was worn by my great-grandmother, my grandmother, and my mother." Grace's eyes fell to the diamond as she wiped a tear away.

"Oh, Noah. This makes it all the more special."

Wrapping her arms around my neck, Grace held onto me so tightly I was afraid she was going to choke me.

"All right, all right. Get up off the floor and let me give my baby girl a hug," Jeff said as Grace and I both stood up. Grace ran into her father's arms as Ari hugged me and gave me a soft kiss on the cheek.

"Well done, sweetheart."

"Thank you," I said with a wink.

Grace hugged her mother as I held my hand out to shake Jeff's. Shaking my hand, he laughed and pulled me in for a bear hug. Stepping back some he said, "You do realize what you're getting yourself into. She's just like her mother."

"Oh stop it," Ari said as Matt came rushing back into the kitchen. With everything that had just happened, I wasn't even sure when he left.

"Oh. Everyone is so happy! Noah, come tell me your

secret. I have my room ready. I'll start your painting today!"

Grace giggled and motioned for me to go. Following Matt, we went into the guest bedroom that was downstairs. Matt often stayed with Jeff and Ari so they converted the guest bedroom for Matt to stay there. Jeff had even built on an addition to give Matt a small studio to paint in.

There was a blank canvas already set up and Matt sat in front of it as he stared at it. We must have stood there a good three minutes before he turned and gave me a funny look.

"Well? Are you just going to stand there and be an assmole or are you going to tell me what you want me to paint."

"Oh!" I said with a soft chuckle. Here I thought Matt was getting into the zone and all he was really doing is waiting on me to tell him what to paint.

"Matt, do you think you could paint me a picture of Grace?"

Matt grinned from ear to ear. "Oh I love painting, Grace. I'll paint her like how I just saw her. She seemed to be very happy. I like a happy Grace. Not a sad Grace."

Feeling my heart drop, I nodded. "I like a happy Grace too, Matt."

Matt picked up his brush and said, "Okay bye, assmole."

"Oh, um, okay. See ya later, Matt."

Stepping out of the bedroom, I turned and headed back to the kitchen. Ari and Jeff were sitting at the table talking. When I walked in, they both stopped talking and stared at me. Giving them an awkward smile, I said, "Matt really is something."

Ari's smile grew bigger. "He really is. Thank you for asking him to do a painting for you. He loves to paint. It calms him."

Rubbing my sweaty palms on my jeans, I said, "It's my pleasure. He's ah . . . he's painting a picture of Grace for me."

Jeff nodded his head and said, "Are you sure you haven't talked to Gunner?"

Looking at Jeff with an inquisitive look, I shook my head. "No, sir, I haven't. Why?"

Ari hit Jeff playfully on the chest as she looked back at me. "Pay no attention to him, Noah. Grace told us to tell you she'll be in the barn."

Slapping my hands together, I said, "Great. Okay, well I'll just go track her down."

Heading toward the back door, Jeff called out for me. Stopping, I turned back at them both. "Thank you, Noah. Thank you for sharing that moment with us."

I gave a quick nod and barely said, "Thank you for inspiring it."

Reaching back for the doorknob, I quickly pulled it open and rushed outside as I dragged in a few deep breaths.

Holy shit. My emotions were all over the fucking place tonight. Looking up, I smiled. "Mom, I hope I made you proud tonight."

Before I looked back at the barn, a shooting star raced across the sky. Smiling, I knew my mother hadn't missed this moment. She had been right there with me the entire time.

Twenty-Three

GRACE

"THANK YOU SO much for stopping by Wild Flower," Alex said as she rested her hand over her belly.

The older lady smiled as she held up two birdfeeders she had bought. "Oh, I'll be back. Don't you worry that pretty little head of yours!"

Alex and I both let out a giggle and walked the older woman to the door. Shutting the door, I quickly locked it as Alex leaned against it.

Following her lead, I leaned against the door as we both turned and looked at each other. I was almost positive my smile matched Alex's. My heart was still racing with the idea that we owned our own nursery. "That was amazing."

Alex nodded her head as tears built up in her eyes. "We did it, Grace. We followed our dreams."

I pushed off the door and began jumping as Alex started laughing. Coming to a stop, my eyes landed on my best friend's pregnant stomach.

Placing my hand on her belly, I bit on my lip to control my emotions. "Yes we did, Alex."

"This day couldn't get any better!" Alex said as we both hugged each other. Turning and looking at Will, Alex made her way over to him with a skip in her step. Wrapping her up in his arms, Will whispered something into her ear and then kissed her. My eyes moved across the room until they found those amazing caramel eyes that caused my heart to skip a beat every time I looked into them.

Noah gave me a quick wink before he focused back on what Colt and Luke were talking to him about. I couldn't help but smile at the whole picture.

Walking over to the open sign, I turned it off and made my way over to Noah. I could hear Colt and Luke trying to talk Noah into stopping by Scott's ranch and talking to him about a new software that tracked income and expenses.

Colt almost seemed to be pleading. "Noah, I'm telling you, Scott would really be interested in talking to you."

Holding up his hands, Noah said, "Guys, I'm focusing on helping the girls run this business. Maybe once we get things up and running, we can talk about me . . . expanding."

Luke pushed Colt out of the way and asked, "What about the stock market today? Thoughts?"

Noah and I both laughed. "It seems like you boys don't know when to leave my man alone."

Luke rolled his eyes at me. "Please, you get him all the time, Grace. I need investment advice. I have a child to put through college. Stow your horny self in a corner or something?"

Dropping my mouth open, I punched Luke in the chest as he screamed out, "Ouch!"

"Fuck you, Luke! I'll show you where you can stow your—"

Will stepped in-between us as Colt and Noah busted out laughing. "Break it up. Come on y'all. We just had an amazing grand opening. Now let's go meet everyone else for dinner."

Pointing to Luke, I said, "This isn't over, vagina face!"

Luke placed his hands over his chest and said, "Oh, Oh . . . that hurt! Not! Is that all you got, dick dancer?"

Frowning, I shook my head in disbelief. "Stupid ass, Meg's the dick dancer." Looking to the right like he was thinking, Luke nodded in agreement. "Shit, that's right."

"Oh my God, y'all, will you please stop it. I'm starving, so can we please head out? We still have to drive to Fredericksburg," Alex said as she grabbed her purse and headed to the front door.

"My baby and I need food, and I'm not afraid to bust someone's nuts if I have to wait much longer."

Placing my hand over my heart, I smiled and said, "See. That's the Alex I love and adore."

Colt laughed and jogged over to the front door. "I'm here! I'm here. Gesh, I should have rode with Lauren and her parents."

Will unlocked the door and held it open for Alex and Colt. "Lock it after we walk out. Don't forget to set the alarm to away, Grace."

Pushing him out the door, I said, "Yes, Mom."

The door shut and I locked it.

A few minutes later, Noah, Luke, and I were following Will, Alex, and Colt to Cabernet Grill. As we drove, we talked about how amazing the first day of Wild Flower's grand opening was.

"I'm thinking once the word really gets out, business will pick up even more. Everyone is going to want to start getting their spring gardens going."

"I still can't believe my little sister is a business owner," Luke said as I glanced at him in the backseat.

Grinning like a fool, I said, "I know! Me either!"

Turning back, I looked over at Noah and noticed he was frowning. "What's wrong?"

Noah slowly shook his head. "Will's swerving all over

the place."

Looking out the front window, my mouth dropped open. "What's he doing?" Pulling out my phone, I called Alex's cell phone but she didn't answer.

"She's not answering," I said as fear engulfed my whole body.

"I'm calling Colt right now to see what's going on," Luke said from the backseat. "Colt, what in the hell is Will doing? He's going to wreck with the way he's driving!"

My heart rate must have increased a hundred percent. Something was wrong. Something was very wrong.

"What? Are you sure?"

I turned to face Luke. "What's wrong?" I asked.

Holding up his finger, Luke kept talking to Colt. "Have Will pull the fuck over so you can drive. Get Alex into the back seat." Luke looked at me and said, "Grace, call Dr. Johnson's office. Tell them we're on our way to the hospital. Alex's water just broke."

Staring at Luke, I tried to let his words process as Noah pulled over on the side of the road behind Will's truck.

"Grace!" Luke shouted. "Did you hear me?"

Nodding my head, I looked up the number and called the after hours emergency line.

My vision became blurry as I watched Will and Colt help Alex into the back of the truck. She looked over and gave me a weak smile as I tried to smile back. "It's okay, Alex," I whispered.

"Dr. Johnson's after hours line. How may I help you?"

"Um . . . yes . . . my name is Grace Johnson, Alex Hayes is my cousin. She's in the truck in front of us and her water just broke." Wiping my tears away, I waited for them to tell us what to do.

"When is her due date?"

A small sob escaped from my mouth as I said, "She's not due for another month. March seventeenth."

"I'll page Dr. Johnson right now. Take her to the

emergency room. They'll know to expect her. Just keep her calm and let her know everything is going to be okay."

"O-O-Okay . . . I'll tell them," I said as I watched Colt pull back out onto the highway and take off toward Fredericksburg.

Turning to Luke, I said, "Tell them the doctors been paged and to go straight to the emergency room. They also said to keep Alex calm and to tell her . . . to tell her . . ."

Luke's eyes widened as he shouted, "Tell her what, Grace?"

Attempting to keep myself from crying out of sheer fear, I fought to talk, "That everything is going to be okay."

Luke's face pained as he repeated everything I told him to Colt.

Noah took my hand and kissed the back of it as he concentrated on driving. "How can they say that?"

Noah glanced quickly at me and asked, "Say what?"

Shaking my head, I stared back at Will's truck. Trying to imagine how scared Alex was. If I knew her, she was blaming herself and saying it must have been something she did.

"How can they say it's going to be okay? They don't know if it's going to be okay? They have no damn clue if Alex or the baby is going to be okay."

Noah squeezed my hand gently as he spoke softly. "Grace, I know you're scared right now baby, but trust me, babies are born prematurely all the time. Let's just take a deep breath, say some prayers and be there for Will and Alex."

Slowly nodding my head, I said, "Okay."

A few seconds of silence passed by before Luke said, "Shit. I better call Gunner and Ellie."

"I'll call Mom and Dad, even though I'm sure they're all together."

My father's phone went to voicemail which wasn't surprising and my mother's only rang twice when she answered in a panicked voice. "Grace! What's happening? Gunner is talking to Luke and Ellie is freaking out."

"Mom, calm down. Alex's water broke."

I could hear my mother put her hand over the phone and said, "Alex's water broke."

"Mom, Colt is driving her and Will to the emergency room, and Alex's doctor is meeting them there."

I could hear Gunner and my mother say at the same time, "The emergency room."

Turning around, I looked at Luke. He was staring straight ahead as he talked to Gunner. "Okay, you'll be there before us. The doctor's office said we needed to keep Alex calm."

Luke nodded his head at something Gunner told him. "Yes, sir. We will. Bye."

"Gunner told us to be careful and make sure Colt doesn't speed. Josh and Heather weren't at the restaurant yet, so Gunner asked if we would call them."

After calling Josh and Heather and telling them everything I told my mother, we drove in silence. I knew each of us was saying our own silent prayers. Covering my mouth, I cried. Noah placed his hand on my shoulder and I knew he was feeling helpless. Just like I was.

"The other day Alex told me she had a weird feeling something was wrong. I brushed it off to nerves. What if something was wrong and I'm the reason she ignored it?"

"That's crazy, Grace. Don't sit here and blame yourself. Let's get to the hospital and see what's going on before we start thinking the worse."

"Luke is right, Grace. Baby, just take in some deeps breaths. We're almost there.

Leaning my head back against the headrest, I prayed harder than I ever have before for Alex and the baby.

Please let her and the baby be all right. Please.

Twenty-Four

GRACE

MY EYES ROAMED the waiting room as I took everyone in. Most of everyone was sitting in silence as we waited for news on Alex and the baby.

Noah walked up and handed me a cup of hot chocolate. I wasn't in the mood for coffee so he went on a search to find me something hot to drink.

"Thank you, babe," I said while my shaking hands took the hot chocolate as Noah kissed me gently on the forehead before sitting next to me. The nurse had already come out and talked to all of us. She said Alex's water did indeed break, but she wasn't going into labor, which was not good. They were going to have to do an emergency C-section. I could see the fear in everyone's eyes as I looked around. Ellie, Gunner, Josh, and Heather were all in another waiting room right outside where they were performing the C-section. My heart broke as I watched Grams and Gramps across the waiting room as they held each other's hands and waited.

Their main concern was the strength of the baby's lungs. Closing my eyes, I leaned my head on Noah's shoulder.

"How many kids do you want?" I asked.

Noah kissed my head and said, "How ever many you want."

"Two. I kind of liked having Luke around. He came in handy when I needed him."

Noah's body rocked me gently as he chuckled. "Yeah, I liked having Em around too. Especially when I needed her to taste something new my mother had cooked."

Smiling, I peeked up at Noah. "That's mean."

Shrugging his shoulders, Noah said, "That's life. She learned quickly not to be such a push over."

I let out a soft chuckle as I looked back over at Grams and Gramps. They both looked so worried. "Can you believe they're waiting for their great-great-grandchild to be born? Can you even imagine?"

Noah's fingers glided across my arm softly as he said, "No, I can't imagine how that must feel."

"The things those two must have seen in their day. How awesome is that?"

Noah pulled my body closer to his. "Colt was telling me about his Grams and Gramps. He said he'd never seen two people so in love after so many years together."

"I think that's what keeps them going so strong. Their love for each other. I would dare to say that when they do pass on . . . they'll probably go together. I couldn't imagine either one of them being happy without the other."

Noah took his finger and placed it on my chin as he brought my lips to his. "That's a forever love."

Whispering, I smiled and said, "Yes it is."

Hearing Taylor let out a gasp, I looked over toward the doors and saw Gunner standing there. Tears were streaming down his face as we all slowly stood up.

"No. Please, God no," I said as I leaned my body into

Noah's.

Smiling a smile so big and bright, Gunner held up his hand as if he was asking for a moment. Ellie came walking out behind him, followed by Josh and Heather.

Heather took a step forward and said, "Bayli Elizabeth Hayes was born about fifteen minutes ago."

Crying, I turned to Noah who held me tightly while Heather kept talking.

"She weighs four pounds one ounce and is seventeen inches long."

Everyone erupted in cheers as they hugged the new grandparents.

Walking up to Ellie, I wiped my tears away as I said, "Ellie, is Alex okay?"

Taking me in her arms, Ellie cried as she said, "Yes! Oh sweetheart, Alex is doing amazing. Will is a little emotional, but I think he is okay." Pulling back some, Ellie pushed a strand of my hair behind my ear. "Bayli is in NICU, but Dr. Johnson thinks she'll only be in there for a few days. The main thing is making sure she can breathe on her own and suck so she can eat."

Closing my eyes, I thanked God for the answered prayers. Opening my eyes, I turned to Gunner as he held me close to him. I stood back and looked between the happy grandparents.

"Um . . . did they say what caused her water to break?"

Ellie shook her head. "It's really hard to say. It was nothing Alex did. Stress might have led to it, but they aren't sure. Sometimes these things just happen. Thankfully though, both Alex and Bayli are doing wonderfully."

Noah wrapped his arm around my waist and said, "Looks like Bayli wanted to make today's grand opening . . . grander!"

Everyone laughed and agreed as the mood in the waiting room shifted and sniffles were replaced with laughter.

"ALEX STOOD OUTSIDE the store front window of Wild Flowers and stared as she rocked Bayli back and forth in her arms.

Rolling my eyes, I said, "Jesus H. Christ, Alex. Bayli's going to be ten by the time you decide if you like the display window or not!"

Alex giggled and handed me her four-month-old baby who had been sleeping in her arms. "Here, take Bayli and let me go change one thing. I want to see if moving that vase to the other side will balance the display more."

Alex rushed back into the store and moved not only the vase, but at least ten other items as well.

Sighing, I walked with Bayli over to the small bench that sat outside our nursery. Sitting, I hummed as Bayli stretched and opened her eyes. Her big, beautiful blue eyes met mine and my heart melted on the spot. Just like it did every time I looked into her eyes.

"Hey, baby girl. Are you awake now that you're not in Mommy's arms?"

Bayli gave me a small smile and closed her eyes again as she quickly drifted back to sleep. Will said his daughter was sharp and I believed it. Even in her sleep, she knew something was different. She wasn't in her momma's arms, so she woke up to check it out.

I began humming again while I slowly rocked back and forth as I studied Bayli's precious face.

I want one.

Wait. What?

Closing my eyes, I shook my head to clear my crazy thoughts. *I can't have a baby! What in the hell am I thinking? I'm getting married in two weeks, I'm part owner of a successful business; I don't have time for a baby.*

Glancing back at the window, I watched as Alex stood in front of the window and looked at all her changes.

Alex does it. Why couldn't I?

No. No stop this Grace.

There will be no babies. No baby making with Noah. Who was really good at what we would need to do to make babies.

Really good. Really . . . *really* good.

I wonder if she'd have green eyes or brown? She'd have brown hair for sure. And my chin and nose. Oh lord, I hope she got Noah's eyebrows and eyelashes because I'd kill to have both. They are perfect.

Smiling, I glanced back at Bayli. *What if I had a boy?* He for sure would have his father's handsome as hell good looks. I bet he'd be just like his daddy.

"Whatcha thinking about, Grace?" Alex asked as she sat next to me, pulling me out of my wonderful daydream.

"Nothing."

"Uh-huh. Cause that goofy, happy look on your face as you gazed at my daughter was a look of nothing."

Handing Bayli back to Alex, I stood up and laughed. "I have no idea what you're talking about. Listen, I need to go in and start thinking about flower designs for the wedding."

Alex pinched her eyebrows together and said, "Whose wedding?"

"Mine of course! You know, the wedding I'm planning that's in two weeks."

Alex stood up and winked at me. "We already planned them out, remember?"

Oh yeah. We did already plan them out.

"We did?" I asked even though I remembered we had done it yesterday.

"Yep. Yesterday to be exact."

Rubbing my hands together, I said, "Well, I need to call the caterer and make sure she is on track."

"It's Jessie. She's on track and I know for a fact because Colt told me his mother-in-law was the most organized person on the planet."

"Hmm . . . well . . . Oh I know! I need to call about Noah's tux."

Alex walked ahead of me as she said, "Done."

"The rest of the guys' tuxes?"

Glancing back over her shoulder, Alex smirked. "Done. Your dress is hanging up in your mother's closet ready for the big day. Your dad has been warned not to threaten Noah's life, and Luke has been told if he tries one prank, Libby will withhold sex for two months. The chairs for the wedding are ordered and set to arrive the day before. I've got all the guys on chair and table duty." My mouth dropped open and before I could even say anything, Alex opened the front door of our store and headed toward the back offices and to Bayli's room.

"Meagan flies in two days before the wedding after she made it clear she was not to be on the same flight as Noah's cousin Grayson, who I still can't believe was the stripper that Lauren snagged his number from." Setting Bayli gently in her crib, Alex turned and walked out of the room, shutting the door quietly. "Oh, speaking of, Grayson will be flying home two days before the wedding, on the same flight as Meg but we've kept that little bit information from her."

Alex grabbed a birdfeeder and turned and put it on one of the displays as she continued talking. "The cakes have been triple-confirmed and will be delivered four hours before the wedding."

Stopping in front of me, Alex grinned from ear to ear. "You see. Everything is taken care of and on schedule. So, now will you tell me what you were really thinking about outside."

Feeling my stomach drop, I was about to tell Alex when the bell rang on the front door and Noah and Will walked in. Both of them were covered in sweat with their T-shirts plastered to their chest. My eyes landed on Noah's perfectly chiseled chest as my libido kicked into overdrive.

"Holy hell," I whispered.

"Lord, please let Bayli nap extra long today," Alex said next to me.

Turning my head to look at Alex, I gave her a shocked expression. Alex waved me off. "Please, don't even look at me like that. I've been dying to break in my office furniture."

Slamming my hands over my ears, I said, "Ew! I didn't need that visual, you bitch!"

Will walked up to Alex and kissed her as she grabbed him by the shirt and said, "I need to talk to you alone in my office."

Will glanced at Noah and wiggled his eyebrows as Noah laughed and called out, "Have fun kids!"

Watching Alex and Will walk toward the back, I quickly turned back and let my eyes take in the handsome man standing in front of me.

His brown hair was wet and a mess on top of his head. His caramel eyes danced with a desire that had my body literally aching to feel him inside of me. His perfectly plump lips demanded to be kissed by mine.

"Baby, if you keep looking at me like that, I'm going to bend you over the counter and fuck you hard and fast."

A soft low moan escaped my lips as I quickly reached behind the counter and grabbed my purse. "We really need to get you home, so you can shower," I said as I walked past Noah and locked the front door. Turning off the open sign, I placed the out to lunch sign in the door and grabbed Noah's hand as I led him to the back door and to his truck.

Once we moved to Mason, Noah decided he needed a truck. He traded his Nissan sports car in for a Chevy truck. I'd never seen anyone as excited as he was when he drove it home for the first time. We barely made it into

Mason County before Noah pulled down a dirt road and parked. Claiming we needed to break the truck in ASAP, he climbed into the bed of his truck and dragged me with him. We quickly got lost in each other and stayed in that field for three hours. Talking, making love, and talking some more. It had been the perfect way to celebrate our moving to Mason.

"Grace, you're not even going to tell Alex you're leaving?"

"Nope," I said as I opened the driver's side door and pushed Noah in. "I need to be with you. Now."

Noah licked his lips as he quickly motioned for me to get in the truck. Running around the front, I climbed in and quickly unbuttoned his jeans.

"Grace, baby I've been working in the field loading hay bales. The sweat on my balls has sweat on it."

"Don't care," I said as I quickly found what I was looking for. "Drive Noah."

"How in the hell do you expect me to . . . holy fuck!"

Wrapping my lips around his dick, I began sucking. Noah's hand went to my head where he grabbed a handful of hair and guided my head to the motion he wanted. "Mother of God, that feels amazing," Noah hissed between gritted teeth.

Pulling my lips off of him, I looked at him and said, "Drive. Noah."

Putting the truck into reverse, Noah, backed up and then headed to our three-bedroom house we had bought after Noah and Em sold the house in Austin they grew up in. They split the money, and Noah and I used his half to put down on our little piece of heaven here in Mason. It was perfect. Six miles from the shop, and only ten minutes from my parents' ranch.

"Oh God, Grace, baby, you better stop or I'm going to come."

Smiling, I slowly started to sit up when Noah pushed

my head back down on his dick, nearly causing me to gag and throw up.

"Holy fuck! Your dad. Your dad is behind me! No! No! No!"

Pushing his hand off my head, I raised up slightly. "What?"

"He's pulling up next to me. Oh for the love of God! Why?"

"Don't look at him. Speed up. Go faster!"

"Fucking hell, Grace. Don't say shit like that. All I can think of is fucking you right now and my dick is about to explode."

Biting on my lip, I said, "Oh really?" Running my tongue along his shaft, Noah sucked in air through his teeth and moaned.

"Stop. Grace. Your father is . . . oh God . . . oh yeah, baby."

Slipping him into my mouth again, I went to town. "No! Grace, your head is fucking bopping up and down. Have. To. Stop."

As I moaned against his dick, Noah dropped his head back onto the headrest. "Fuck, I'm going to die before I even had chance to marry you."

Hearing my father's truck move up further next to Noah, I slid off his dick and managed to move my body to where it looked like I was laying against the passenger side door sleeping."

Noah laughed and said, "This is why I'm marrying you. You're fast on your feet."

Smiling, I kept my head down so it would appear I was sleeping. My father honked the horn to get Noah's attention.

"Oh hey there, Grace's dad, who is driving along next to me while my dick is exposed. At least the sight of your dad made it go down."

Busting out laughing, I slowly sat up and appeared to

look like I just woke up. Turning to look, I fought like hell not to laugh. Noah had been waving as my dad was waving back. Pointing in front of him, he mouthed something.

"What . . . what did he say?" Noah asked.

Panic raced through my body as I dug through my purse for my phone. Hitting his number I waited for him to answer.

"Hey, Grace. Are y'all headed home for lunch?"

"Um . . . well Noah needed to shower and I needed to grab something that was at the house for the display window we're working on for the Fourth of July."

"How awesome. Should I stop by and visit?"

"No!" I shouted. My father had already pulled ahead of Noah and was now in front of us.

"Why not?"

Swallowing hard, I tried to think quickly. "Well, I'm just going to grab the little stool and then head back in my car."

"Want me to drive you back? That way, Noah can come get you in his truck."

"Awe, Daddy, you're so sweet, but that's okay."

Hearing him let out a breath, he finally said, "Well, do you think I'm going to get to spend some time with you before I lose you to Noah?"

My heart broke as I heard the sadness in his voice. "Oh, Daddy. You're not losing me to Noah."

Noah looked over at me and smiled as he took my hand and kissed the back of it.

"I am, Grace. He's taking my little girl from me and there isn't a damn thing I can do about it."

Feeling a sense of warmth rush through my body, I said, "How about this. You and I spend the entire day together tomorrow."

"Will you go fishing?"

Letting out a chortle, I said, "Yes. I'll even go fishing with you."

"The whole day? You and me. No Noah at all?"

Peeking over to Noah, I smiled and said, "Yes, Daddy. You and me, and no Noah."

"Hey," Noah said playfully with a pout that had me instantly turned on again.

"Okay. It's a deal. Then dinner at our house, and I guess that little bastard can come too."

Shaking my head, I reached over and played with Noah's dick again as his eyes grew wider. "Dinner at the house with you and Mom. Got it. Love you, Daddy."

"Love you back, baby girl. Do me a favor, put Noah on the phone."

The fact that my father just busted out and asked to speak with Noah should have had me worried, but I figured he was going to give Noah hell about the wedding coming up. "Okay, here he is." Handing the phone to Noah, I said, "He wants to talk to you."

Noah pushed my hand off his dick as I giggled and pouted. Taking the phone from me, Noah said, "Hey Jeff, what's up?"

Noah's face instantly turned white as he let his foot off the gas some before applying pressure again.

Noah nodded his head and said, "Yep. Okay got it, thanks for taking care of that for me. Yes, sir. Bye."

Handing me the phone back, Noah ran his hand through his hair and said, "Holy fucking hell. I can't believe this shit."

Pinching my brows together, I asked, "What's wrong?"

Noah pulled down our driveway and stopped at our gate as he hit the button and waited for it to open. "I need a second, Grace."

Once the gate opened, he hit the gas and flew down the driveway. The entire time he kept mumbling something over and over again.

As we approached our house, I saw a car parked in our driveway. "Who is that and how did they get in?"

Noah stopped the truck behind the white Mercedes and let out a deep breath. "Your dad let her in."

Turning to look at Noah, I asked, "Well who in the hell is she?"

Closing his eyes, Noah said, "The girl I dated before you."

Feeling a lump in my throat, I turned and looked back toward the house. A girl with blonde hair that was pulled back in a ponytail stood on our front porch. "The girl you dated in high school and college?"

Noah grabbed my hands and pulled on them to get me to look at him. "Yes. Your dad drove by and saw her sitting outside the gate trying to dial to see if anyone was home. He let her in after she told him who she was. Jeff said he left me a message on my cell phone."

"Why would my dad let some stranger in, Noah? Regardless if she told him she dated you, that doesn't make sense."

Noah's eyes flashed back over to the blonde and then back to me. "She told him she was looking for her old fiancé, tracked him down and found out he lived here. Then she told him my name."

My mouth dropped open as I pulled my hands from Noah's. "You bastard. You were engaged to her?"

"Wait, Grace, you don't understand and you need to let me explain all of this, after I find out what she wants."

Turning back to her, my heart raced. Holy shit. Please don't let the past be showing up on my doorstep.

Pushing the door to the truck open, I jumped out and headed to toward the blonde.

I could hear Noah trying to get out of the truck. He probably remembered his pants were undone and that's why he was further behind than I was.

Walking up to the steps, I plastered on a fake smile. "Howdy. May I ask who you are and what you're doing on my front porch?"

The blonde's smile faded some, as she quickly looked at Noah who was now coming up behind me.

"Jade. What in the world are you doing here?"

Jade. Ugh what a trampy name.

Jade quickly looked to me and then back to Noah. "Noah, I've been trying to locate you ever since I got your letter about your mother."

Letter? Holy hell. Noah had talked to her recently? Why didn't he tell me? What reason would he have keeping it a secret?

Balling my fists up, I tried not to read into this too much. This is what happened last time. I read the entire situation wrong.

"Um . . . Jade, what's going on? Why in the world would you need to track me down?"

A million things went through my head. She'd had Noah's baby. Or maybe she had some sexually transmitted disease and she had to tell him about it. Maybe she wanted him back and him sending her a letter gave her hope?

Jade took a step closer to Noah and asked, "Is there somewhere we can talk . . . alone?"

Oh, she didn't. She. Did. Not. That . . . that . . . bitch!

Keeping my cool, I slowly let out a breath and said, "I'll just step inside and take care of some things that needed taken care of a few minutes ago."

Noah looked at me and went to talk, but shut his mouth quickly. As I made my way to the front door, I pulled out the house key. As I slid it in, Jade began talking. "Wow, you're still looking hot as ever."

Squeezing my eyes shut, I pushed the door open and turned to face Noah. He was staring directly at me, trying to get a read on what I was thinking. His face was blank, like he was just as taken off guard by this woman showing up on our doorstep as I was.

Shutting the door, I leaned my forehead against it and let out the breath I'd been holding in.

Turning, I propped myself against the door and slowly slid to the floor as I looked at the engagement ring on my finger.

Dropping my head back, I whispered, "Please don't let this all be too good to be true. Please."

Twenty-Five

NOAH

STANDING THERE, I stared at the door. I could see it written all over Grace's face. Panic. Fear. Uncertainty as to why the one and only other girl I'd ever been with was standing on our front porch. Jeff's words filled my head.

"I swear to God, if you hurt my daughter, I'm going to hurt you."

Jade had written me a few letters over the years, but after I met Grace, I threw them out. I never even read one after Grace came into my life. Jade was my past and as far as I was concerned, Grace was my future. Even when she pushed me away, my heart belonged to Grace.

Clearing my throat, I glanced over to Jade and said, "So are you going to tell me why you're here, Jade?"

Frowning, Jade shook her head and said, "Is that any way to treat your ex-fiancé? Does she know about us?"

Pushing both hands threw my hair; I scrubbed them down my face and let out a frustrated moan. "Jade, there is no us, there hasn't been for years and we were never engaged."

"That's a lie, Noah. You asked me that one night we were at the beach."

Letting out a laugh, I couldn't believe she was holding on to something like this. "Jade, I was drunk for Christ's sake and it was on a dare. I told you that the next morning. That's when we decided to go our separate ways."

Pointing to me, Jade's eyes grew dark. "No. That's when you decided to go your own way and you left me heartbroken."

"For fucks sake, Jade. All we ever did was fight; you cheated on me! Do you remember that?"

"Mistake. It was a mistake, Noah."

"Nothing was a mistake. It was all done with the knowledge of what the consequences would be, Jade."

Jade took another step closer to me as she let a smile play across her face. "Noah, if you didn't care about me, why did you send me a letter?"

Shaking my head, I couldn't believe what was happening. "Because no matter what happened between us, we were still together for five years, Jade. My mother liked you and you liked my mother. I was only doing the polite thing by sending you the letter to let you know my mother passed away. I sent them to a few people, not just you."

Jade's face filled with disappointment. "Did you read any of the letters I sent?"

Looking away, I softly spoke, "No."

"Not one, Noah. Not one single letter? Why?"

Blowing air out forcefully from my mouth, I looked back at Jade. "I don't want to hurt you again, Jade. But you showing up here and doing all of this, you leave me no choice. I didn't read the letters because there was nothing there for me to read. No matter what you had said in them, it wouldn't have changed my mind. Once I met Grace, everything changed. She's my entire world. When I think of my future, I only see Grace."

Jade stood a little taller and titled her head some as she stared at me. "I see. Well, this was all just a waste of time. I guess I'll be getting married this Saturday knowing there will never be an us again."

This Saturday she's getting married? Wow. That poor bastard had no idea what he was getting into.

"You're getting married this weekend and you're standing here asking about us?"

Jade smiled. "Noah, we were together a long time. You can't deny we didn't have some wild and crazy times. I miss you. I had given up hope of us ever getting back together until you sent me that letter. It took courage to seek you out and when I did, the house had been sold and you were gone. I had to find you."

Shaking my head, I looked into Jade's eyes. "Jade, we were young. There isn't anything there between us. There hasn't been in a very long time. Maybe you're just nervous about the idea of getting married."

Throwing her head back, Jade laughed. "Trust me . . . I'm going to be set for life, Noah." Jade took a few steps closer to me as she licked her lips.

Nothing. I felt absolutely nothing.

"So you're sure there's no chance we can go out to dinner. See if there is anything there that once was?" Lowering her voice she said, "Maybe a roll in the hay for old times sake, Noah?"

I actually felt sorry for Jade. She clearly didn't love the man she was engaged to. If she had, she wouldn't have tried so hard to track me down. Especially when she was getting married in a couple of days.

"Sorry, Jade. I'm very much in love with Grace."

Pursing her lips, she said, "You're kidding, right? I'm practically throwing myself at you, Noah, and you're turning me down?"

"I'm beginning to remember why we broke things off,

Jade. I think the best thing for you to do is leave."

Swallowing hard, a look of anger moved across Jade's face before she smiled and laughed. "Now I know why I cheated on you. You always were a bit boring. In and out of bed."

My eyes drifted over toward the door as I looked back at Jade. "I guess I was saving the best for the woman I loved and wanted to spend the rest of my life with. The woman I'm marrying in two weeks."

Pushing past me, Jade headed to her car, got in and slammed the door shut. She quickly headed down the driveway as I stood there still in shock somewhat that she had even been there.

The door to the house opened and I quickly turned around to see Grace standing there. She wore a smile so big it caused me to smile.

Before I could even say a word, Grace jumped into my arms and wrapped her legs around me as she pressed her lips against mine. Walking her back into the house, Grace spoke against my lips. "I'm so sorry. I eavesdropped, but I'm so glad I did. I love you. I love you so much, Noah."

Pushing Grace against the wall, I gazed into her eyes. "You're the one for me, Grace. You always were and you'll always be."

Grace placed her hand on the side of my face and ran her fingers over my two-day-old stubble. "I've changed my mind."

"About?"

The way Grace was looking at me had my stomach doing all kinds of crazy flips. The love in her eyes was the only thing I ever wanted to see there. Licking her lips, Grace said, "Make love to me, Noah. Slowly."

Just when I didn't think I could love this woman anymore than I already did, she proved me wrong. "My pleasure, baby," I said as I kissed her gently on the lips.

Taking Grace into our bedroom, I slowly placed her

back onto the floor. Just thinking about being with Grace had my pulse speeding up. Taking my time, I undressed her as I took in every inch of her beautiful curvy body.

"Noah," Grace gasped as her hands went to my hair. Cupping her breast with my hands, Grace dropped her head back and released a sigh of contentment. "God, you're beautiful," I whispered as I took a hard nipple into my mouth.

Moving my mouth to her other nipple, my hand slowly slid down her stomach as I felt her entire body shudder. Slipping my hand between her legs, I slipped in two fingers as Grace called out my name. "Oh God, Noah."

Smiling, I sucked and pulled her nipple until it couldn't get any harder. The urge to push her against the wall and fuck her hard was a battle I was trying to defeat as I went painfully slow with every move I made.

"Grace, your body turns me on so fucking much." I spoke against her ear as I kissed along her neck. Grace's hips began pumping and grinding as she demanded more from my fingers.

Smiling, I pulled back and looked into her needy eyes. "You said slowly, baby."

Shaking her head quickly, Grace panted out. "Changed. My. Mind."

Slowly pulling my fingers out from Grace's body, she protested by grabbing my ass and pulling me closer to her.

I was still dressed and wanted desperately to feel my skin up against, Grace's. But I was going to take this painfully slow. Stepping away from her, Grace jetted her lips out and gave me the cutest damn pout I'd ever seen.

Attempting to speak without sounding like a fifteen-year-old boy going through puberty, I said, "Lay on the bed, Grace."

Biting hard on her lower lip, her eyes raked over my body. "But you're still dressed."

Lifting my shirt up and over my head, I tossed it to

the ground as Grace whimpered. I ever so slowly took off the rest of my clothes, never taking my eyes off of Grace. When I slipped my boxer briefs off, my hard dick jumped. Ready for the attention it was about to receive. Grace's eyes locked onto it as I smiled. I loved the way she looked at me like she would never be able to get enough of me.

Taking my dick in my hand, I slowly worked it as Grace sucked in a breath.

"So damn hot," she whispered as she quickly moved to the bed and sat.

I knew she wanted to take me in her mouth, but this time, it was all about pleasuring her. Dropping in front of her, Grace's eyes lit up as I lifted her legs, causing her to fall backward. Leaning up on her elbows she watched my every move as I held her legs up and kissed the inside of her thigh. Ever so slowly making my way to her wet pussy.

My eyes quickly landed on Grace's as I smiled and then swiped my tongue across her clit.

"Oh God!" She called out as her body jerked. She was so turned on I knew it would only be a matter of a few licks and she'd be falling apart.

"Does that feel good, baby?"

Grace nodded her head frantically. "More. Noah, for fucks sake, give me more!"

"My little demanding, Grace."

Grabbing my head, Grace took a handful of hair and pushed my face into her. Giving in to her demands, I sucked and licked as Grace let out whimpers and mews.

"Noah, yes!" Grace trembled as her orgasm rolled through her body. I had to fight like hell to keep from coming at the same time. Grace tasted like heaven and I wanted more than anything to dive back into her.

"Noah . . . please I need you inside of me."

Kissing along her lower stomach, I smiled as I watched goose bumps engulf Grace's body. Giving more attention to her breasts, I kissed along her neck and finally took her lips with my mouth.

Grace wrapped her legs around me and pulled me toward her pulsing pussy. I'd never be tired of being with Grace. Every time felt like the first time. I could explore her body for hours upon hours.

Our kiss turned frantic and the plan to go slow quickly flew out the window as I lined my dick up at her entrance and pushed in fast and hard. Never breaking our kiss, I moved in and out of Grace as if my life depended on it.

Pulling her lips from mine, Grace captured my eyes and smiled. "Harder, Noah. I want to feel you for the rest of the day."

Giving her what she asked for, I grabbed her hips and pulled another orgasm from her as I hit the spot I knew was her undoing over and over. The moment I felt her squeeze on my dick, I exploded. It was almost as if time stopped and I was trapped in a lovemaking euphoria.

It was paradise.

STANDING AT THE end of what would be the aisle Grace was supposed to walk down in two hours; I stood there in silence as I listened to everything that had gone wrong since this morning.

The guy who was delivering the cake tripped, falling on the cake, thus destroying it.

The florist, who had designed all of the flowers, was in an accident on the way to delivering the flowers. She was okay, but our flowers were spread across the highway. Apparently, there were three cows in the middle of the highway and when she tried to avoid them, she swerved too much and flipped her van. She walked away without a scratch, thank God, but we wouldn't be having flowers for the wedding or the reception.

The pastor who was going to do the ceremony was stuck in Austin on the side of the road. His truck overheated and he was waiting on someone to come help him.

The band that was going to play at the reception all came down with strep throat. Yes. The entire fucking band all had strep. Colt was scrambling to find someone to step in. Jeff and Gunner offered to play a few tunes, but apparently, Grace threw a shoe at both of them when they told her their idea.

Scrubbing my hands over my face, I asked. "Is there anything else that's gone wrong?"

Alex scrunched up her nose and said, "Yes."

Grayson was standing next to me as he murmured, "Oh shit."

Rolling my eyes, I whispered, "Hit me with it."

Alex sucked in a long deep breath as she slowly blew it out. "I called St. Regis to confirm your honeymoon package and they said they didn't have you coming in until next week."

My mouth dropped open. "What?"

Nodding her head, she said, "Yep. Grace has the confirmation email with the correct dates, but honestly, I'm too afraid to even ask her for it. If she finds out this is going on . . . she may lose her shit. She's been pretty calm so far."

Holy fucking shit. Shaking my head, I said, "It's like someone doesn't want this marriage to happen." Turning slowly, my eyes searched for him.

Jeff.

Narrowing my eye, I shot daggers at him.

Alex hit me on the chest and said, "Stop it, Noah. I see it all over your face and Jeff didn't do this. Y'all have just had a series of misfortunes."

Glancing back at Alex, I said, "Misfortunes? Alex, this is a fucking nightmare."

Turning away from Alex and Grayson, I paced back and forth. *What could I do to fix this?* I wasn't about to let our wedding day go down like this. Not without a fight.

Stopping, I let a small smile play across my face. Turning to Alex and Will, I said, "I need to run to Wild Flower."

Alex pulled her head back in shock and asked, "Why?"

Giving her a wink, I started walking backward. "Don't tell Grace about the honeymoon just yet. Make sure Colt has the pastor secure and set. Will, Gray . . . I need y'all to come with me. I'm going to need help."

Will glanced over to Alex and shrugged his shoulders as Grayson followed me. "I guess we'll be back in a few", Will said as he kissed Alex quickly on the lips.

Making my way to my truck, Grayson grabbed my arm. "Dude, do you have plan?"

Smiling, I nodded my head. "I have a plan." Will walked up next to me as I looked over at him. "Will, I need you to go to my house. In my office closet is a guitar case. I need you to get it and bring it back here. Grayson and I are going to get some things from the nursery."

Will gave me wide smile as he asked, "A guitar case?"

Nodding my head, I said, "Yep. That's what I said."

"Okay, I'm on it," Will said as he took off jogging over to his truck.

Grayson and I walked up to my truck and got in. Starting my truck, he asked, "Noah, dude, your wedding day is falling to shit and you've got Will getting a guitar and we're headed to a damn flower store. Please tell me you haven't lost your mind."

Turning to Grayson, I gave him a serious look. "I haven't lost my mind, Gray. I'm giving my bride to be the only thing she said she ever needed."

Grayson stared at me for a few seconds before a smile spread from ear to ear. "Holy shit. Dude, you have a determined look on your face."

Pressing on the gas, I looked straight and said, "Grace is going to have the best damn wedding day even if it kills me."

Letting out a laugh, Grayson let out a hell yeah as we drove toward the nursery.

Twenty-Six

GRACE

"WHAT DO YOU mean, Noah left?" I asked as I stood there staring at Alex.

"He said he had to go take care of something really quick and he'd be back. Grace, let's just get your dress on."

Falling back onto the bed, I didn't even care if my hair got messed up. It was half up and half down. No one would ever know the difference.

"Why?" I said as I squeezed my eyes shut. "My wedding day is falling apart before my very eyes and there is nothing I can do about it. Nothing."

"Bullshit," Meagan said as I opened my eyes and leaned up on my elbows.

"What did you say, Meg?" I asked as I narrowed my eye at her.

Giving me a smirk smile, Meagan flopped on the chair from my desk and said, "You heard me. If that was me sitting on that bed, you'd be telling me to get my damn ass up and make the most of it. Well, I'm telling you, it's bullshit that you're giving up on your wedding day. Noah isn't."

My mouth hung open as I stared at her. "He's not even here! He left!" I shouted as Alex jumped with Taylor over at the window. "What?" I asked, jumping up and pushing them out of the way. All I saw was Libby with the baby. It looked like she was directing someone over to the altar.

I let out a frustrated exhale and went to turn away from the window when I saw Noah and Grayson carrying a bench from Wild Flower. Tilting my head, I whispered, "What in the hell is he doing? Does he plan on napping or something?"

Alex spun around and pushed me away from the window, causing me to stumble backward. Trying to catch myself, I moved at an awkward angle and twisted my foot and went down hard.

"Holy son-of-a-bitch, fuck the mother living duck, crack head jerk off, shit that hurts!" I screamed as I grabbed my ankle.

Alex's face turned white as Taylor dropped down and took my ankle in her hand. "Oh no. Grace, I think you sprained your ankle."

"Crack head jerk off? Where in the hell did that come from?" Meagan asked as I shot her a dirty look.

My heart fell. That was it. I was done. The heavens were telling me that I wasn't supposed to marry Noah. Everything that could go wrong, went wrong. Glancing at my ankle, I watched as it grew bigger and bigger. "Holy hell. Who knew it could swell up that fast?" I whispered as I felt the throbbing in my ankle.

Alex was by my side as Taylor yelled out she was going to get ice. "Oh my God, Grace. I didn't mean to push you so hard. Oh no! Oh shit! This is all my fault."

Tears began building in her eyes as I gave her a warm smile. "Alex, it's not your fault. Clearly Noah was trying to set something up for the wedding and you didn't want me to see it. You didn't know I was going to twist my ankle."

Hearing Meagan let out a chuckle, I slowly turned my head to see her sitting on the end of my bed. "You know what this is? This is karma for putting me on the same damn flight as stripper boy."

Rolling my eyes, I tried to ignore the fact that my heartbeat was now residing in my ankle and pounding so hard that I could feel my ankle grow bigger with each beat.

"Stop calling him that. Did you know Gray is now a detective for the Durango Police Department? That's kind of sexy don't you think?" I asked as I wagged my eyebrows.

A look passed over Meagan's face as she glanced away. "So what, he'll always be a stripper to me."

Taylor came running in with ice. "I've got ice!"

Alex motioned for Taylor to sit next to her. Alex lifted my ankle and moved it some as I yelled out, "Ouch!"

"That hurts?" Alex asked as concern wore heavy on her face while she motioned for Taylor to put the ice on my ankle.

"No Alex, I just felt like screaming out ouch for the hell of it." Dropping down onto the floor, I covered my face as I let out a scream. Letting my hands down to my sides, I said, "Just tell Noah the weddings off. It's no use in trying anymore."

"That would really suck considering I had the most amazing wedding day planned for us."

His voice moved over my body like a silk blanket. I'd never tire of hearing it. Turning my head, I looked up at Noah towering over me. His smile lit up the entire room and I instantly forgot about my ankle. And the flowers. And the cake. Oh let's not forget the pastor, the sick band and whatever else went wrong because I could see it in Alex's eyes there was more.

Okay, maybe I hadn't forgotten about my ankle, considering it hurt so bad I wanted nothing more than to rock in a fetal position and cry out *why!*

"Hey," I said as I smiled.

"Baby, why are you on the floor?"

"Alex pushed me and I twisted my ankle," I said with a pout.

Alex jumped up and said, "No. No that's not how it happened. You and Gray were bringing in some stuff from Wild Flower and I didn't want to ruin it so I gave her a little . . . shove."

Letting out a laugh, I looked at Alex and said, "Push. It was a push and sure as hell wasn't little." Lifting my head, I pointed to Meagan and said, "Meg, tell Noah how hard Alex pushed me.

Meagan shrugged her shoulders and said, "Honestly, Grace you did a very over exaggerated twist of your body. It wasn't that big of a push."

Sitting up, I shot Meagan daggers from my eyes as I shook my head and said, "You wait. Pay back is a bitch, Meg."

Letting out a roar of laughter, Meagan stood up and gave me a go to hell look. "Oh, you've already done the worst possible thing to me this weekend, nothing could top it."

Lifting an eyebrow I asked, "Are you sure you're willing to bet on that?"

Meagan's smile dropped as a look of horror crossed over her face. "You wouldn't."

"Oh. Oh, yes I would."

Noah looked between the two of us, as he finally reached down and picked me up. "Hey, Alex, would you mind helping Libby out downstairs? I'm sure Taylor and Meg can help my beautiful bride here with her wedding dress."

Confused and wondering what was going on, I looked at Noah. "But—"

Placing his finger over my lips, Noah slowly shook his

head. "I need you to put your dress on, baby. The pastor is ready and waiting."

A bubble of happiness began to build inside of me. "Pastor?"

Giving me a smile that made my insides tremble, I said, "He showed up?"

"Colt found one and he's ready and able to marry us. I just need you to finish getting ready."

Nodding my head, I smiled. "I love you," I whispered as he held me tighter.

Setting me on my feet, I grimaced in pain. "Damn it, Grace. What do we do about your ankle?" Taylor asked.

Noah pushed a loose curl behind my ear and said, "Leave it to me. I'll take care of it. Get ready, baby."

Kissing me quickly on the lips, Noah turned to Meagan and Taylor and winked at them as he said, "Let's have a wedding, ladies."

Taylor jumped as Meagan tried to hold back her excitement and lost out. Soon both her and Taylor were acting like idiots.

"All right, all right. Let's save the jumping celebrations for when Taylor pops her cherry," I said as I hopped over to the bed.

"Hey!" Taylor said as she placed her hands on her hips.

Meagan and I both let out a giggle as Taylor spun around and took my dress from where it had been hanging up.

I had no idea what Noah was up to, but I sure as hell couldn't wait to find out.

MEAGAN HAD TOUCHED up my makeup as Taylor and Libby took my hair down and started all over again. Libby kept wiping her tears away every time she looked at me.

"Why are you crying so much Libby?" I asked as she shrugged her shoulders and chewed on her lip.

Meagan stood directly in front of me and said, "Lips."

Jetting my lips out, Meagan applied a light pink lipstick to them. Taking a step back, she smiled and said, "Damn. I should be in Hollywood doing all the actors' makeup."

Taylor rolled her eyes and said, "Yeah. Dad would love that."

Meagan let out a gruff laugh and agreed.

Libby added another piece of babies breath to my hair and then stood back to look at me. "Well? How does it look?" I asked.

Covering her mouth with her hand she said, "You look b-b-beautiful!" And busted out into tears . . . again.

"Jesus H. Christ. What in the hell is wrong with you?" I asked as I stared at Libby.

Meagan and I both looked at Libby as Meagan said, "Shit, if I didn't know any better I'd say you were—"

Meagan's voice cut off as she sucked in a breath of air. That's when it hit me.

"Oh. My. God," I said as I stood up and tried to balance on one foot.

"Libby?" I asked as my eyes fell to her stomach and then back up to her face.

Smiling from ear to ear, Libby's cheeks blushed.

"Libby!" I screamed as Alex and Taylor both screamed.

"What? What's happening?" Alex asked as she walked up to me and then looked at Libby.

"Libby's pregnant." I yelled out as I pointed to her.

Alex's mouth dropped open as Taylor quickly wrapped Libby up in a hug. "Oh Libby! Are you really? How far along are you?"

Libby's face glowed. I couldn't believe none of us noticed it until now. "Luke and I didn't want to say anything just yet. We were waiting to say anything, but . . . well . . . my emotions are all over the place!"

Taking her hands in mine, I tried to push away the ping of jealousy I was feeling. I wasn't sure why I was so bothered by this news. I mean, I wasn't bothered, I was happy for Libby and my brother. *Very* happy. But a part of me was envious and that bothered me.

Plastering on a smile, I prayed like hell it didn't look fake as I attempted to push away my sadness as I said, "Libby, you have to tell us. That's my little niece or nephew in there!"

Chewing on her lip, she finally said, "I'm almost three months along. My due date is actually New Year's Day!" Libby said, as happiness spilled from her body.

Everyone took turns giving Libby a hug. Once everything was settled, Libby walked up to me and said, "Grace, I didn't want to say anything until after your wedding. I'm so sorry."

Shaking my head, I instantly felt guilty for how I was feeling earlier. "Oh, Libby. Don't be silly. This is the best news I've heard all day!"

Giggling, Libby pulled me to her. "I'm so glad you found love. And I'm so glad you stood and fought for that love."

Holding her tighter, I whispered, "Thank you, Libby."

A light knock on the door caused me to take a step back and say, "Come in."

My mother walked in and tears immediately filled her eyes. "Girls, it's time. Grace darling, we need to put your dress on. Your father is waiting outside."

"What about my ankle?" I asked as I held up my expensive ass high heel shoes I'd never get to slip my feet into. I guess I could put one on.

My mother winked. "Noah has it covered."

Alex and Libby picked my wedding dress up from the bed and made their way over to me as all four of my best friends helped me get dressed.

The tears in all their eyes as well as my mother's told me I looked good as I stood before them in my wedding gown.

"Noah's going to shit his pants," my mother said as I let out a laugh while trying to hold my own tears back.

Twenty-Seven

GRACE

AFTER MY DRESS and the veil were on, I asked to spend a couple minutes alone. There was a light tap on the door and it slowly opened. Attempting to turn toward the door, I lifted my dress and did a couple of hops on my good foot. My father stood before me as his watery eyes took me in.

"Oh, Grace Hope. I've never seen such a beautiful sight."

My mother stood to his side and dabbed her eyes with a tissue. "I told you," she said to my father.

They both approached me and I took their hands in mine as I rubbed my thumb across their skin. "Thank you for loving, Noah. And for welcoming him into our family like you both have."

My mother smiled and nodded her head as she whispered, "Of course, Grace. You'd have to be a fool not to see how much that boy loves you."

My father cracked his neck and looked out the window. "I never said I loved the little bastard."

Hitting my father on the chest at the same time my mother hit his arm, I said, "Daddy! Stop that. You know you like him."

My father's eyes captured mine as they built with tears. "After seeing what the two of you have been through together, and what that boy did today, yes . . . yes, Grace. I like Noah very much."

Joy swept across my body. "Oh, Daddy. You have no idea how much that means to me."

Placing his hand on the side of my face, I gently leaned into it. "God, do you have any idea how much you look like your mother?"

Peeking over at my mother, I took her in. Her long brown hair was up in a French twist and her green eyes stood out as they sparkled with joy. My mother was breathtaking. Her beauty was flawless and I was blessed to have anyone say I looked like her.

Standing next to my father, my mother gazed upon me with the most adoring eyes. "Grace, I can't believe my sweet little girl is getting married. It seems like it was just yesterday we were in the barn in one of the stalls having a tea party."

Smiling, I shook my head. "Leave it to me to have a tea party in the barn!"

My father and mother both started laughing. "You always did love your horses," Daddy said with a sweet smile.

Exhaling slowly, I asked, "May I ask y'all a question?"

"Of course, Grace. You never have to ask if you can ask us something."

Pressing my lips together tightly, I looked between the two of them. "With all the stuff that's happened today, you don't think it's a bad sign do you?"

My mother slowly shook her head and reached out for me as I fought to hold back my tears. Meagan would kick my ass if I ruined my makeup.

"Grace, sweetheart. Push that right out of your mind.

So you ran into a few problems today. It's not the end to the beginning."

"A few?" I asked as I heard my father chuckle. Pulling back, I glanced over and gave him a dirty look.

"Daddy, seriously. Everything that could have gone wrong, went wrong."

My father's face turned serious as he pushed out a quick breath. "Grace, this is the way I see it. Yes, some things went wrong, did I enjoy seeing Noah freak out like he has, yes, but—"

Dropping my mouth open, I hit him on the shoulder hard as my mother attempted to hide her chuckle.

"Dad!" I said as I narrowed my eyes at him.

Holding up his hands to calm me down, he kept talking. "Like I was saying, but, I think it all happened for a reason. Every day is some sort of struggle with Noah. Last night, when he and I were . . . bonding." My father lifted his eyebrows and smirked as I rolled my eyes. My father had insisted on Noah and him going for drinks alone. I honestly was scared for Noah's well-being.

"Yes, bonding; don't look at me like that, Grace Hope. Anyway, Noah shared something with me."

My interest piqued beyond belief, I whispered, "What?"

"He told me every day when he wakes up, he thinks back to when he was going through the withdrawals and the desire he had to take a pill just so his body could relax and he could go to that place where there were was no pain. No thinking about anything. The pain and hurt that he put you through when all of that was going on kills him, Grace. He told me he made a promise to God that he would live this life making sure he never saw that look in your eyes again."

A single tear escaped and descended down my cheek. My father reached up and gently wiped it away. "Grace, today wasn't a bad sign. Today was about Noah finding his strength."

Pinching my eyebrows together, I asked, "What do you mean, Daddy?"

Nodding his head, my father said, "If ever this was a day to test his strength, today was it. Instead of wanting to run away and take a pill, Noah did something else. He stayed in the game and followed his heart to make this the best day of your life. I truly see how much that boy loves you, Grace. And I've never been so happy for you, sweetheart."

My body trembled as I felt the onslaught of emotions. Launching myself at my father the best I could on one foot, he wrapped his arms around me and held me tight. "Just know, you'll always be my little girl and I know someone who knows someone who will take Noah out if need be."

Laughing, I reached over his shoulder and wiped my tears away.

"Oh lord. You ruined her makeup," my mother said.

Stepping away, I gently attempted to dab the tears away as my mother grabbed my hand and pulled me over and sat me down. "Really quick, let's fix this. Thank goodness, Meagan used waterproof mascara."

Smiling, I watched my mother's face as she touched up my makeup. Nothing in this world would ever top this day.

Standing up straight, my mother smiled. "All right. Let's do this shall we?"

Nodding my head, I stood up and adjusted my dress. My mother kissed me gently on the cheek. "Deep breaths. You look beautiful."

Barely finding the words to speak, I managed to push out three words. "Thank you, Mom."

Giving me a small nod, my mother turned and kissed my father gently on the cheek.

When the door shut, my father and I stood staring at each other. "Now I know how your Grandpa Mark felt the day he had to give your mother away to me."

Feeling my stomach dip, I pressed my lips together.

"I don't want to let you go, Grace."

Reaching for my father's hands, I squeezed them. "You're not. You're just letting Noah borrow me."

Grinning from ear to ear, he nodded his head. "I do have a surprise for you."

Lifting my eyebrows, I said, "I do love surprises."

"Grandma and Philip were able to catch another flight and they're here for the wedding."

Feeling like a bubble of happiness busted inside of me, I let out a scream as I covered my mouth. "Oh, Daddy! This is perfect! Everyone is here!"

My father's parents had been divorced for many years. Philip was my father's step dad. His real dad, Brian, had fought a long and hard battle with lung cancer and won. He now lived in Alaska running a hunting tour guide company with his wife of ten years, Jessica. They flew in three days ago to spend some time with everyone. It had been wonderful having everyone there.

"And waiting!" Daddy said with a chortle.

Picking up my dress, I showed my father my one foot that had my expensive ass shoe on it. Laughing, he shook his head. "I get to do one thing I haven't done in a very long time, sweetheart. Let's just get you downstairs; everyone is waiting on us."

Letting out a halfhearted laugh, I said, "What are you going to do, Daddy. Carry me down the aisle."

Giving me a wink, he said, "Not down the aisle, but to your chariot. Well, a makeshift one anyway."

STANDING IN THE living room, I watched as Taylor, Meagan and Ellie all headed out the front door. Making their way to where everything was set up. My heart was pounding and my hands were sweating so bad I had to keep wiping them on my father's jacket. Each time I did it he looked at me and frowned.

Libby handed Mireya the basket filled with rose petals as Mireya jumped with excitement. I couldn't help but laugh at my precious little niece."

Daddy leaned over and said, "Hard to believe she'll be two in November. I miss her being a baby."

Biting on my lower lip, I realized Luke and Libby hadn't told my parents about the new baby.

"Yeah, me too. But she is so much fun at this age," I said as I looked over at my father and Mireya.

Libby called out and told Mireya to follow behind her. Giving me a wave, she took off out of the door

Inhaling a deep breath in, I slowly blew it out. "Ready?" my father asked.

Turning to him, I smiled and said, "So ready."

Reaching down, Daddy picked me and held me as tears filled his eyes. He slowly made his way out the door and down the steps. "Jesus, Daddy. Don't fall. If you break your leg you're going to screw up my whole wedding day."

My father looked at me with a stunned look as we both busted out laughing. When he turned the corner, I glanced up and saw Jack, one of my horses saddled up in a beautiful white saddle. Wiping my tears away, my father lifted me up and helped me climb up onto Jack. "I can't believe I'm walking you *and* a horse down the aisle. I'm sure Noah is loving this."

Laughing, I looked over to where everyone was and the first thing I saw was the love of my life standing at the end of the aisle. The song "Giving It All (To You)" played as Daddy slowly made his way down the aisle as he led Jack. Trying to pull my eyes from Noah so I could look at everyone else, I couldn't help but notice how freaking handsome he was.

Damn I'm a lucky girl.

I quickly glanced around as I smiled and said, "He'll be

offering guided kiddy rides after the ceremony for anyone interested."

Laughter erupted and I could feel my father's eyes on me.

"Funny," he whispered. When we got to the end of the aisle, my father helped me off of Jack and slowly set me down. The pain immediately pounded in my ankle and I let a small whimper slip from my lips. Noah was by my side and had his arm wrapped around my waist before my father could even react.

"I've got you, baby," he said as he gave me a drop-dead gorgeous smile. My heart melted on the spot and I fell in love with him more. If that was even possible.

"I've got this, Noah," my father said as he gave Noah a small push away.

Giggles could be heard all around me as I looked between the two favorite men in my life. "No, really, sir. I've got it from here."

Feeling my cheeks blush, I turned to my father who was glaring at Noah. Pointing a finger at him, my father said, "You're only borrowing her, Noah."

Noah nodded and said, "Yes, sir. Got it."

My father pointed again. "I know people, who know people who will take you out."

Noah's eyes widened as he slowly nodded his head and said, "Yes, sir. You've mentioned that a time or two."

Grandpa Mark let out a chuckle as he said, "Paybacks. Oh man I love paybacks."

"Oh Lord help this family."

My eyes snapped over to Pastor Roberts. I hadn't even seen him standing there. Letting out a chuckle, I wondered how Colt ever talked this poor man into doing another one of our family's weddings.

My eyes then caught the little teal and brown bench I'd found at an antiques store in Fredericksburg. It had been in the front display window of Wild Flowers. Turning to

Noah, I asked, "What's the bench for?"

Noah's eyes moved to it as he smiled and took my hand. Alex and Libby helped with my dress and train as I sat on the bench. I was looking back at everyone and my heart was overcome as my eyes looked over my friends and family. Matt sat next to my mother holding a painting that was wrapped up in wrapping paper. I lifted my hand and waved to him as he waved back and shouted. "Hey, Grace! Want to go fishing?"

Grinning, I said, "I'd love to, but we'll have to wait a few days."

Matt gave me a thumbs-up and said, "Okay, Grace!"

As my eyes scanned everyone sitting, I saw my grandparents . . . all of them . . . smiling back at me with tears in their eyes. I saw my friends and family as they each looked upon me with loving eyes.

My eyes soon found Emily and her husband. They had flown in a week ago to spend time with Noah and me. Emily's hands rested on her swollen belly. She was six months pregnant with twins. She wiped a tear away as her husband, Mitch, took her hand in his.

Finally, my eyes focused back on Noah. He was standing in front of me with the goofiest smile on his face. He peeked over to Alex who walked up and pointed to my bouquet as she said, "Can I trade your bouquet for something else?"

She was holding her hand out for my bouquet. I held my flowers away from her and said, "Hell no."

Laughing, she pulled out a single sunflower and held it in front of me. My heart felt as if it had skipped a beat as I sat there staring at the sunflower. Slowly reaching up for it, I handed her my flowers as she winked and stood back in line next to Libby.

Glancing back to the front, I let out a gasp as I watched Noah sit on the ground as Will handed him the teal guitar Noah had bought off the street vendor.

Tears flowed freely now and I didn't give two shits about my makeup. Noah was bringing me back to the day I knew my heart would forever belong to him.

Best. Day. Ever.

Twenty-Eight

NOAH

A LUMP FORMED in my throat as I watched Grace begin crying. Meagan let out a gasp as I heard her say under her breath, "Thank God I used waterproof mascara!"

Chuckling, I shook my head as I dragged in a deep breath. I couldn't believe what I was about to do. Not only was I about to speak in front of everyone, I was also going to sing to my beautiful bride on our wedding day, but in front of everyone else as well.

Clearing my throat, I dug deep inside and found my voice.

"Once upon a time, I met a beautiful princess. She ran into me so hard, she knocked herself down to the ground."

Small chuckles played around me as I watched Grace smile even bigger.

"If only she had known, I was the one who was knocked off my feet. But she got up, dusted herself off and quickly walked away. I stood there like a fool and watched her leave. Then I ran into the beautiful princess again. This time, I was smart enough to get her number."

Everyone laughed again as a small sob escaped Grace's lips as she shook her head at me.

"It was hard winning the princess over. It was obvious; she'd been hurt before. I wouldn't give up on the idea of us though. We spent countless nights texting back and forth. At the time I thought it was odd she didn't tell her friends about me, but I soon learned this was her way of keeping me just one step away from being too close."

Grace wiped her tears away as she pressed her lips together. "But I made a promise to myself—I wouldn't let her go. She pushed me away and for a brief time, I was a stupid fool and let her. Until one day, she ran into me again. Third time is the charm my mother always said."

Small giggles let out around me as I stared into Grace's eyes. "I knew this time, I was not ever going to let her push me away again. I loved this girl and I knew I had loved her from the first moment she ran into me. Knocking us both off our feet."

"Noah," Grace whispered as she started to cry.

"Then, I lost myself. I lost myself to a dark world after my mother passed away."

Emily's crying could be heard from my left side. Turning, I gave her a wink and she barely smiled as Mitch wrapped his arm around her. Glancing back toward the front, I captured Grace's eyes. "I pushed you away, Grace. So many times I pushed you away, but you never left my side. You were the one to find me again, Grace. You brought me back to life. Each morning I wake up to your beautiful smile is a testament to the love that we share. We might have taken the long road getting here, but I'm so glad that road was traveled with you, Grace."

Grace and I had picked out an oldie but goodie for our wedding song, Tim McGraw's "My Best Friend".

I started playing the cords to the song and said, "Since

our wedding day has been far from the normal side of things, and since you can't really dance to our wedding song," Grace and I both looked at Alex.

Alex dropped her mouth open and said, "It was a just a small push!"

Winking at Alex, I looked back at Grace. "I thought I would do our wedding song a bit differently. Take us back to that day in the park. Do you remember that day, Grace?"

Grace nodded her head as I sung the words to her. I fought like hell to keep my voice strong and steady as I heard sniffles and cries erupt all around me.

Focusing only on Grace, I kept my eyes locked on hers. In this moment, it was just the two of us.

Finding Grace was truly finding my life . . . my very existence.

BY THE TIME Grace and I finally stood in front of Pastor Roberts, my nerves were settled and I had fallen in love even more with the breathtaking woman standing beside me. Pastor Roberts' cleared his throat and said, "Never a dull moment with this crowd."

Laughter erupted as he continued on with the ceremony. I wasn't even sure I heard a word he said as Grace and I stared into each other's eyes. The only thing I was sure I heard was, "I know pronounce you Mr. and Mrs. Noah Bennet. You may kiss your bride."

Cupping Grace's face gently with my hands, I brushed my lips against hers as I whispered, "I have just one little bit of bad news."

Grace laughed and said, "Hit me with it."

"The hotel messed up our reservations. We don't have rooms booked until next week."

Closing her eyes, Grace inhaled very slowly through

her nose before opening her eyes again and giggled. "Looks like we'll have to find something to do before then."

"Kiss her already!" Luke shouted.

Giving her a wink, I said, "Oh, I can arrange that." Pressing my lips to hers, Grace wrapped her arms around my neck as we quickly got lost in our kiss. Feeling someone tap my shoulder, I pulled my lips back.

"Dude, my dad looks like he's ready to step in and break y'all apart, so I'd wrap it up."

Pushing Luke out of the way, I kissed Grace quickly on the lips again. Pastor Roberts motioned of us to turn around. Facing our friends and family he said, "Ladies and gentleman may I introduce, *finally*, Mr. and Mrs. Noah Bennet."

Everyone stood up and started clapping. Seeing my sister standing there with her hand on her stomach caused my heart to feel as if it had stopped for a moment. I glanced over to Luke who was clapping. I could see how happy he was just by the smile on his face. He told me this morning that he and Libby were expecting another baby. My eyes then fell on Grace.

God she was beautiful. And mine. She would always be mine.

Grace turned to me and said, "Should I hop down the aisle or have my father carry me again?"

Frowning, I said, "He won't give you back." Leaning down, I scooped her up into my arms and walked down the aisle with her. As we neared the end of it, I took a deep breath and decided to be honest with Grace. I wasn't sure if now was the time to spring this on her or not.

Walking Grace up and into the house, she looked back and said, "Noah we need to do pictures!"

Setting her down in the living room, I dragged in a deep breath. "Grace, now might not be the best time to talk to you about this."

Narrowing her eye at me, Grace said, "Holy hell. You

better hope what you're about to say is not more bad news."

Letting out a nervous chuckle, I said, "No. It's just, well I've been thinking about this a lot lately and seeing Emily and then Luke telling me that him and Libby are pregnant."

Graces eyes lit up and she smiled the brightest smile I'd ever seen. My heart pumped hard and fast in my chest and I was too scared to even hope that she might feel the same way.

"Keep going," Grace said.

Lifting my hand up, I pushed a loose strand of hair behind Grace's ear. "Grace, I want to have a baby. Like now. I mean I know we can't have one right now, now. I mean like can we start trying for one . . . now."

Grace's emerald eyes were filled with a pool of tears. "Now now? You want to start right now? Like you want to have sex right now?"

My body came to attention as I watched Grace lick her lips. "Holy fuck, if you can make that happen, I'd give you anything you want."

Grace's eyes turned dark as she grabbed my hand and hobbled through the house. "Where are we going?" I asked.

"To the barn!"

Pulling her to a stop, I asked, "The barn? Are you insane? There are people all gathered up outside waiting for us and you want to sneak off to the barn to have sex!"

Placing her hands on her hips, Grace tilted her head at me. "Hold up. You were the one who just said if I could make sex happen right this minute you'd give me anything. I want sex right this minute."

Swallowing hard, I thought about Jeff and Luke just right outside. "What if we get caught?"

Grace placed her hands on my chest as she slowly moved them out and wrapped her arms around my neck. "We're married now, Noah. There is nothing they can do about it."

Letting her words soak in, I leaned down and picked her up as I carried her through the house and out the back door. Grace looked around. "Stop!" she said as I came to an abrupt stop. "Fuck a duck. Luke and Will are headed to the barn. To the trees!"

Giving her a dumbfounded look, I whispered, "What? To the trees?"

"Noah. I want you now. You have no idea how much I need to come right now. It's been a stressful day, baby," Grace said as she gave me a pout.

Licking my lips, I headed to the trees as Grace giggled. "Don't mess up my dress, or my hair, or they'll know what we've been up to."

"Right," I said as I carried my bride through the trees and deep enough in where no one could see us.

Stopping, I gently set Grace down. Her chest was heavy as the anticipation built up. Cupping her face with my hands, I kissed her with everything I had as I pushed her up against an elm tree. Dropping to my knees, I lifted Grace's dress as she hissed through her teeth, "Oh God, Noah yes."

"Mother of God", I whispered as I saw her lingerie. My hands moved up her thighs as her whole body trembled with anticipation.

Lifting her leg with the sprained ankle, I put it over my shoulder, as I pushed her white lace panties to the side and licked all the way up her pussy.

Jesus she tasted like heaven. "Oh hell," Grace panted out as she pushed her hips out and said, "More."

Smiling, I spread her swollen lips apart and buried my tongue inside of her as her hips fucked my face.

Slipping two fingers inside of her, I massaged the inside of her wall, bringing her closer and closer to release. Moving my lips up, I sucked and flicked her clit with my tongue. Grace called out my name as her entire body shook with her orgasm.

"Yes, oh God yes! Noah!"

My dick was throbbing so hard, I about came in my pants. Lifting Grace's dress over my head, I stood up and unzipped my pants as Grace's hands shook as she helped.

She went to drop down on her knees when I took her by the arms and said, "Fuck that. I want inside of you."

Her eyes lit up as she lifted her dress. Positioning myself at her entrance, I pushed in as we both let out a moan.

"Fuck I'm not going to last long," I said as I pulled out and pushed back into her.

"Noah, don't stop. Move faster."

Doing as my bride asked, I pulled out and pushed back into Grace over and over until I felt my balls sucking up. Grace grabbed my shoulders and said, "I'm going to come again!"

The moment she clamped down on my dick, I lost it. It felt like I came forever as I closed my eyes and watched as stars danced behind my eyelids.

Slowly pulling out of her, I took the hankie from my jacket and went back under her dress where I cleaned her up as we both attempted to get our breathing under control.

Standing back up, I looked at Grace and we both started laughing. "You horny bastard!" she said as she launched herself into my arms. Picking her up, I held onto her tightly as I said, "Being with you is like the first time every time, Grace."

"Grace? Noah? Where in the hell are you two?" Meagan called out.

"Noah! Asshole where are you?" Grayson said.

Grace lifted her eyebrows and said, "That's an unlikely search party pair."

Laughing, I placed my hand on the back of Grace's neck and pulled her to me. Kissing her fast and hard, I said, "I love you, Grace Bennet."

Giving me a smile that made my knees weak, Grace

replied back, "I love you the most, Noah Bennet."

This. Life couldn't get any better than this.

As we made our way out of the trees, we came face to face with Meagan and Grayson. The two of them glared at us.

"Oh. My. God. You had sex, didn't you?" Meagan asked as she looked between us. Smiling, I glanced over to Grace who wore a beautiful shade of pink on her cheeks.

Grayson laughed and said, "You lucky son-of-a-bitch. I want your life."

Meagan shot a look over to Grayson. I wasn't sure how to read it. She quickly rolled her eyes and pointed to Grace. "Slut!"

Turning on her heels, she started off toward the house again as Grace called out, "Whore!"

Meagan lifted her hand and waved it as she said, "You taught me well, Grace!"

Letting out a chuckle, Grace turned to Grayson. "I'd say someone was sexually frustrated. You should go after her, Gray."

Letting out a gruff laugh, Grayson said, "Fuck that. Been there done that. No thanks." Turning, Grayson followed Meagan.

"Wow, I'm sensing deep issues between those two," I said as I picked Grace up and threw her over my shoulder as she screamed out in protest."

Meagan turned around and screamed, "If you ruin her hair before pictures, Noah Bennet I'm kicking you in the balls!"

As we walked back up to join everyone, I took a chance and looked over at Jeff. He was shooting me daggers so I looked away. Matt walked up and handed Grace the painting that was wrapped up. "Assmole Noah had me make you this. It's his wedding gift to you, Grace. Open it now!"

The excitement in his voice made me smile as Grace took the painting and sat on a chair. When she opened it, she let out a gasp. It was a portrait of Grace. A beautiful one at that. “Matt, this is beautiful. I’m in the kitchen at home!” Grace turned and looked at me and then back at Matt.

Nodding his head, Matt said. “You said yes.”

At first Grace was confused before she looked back at the picture. “Oh my goodness. The day Noah asked me to marry him. Matt, you’re amazing.”

Matt smiled a smile so big and bright. “You are amazing, Grace.”

Tears fell from my eyes and Grace’s eyes. “Matt, may I hug you?” Grace asked as Matt nodded his head.

After a quick hug, Matt looked at me and said, “Come play Frisbee with me, assmole.”

Yep. This day was beyond perfect.

Twenty-Nine

GRACE

I HATED THE month of September. It was hot and today I wasn't in the mood for hot. October was in one week and I couldn't wait to do the Halloween display in the front window of Wild Flower.

"Hey," Alex said as she walked up with Bayli on her hip.

Wiping the sweat from my forehead, I stood from where I had been digging in the small garden in the back of the nursery. It was only there for Alex and me to play around in. Something about digging in the dirt calmed me and today, I felt like I needed calming. I smiled when I saw Bayli hold her arms out for me to take her. "Hey, baby girl. Oh, look at my big girl."

Bayli gave me a huge grin, and I couldn't help but feel butterflies in my stomach. I wanted a baby desperately.

Because of the Fragile X gene being in the family, I had already been tested to see if I was a carrier of the gene and

I wasn't. As soon as I got that result back, I stopped taking my birth control pills. Noah and I decided not to stress about it. We'd let it happen when it happened. We'd only been married for almost three months, and I honestly was enjoying the time we got to spend together.

"Grace, are you feeling okay?"

Shaking my head, I said, "No. I think I'm getting sick. I feel like shit and this morning I threw up."

Alex stood there staring at me. "Why are you looking at me like that you freak? I'm not going to get y'all sick. I think it was something I ate."

Alex slowly shook her head and said, "Grace! You're pregnant!"

Tossing my head back, I said, "No way, Alex. I just got off the pill a few months ago."

Pulling her cell phone out of her back pocket, Alex hit a number. "Libby? We have a code baby bundle."

"Baby bundle?" I asked as Alex rolled her eyes. Apparently, Libby didn't know what that meant either.

"Oh my gosh. I declare a new code word. Baby bundle is now the code name of when we have a possible pregnancy." Alex giggled. "Nope, not me. Grace."

I heard Libby scream and I couldn't help but chuckle. "I'm not pregnant. I'd know if I was, Alex. I'd feel it."

"Ha!" Alex said as she turned and walked toward the door that led into the back office of Wild Flower. "Okay, we'll be there in thirty minutes."

Shaking my head, I looked at Bayli. "Your mommy is crazy, Bayli. Do you know that?" Bayli let out a giggle and then blew bubbles as she made funny sounds. "Come on, little bit. Let's go prove her wrong. That is Aunt Grace's favorite thing to do, prove your mommy wrong."

Bayli kicked her legs and waved her arms. "Oh, you too, huh? I knew I liked you for a reason."

An hour later I found myself standing in Libby's bathroom staring down at a pregnancy test. The plus sign was like a flashing beacon. A warning sign that kept saying over and over, Pregnant. Pregnant. Pregnant.

The soft knock at the door caused me to jump and let out a gasp. "Grace? Can I come in?" Alex's voice was soft and gentle.

Reaching over, I unlocked the bathroom door as Alex slowly opened it. Looking over at her, a single tear rolled down my cheek. "Oh Grace. I'm so sorry honey. I thought for sure you were."

Wiping the tear away, I held the stick up to her as her mouth dropped open and she let out a gasp. Then her smile faded. "Grace, are you not happy about this?"

Nodding my head, I said, "No. I mean, yes! I guess I'm just in shock. Why don't I feel pregnant? Shouldn't I feel it?"

Alex took my hand in hers and smiled sweetly. "Oh, Grace honey. I didn't know either the first time. I think most women probably think they're sick, just like you did. I'm so happy for you!" Alex pulled me to her as I wrapped my arms around her. Libby walked up and started jumping and pretended to scream. One of the girls must have been asleep.

When Alex let me go, Libby took her turn with the hugging. "Call Dr. Johnson's office right now and make an appointment. He's starting to cut back on patients. My mom said he's retiring this year. Grace, he has to deliver your baby. He's delivered most of us! It's tradition!"

Nodding my head in agreement, I pulled out my phone. "Oh wait! I need to tell Noah!"

Well fell into a fit of laughter until Libby put her hand up to her lips. "The girls are both napping. Come on, I'll grab the monitor and let's go sit on the front porch. Grace, you can call and make the appointment at least!"

Alex agreed and shoved my phone into my chest.

I spent the rest of the afternoon with Alex, Libby, Mireya, and Bayli. It was one of the best afternoon's I'd had in a long time. It was full of laughter, chasing my precious little niece and holding Bayli until Alex demanded I give her back.

Pulling my phone out of my pocket, I saw Noah had sent a text.

> *Noah: Hey babe! I'm exhausted from helping Will and Luke today. Jesus how do they do this whole cowboy shit every day?*

Grinning, I hit reply.

> *Me: My poor baby. I'll treat you right tonight. Let's head into Fredericksburg for dinner. I have a surprise for you.*

It didn't take Noah long before he called.

"Hey, handsome."

"Surprise huh? What is it? Something sexy?"

Standing up, I made my way down the porch steps as I purred back into the phone. "Yep. Very sexy."

"I'm five minutes from home. Where are you?"

Giggling, I said, "Libby and Luke's. I'll leave now. See you at home."

Hitting End, I turned and saw Libby and Alex both standing there with silly looks on their faces. "Oh for Pete's sake. The both of you clearly need to get laid."

Alex shook her head and said, "Well we know who will for sure tonight!"

Giving them a wink, I said, "Hell yeah, I will be. I'm going to head home. Bye y'all."

"Love you, Grace. Be careful and tell Noah congratulations!" Libby called out.

Happiness bubbled up inside of me, but for some reason, doubt plagued my thoughts. *Could this really be happening?* I had wanted a baby so badly, but I'd kept it to myself for so long. Then when Noah mentioned it, I didn't want to be a freak and tell him I'd wanted one since the moment his eyes looked my body over. Now, my dream could very well be coming true. My entire body broke out in goose bumps and I couldn't wipe the smile from my face if I tried.

Climbing into my car, I took a deep breath in and exhaled it as I calmed my nerves down.

I knew Noah was going to be beyond thrilled.

I'm pregnant.

I'm having Noah's baby.

The closer I got to home, the more excited I was to tell Noah.

NOAH'S HAND WAS on my lower back as he led me into August E's. It was one of his favorite restaurants in Fredericksburg.

The hostess asked if we were celebrating anything and I had to bit hard on my lip before I busted out and screamed to the world that I was pregnant.

"Nope. Just a night out with my beautiful wife," Noah said as he slipped his arm around my waist. My heart was beating so hard in my chest I was sure everyone could hear it.

As we sat, the hostess went over the specials as she handed us the menus. Noah and I stared at the menus for a couple of minutes as the waitress came and took our drink orders. Putting his menu down, Noah said, "I know what I'm getting. What about you, baby?"

Baby. He said baby.

Setting my menu down, I smiled and went to tell him what my order was going to be. Except the only thing I heard coming out of my mouth were the words, "I'm pregnant."

I'm pregnant. Holy hell! I'm pregnant and I totally just

blurted it out at Noah.

Making a funny laugh, Noah let out a chuckle and then his face went serious. Pinching my eyebrows together, I shook my head. *Way to be romantic, Grace.*

Noah shut his eyes, and shook his head quickly. "W-what did you just say, Grace?"

My mouth opened, but nothing came out. My hands began sweating as my heartbeat kicked up about ten notches.

Attempting to speak, I smiled instead. "We're having a baby," I whispered.

Noah quickly stood up, came to my side and pulled me into a standing position. "Grace," he said in the most amazing voice I'd ever heard. His eyes locked onto mine and when I saw the tears, my knees about buckled. If he hadn't been holding me up, I was almost positive I would have fallen to the ground.

"We're having a baby?" Noah asked in a stunned voice

Nodding my head, I said, "Yep. I've got a bun in the oven."

Noah's eyes moved quickly about my face before they landed on my lips. Licking them instinctively, Noah pressed his lips to mine as he kissed me deeply as we stood in the middle of the restaurant. Pulling his lips back, he spoke against my lips.

"Holy shit. We're gonna be parents."

Giggling, I placed my head on his chest as he hugged me tightly.

"We're having a baby!" Noah shouted as I buried my face in his chest and laughed.

Applause erupted around the room as people started congratulating us. A few people stood and gave us each a hug, which I thought was so sweet. When we finally sat, Noah reached across the table and took my hand in his.

"When did you find out?"

My cheeks were beginning to hurt from smiling so big. "Earlier today. Alex had a hunch and forced me to take a home pregnancy test. It dawned on me I was late, but I guess I figured my period was messed up from getting off of birth control."

Noah's eyes filled with tears as he leaned forward and kissed my hand. "Grace, you've just made me the happiest man in the world."

My stomach felt as if a million butterflies were flying around in there. "I um, I called the doctor's office and made an appointment. Alex and Libby said the doctor will do another test and then do a sonogram."

Noah's grin grew bigger. "When is it?"

"Tomorrow at nine."

"Damn, I'm supposed to do a conference call with one of the suppliers for the new fertilizer we have coming in the store. Let me reschedule it right now."

Before I could even say a word, Noah got up and pulled his phone out and called someone as he walked out of the restaurant. I watched him through the window as he talked to whomever he was supposed to be talking to tomorrow. The waitress came over and set our drinks down as she gave me a sweet smile and a wink. "You're so lucky he is willing to drop work to go with you. My husband has yet to come to one appointment with me."

My heart broke for the poor girl standing before me, when I glanced down it was then I noticed she was pregnant. Looking back up into her eyes, I gave her a weak smile and said, "How far along are you?"

Placing her hands over her stomach, she grinned from ear to ear and said, "Twenty-four weeks."

"Congratulations. I hope your husband wakes up soon and realizes what he's missing out on."

Her smile faded, as she slowly nodded her head. "Yeah. Here's hoping." Shrugging her shoulders, she put a fake smile on and said, "I'll be back to take your order when your husband comes back in."

Nodding, I said, "Okay. Thank you."

Noah walked back into the restaurant and threw two twenty-dollar bills down on the table and reached for my hand. Pulling me up, he brought his lips to my ears and said, "I need to get you home. Now. We'll pick up something to eat on the way home."

Giggling, I turned to see our waitress laughing. She lifted her hand and waved goodbye. Giving her a wave back, I tried to push away the weird feeling that swept over my body.

Thirty

NOAH

TAKING A HOLD of Grace's hand, I pushed the door open to Dr. Johnson's office. Grace walked in first as she made her way over to the receptionist and signed in. After giving the receptionist everything she needed, they called Grace back to pee in a cup and to draw some blood.

I sat in the waiting room and tried to calm my nerves down. My stomach felt as if I'd eaten something that was not agreeing with me. The moment the door opened from the back and a nurse called for me, I jumped up and quickly followed her.

"Your wife is in here. Dr. Johnson will be joining y'all in just a few minutes."

Smiling, I nodded and said, "Thank you so much."

Grace was sitting on the table biting on her thumbnail. Walking up to her, I pulled her thumb out of her mouth and brushed my lips across hers. "Stop that. Why are you nervous?"

Exhaling a deep breath, Grace closed her eyes and said, "We're going to see our baby for the first time, Noah. I'm so scared. What if I'm not a good mom? What if they were wrong about the Fragile X testing?"

Standing in front of Grace, I pulled her into my arms and kissed the top of her head. "Baby, settle down. Take a deep breath and blow it out. First off, you're going to be an amazing mother. They didn't mess up on the testing so stop worrying."

Placing my finger on her chin, I gave her a wink. "Everything's going to be fine."

Grace smiled and dropped her head against my chest. "Okay. You're right. Deep breaths."

There was a light knock on the door before it opened and a doctor I was guessing was Dr. Johnson came walking in with a smile on his face. Holding my hand out, I said, "Good morning, I'm Grace's husband, Noah Bennet."

Dr. Johnson smiled and said, "Pleasure to meet you." Turning to Grace, the doctor smiled bigger. "Grace, it's hard to believe you're sitting in my office. Feels like just yesterday you were born."

Blushing, Grace peeked over to me and smiled.

Dr. Johnson opened up Grace's file and read over it quickly. "Okay. Well it looks like your tests have all come back positive. Let's take a look at our little peanut shall we?"

My heart felt as if it dropped to the floor as Grace reached out for my hand.

"Move on back and lay down, Grace. We're going to do a vaginal sonogram since the baby will be smaller. By the date of your last period, I'd be willing to guess you're about nine weeks or so along."

"O-okay," Grace whispered as she did as Doctor Johnson asked.

A few seconds later and we were looking at something on the monitor. Dr. Johnson said, "There he or she is."

Looking at Grace, I saw the tears in her eyes. Wiping my eyes quickly, I looked back at the monitor. Dr. Johnson tilted his head as he moved the wand around. Leaning forward I looked for some sign of something from our child. I figured I'd be seeing a little heart beating quickly. All I saw was a black spot. Then again, I wasn't really sure what I was supposed to be seeing.

"Where is the baby?" Grace asked.

Dr. Johnson clicked a few times on the screen, like he was taking measurements.

Pointing, Dr. Johnson said, "The baby is right here."

Looking closely all I could see was a peanut looking thing. My gut told me something was wrong.

After taking a few more measurements, Dr. Johnson did a few other things before he turned back to, Grace. I didn't even need to hear what he was going to say. Somehow I already knew by looking into his eyes. Clearing his throat, Dr. Johnson started to talk as he looked at Grace and then me.

"Grace, I'm not picking up a heartbeat."

Grace's smile vanished as she shook her head and whispered, "What?"

Squeezing her hand, I sat next to the bed and stared at our child.

"It appears the baby passed away maybe a few days ago, possibly even a week ago."

A sob escaped Grace's mouth as she slammed her hand over her mouth. "How . . . um . . . how do you know that, Dr. Johnson."

"The measurements of the baby show he was about seven to eight weeks."

Grace closed her eyes and shook her head. "What if you're wrong? What if there is a heartbeat and you just can't see it?"

Dr. Johnson looked lovingly at Grace as he swallowed hard. This had to be hard on him as well. "Grace,

I'm so sorry, but it's very evident that you've suffered a miscarriage."

Looking away, I fought to hold down my breakfast. Closing my eyes, I counted to ten before turning back and focusing on Grace.

Tears poured down Grace's face. "No. Dr. Johnson. Please tell me you're wrong. *Please*."

"Oh Grace, I'd give anything not to tell a parent this type of thing. Grace, I'm so very sorry, but the baby is gone."

Grace's body shook as she sobbed and asked, "What did I do wrong?"

At this point, the doctor had removed the wand and was motioning for me to help Grace sit up. Doing so, I helped her sit up as she stared at the screen and repeated. "What did I do wrong?"

"Grace, you didn't do anything wrong. This unfortunately is not an uncommon thing to see. This is nature's way of saying something was wrong with the fetus."

Grace wrapped her arms around her waist and looked up at me. "Noah. We didn't even get to see him alive. I didn't even know he was there!"

Pulling Grace into my arms, I held her as Dr. Johnson said, "Let me step outside for a few minutes. I'll be back in to go over some things with y'all."

Nodding my head, I turned and pressed my lips on the top of Grace's head. Her body was beginning to shake violently as she lost all control and started crying harder.

"Our baby. Noah, our baby."

Squeezing my eyes shut, I wanted to cry. I wanted to join Grace and fall apart at the news of our child passing away but I knew I had to be here for Grace.

I slowly rocked Grace as I said, "I know, sweetheart, I know."

Grace cried for a good ten minutes before she finally lifted her face from my chest. Cupping her face within my hands, I wiped her tear soaked face with my thumbs. Our eyes locked and I wanted to let out a scream. The hurt I saw in them about killed me.

A small knock and then the door opening, revealed Dr. Johnson again. "Grace, Noah, we need to talk about what happens next. "Grace, your body still thinks you're pregnant. We have two options. You can leave today, and wait for your body to expel the baby naturally."

Grace's eyes widened. "H-how l-long would that be?" She asked as she barely spoke between her small sobs.

Shaking his head, Dr. Johnson said, "It could be tomorrow or three weeks from now."

"You mean she'd have to carry him around for a few weeks knowing . . . knowing . . ." I couldn't even finish my sentence for fear I would break down.

Dr. Johnson nodded slowly at me before looking back at Grace. "Or, we do a surgical procedure where we removed the deceased fetus."

"Baby. Please don't call him a fetus."

Resting his hand on Grace's, Dr. Johnson gave her a weak smile. "If we do the surgical procedure, you'll have to stay overnight, but there will be less bleeding."

Grace wiped her tears away and said, "I can't carry him knowing he isn't really there. I don't think I can do that." Looking at me, her eyes pleaded with me. Almost as if she thought I wanted her to carry the baby.

Leaning over, I kissed her forehead. Pulling back, I turned to Dr. Johnson. "What do we need to do next for the surgery?"

I could see the agony on his face. As if each and every time he had to do this, it destroyed a small piece of him as well.

Sitting there, I felt numb as Dr. Johnson explained what would happen next. All I could hear was Grace sniffling. Even now, she tried to stay strong when I knew all she wanted to do was fall apart.

The nurse walked into the room and said they had already begun the process of admitting her as they brought a wheelchair in to bring Grace up to her room.

Once we got to our room, Grace stared out the window as I sat next to her. My heart ached as I fought for the words I wanted to say. There wasn't a damn thing I could say to make her feel better. Nothing I could do to take away her pain.

Standing, I walked around to the other side of the bed. Grace's eyes moved slowly up my body before they locked onto mine. "I can't think of one damn thing to say right now, Grace, other than I love you. I love you so much."

A tear rolled down her cheek as she gave me a slight smile. "I love you too, Noah and that's all I need to hear."

The door opened as Grace and I both turned to see two nurses walking in.

It was time.

Just when we found out we were having a child, he was taken away from us. We'd never know if it was a boy or a girl. Would she have had Grace's beautiful eyes?

I fought to find air to breathe. Grace squeezed my hands. "I'm thinking the same things you are," she whispered.

Before they went through the doors that lead to the surgery rooms, I leaned over and kissed her. "I'll be here when you get out."

Smiling, Grace pressed her lips together and nodded. "You and me?"

A lump formed in my throat as I forced the words out. "You and me."

The moment they took Grace back and the doors closed, I turned on my heels and practically ran through the hospital to get outside. The fresh air hit me like a brick wall as I leaned over and cried out, "Why? Why God, why Grace?"

Dropping to my knees, I buried my face in my hands and finally let go. I wasn't sure how long I sat there until I felt a hand on my shoulder and strong arms lifting me up. When I opened my eyes, Jeff was standing in front of me with Ari behind him.

Tears flowed freely from my eyes as I said, "I don't know what to do now."

Ari walked up and wrapped her arms around me as Jeff squeezed my shoulder and looked away for a brief moment.

I wanted to run as far away as I could. The urge to drink something and take a pill to forget everything washed over me as I quickly fought it and pushed it aside.

Ari pulled back and looked into my eyes. "How is she?"

Swallowing hard, I said, "She's trying to be strong. She keeps staring off in the distance. I don't know if I should let her be, or try to get her to talk to me." Shaking my head, I whispered, "I don't know what to do for her."

Ari nodded her head and laced her arm through mine as the three of us started to walk. "I know Grace has told you that Jeff and I lost our first child as well."

Slowly nodding, I felt like a heel for not remembering. "Don't give me that look. I didn't expect you to remember after what just happened, Noah. But, I can tell you, Grace is going to push you away. If she's anything like me, which I've been told a time or two she is."

I let a small laugh escape my lips. "What do I do if she does?"

Ari looked at Jeff as they both smiled. Jeff cleared his throat and said, "You give her some space, leave her with her thoughts but not for long. She needs to know you feel the same way. Noah, you've both lost a child. You're both going to grieve and if someone tells you that you weren't that far along, bullshit. The moment you found out Grace was carrying your baby, you fell in love."

My chin trembled as I thought back to last night when Grace blurted it out she was pregnant. In that moment I made a vow to always protect our baby. I fell in love . . . instantly.

"She's going to blame herself," I said with sadness lacing my voice. "She already asked what she did wrong."

Ari covered her mouth and cried as Jeff wrapped her in his arms. "My poor baby. Oh God, Jeff. Why did this have to happen to our, Grace? Why our Grace?"

Jeff ran his hand over Ari's head as he repeated, "Shh," as he gently kissed her head.

After a few moments had passed, Ari seemed to regain herself. She stood up taller and looked between Jeff and me. "She's going to be devastated, then confused, and then she's going to be pissed. Noah, I want honesty right now. How are you feeling, sweetheart?"

Dragging in a deep and shaky breath, I slowly blew it out. "Earlier, I'd have given anything for a beer and something to make me feel numb. But I pushed it aside and focused on Grace. Her love and the fact that she needs me, is stronger than the urge."

Ari smiled and Jeff slapped my back lightly. "If you feel the urge growing, you know what to do, right?" Jeff asked.

Nodding my head, I said, "Yes, sir. I called Brad after I called y'all. He told me if I was struggling, to call him or you."

Jeff gave me a wink. "Come on, let's go get some coffee and head up and wait for Dr. Johnson."

Jeff wrapped his arm around Ari's waist and led her into the hospital as I quickly said a prayer that everything went okay and that Grace would find the strength she was going to need to get through this.

Thirty-One

GRACE

THE WARMTH OF the sun shining through the window warmed my face as I laid there, too afraid to open my eyes. If I opened them, I'd have to face my reality.

Slowly opening my eyes, I saw my mother sitting in the corner with her knees pulled up and her head resting on them. My eyes filled with tears as I watched her. Turning my head, I saw Noah in the other chair with his head rested against the wall. My heart skipped a beat knowing that he was here. Not that I didn't think he would be, but I knew the moment they brought me back into this room, he probably never left.

Glancing back over to my mother, I whispered, "Mom."

My mother's head popped up and her eyes met mine. There was an instant recognition there. She knew exactly how I felt.

She knew the feeling of loss.

Loss of your child.

Slowly standing up, my mother glanced over to Noah, then quickly looked back at me. "Hey, baby girl. How are you feeling?"

Pressing my lips together to keep from crying, I finally said, "Empty."

Slowly shaking her head, my mother took my hand in hers and brought it up to her lips where she gently kissed it. "I know, sweetheart. I know."

"Mom, why? Why do you think this happened to us?"

I couldn't say me, because this happened to Noah and me. I knew he felt the loss as much as I did. I saw it in his eyes. I felt it in his kiss and I heard it in his voice.

Wiping a tear from her cheek, my mother said, "Grace, I asked that same question. Only God knows the answer. The only thing I can wrap my head around is that sweet little baby wouldn't have been able to make it. It's a cruel, cruel thing to have to experience and no words will ever make you feel better."

"The moment I saw the little plus sign, I felt such a strong love, Mom. I don't think I'd ever be able to explain it. It was like he had been growing in my stomach for months."

Looking over at Noah, I couldn't hold back the sob that slipped through. "He wants a baby so bad, and I wasn't able to give him one."

Placing her finger on my chin, my mother pulled my eyes back to hers. "Stop that right now. This was not your fault and you will be able to give him a child, Grace. I went on and had your brother and you."

Shaking my head, I said, "No. I'm never going to risk feeling like this again. Ever."

Closing her eyes, she took in a shallow breath before opening them again. "Grace, if anyone knows how much you're hurting right now, it's me. But please don't let that fear guide your feelings about children. One day, you and Noah are going to be blessed with a beautiful baby I promise you, darling."

My body came to life when I felt his touch. Turning, smiled when I saw Noah standing by my side. Smiling, h leaned over and brushed his lips gently across mine my stomach dipped. Even though the kiss was soft, I fe Noah's love pouring into my body and in that moment, knew we were going to be okay. It was going to be a lor road, but with Noah by my side it was a journey I knew w could make.

Together.

Pulling away slightly, Noah gazed into my eyes. "Grac Hope Bennet, you're my everything. You always have bee and you always will be."

Placing my hand on the side of Noah's face, I fought pull the words from my lips. "Don't ever leave my side."

Smiling a smile that took my breath away, Noah sai "Never."

My smile faded as I softly spoke. "I feel so lost now."

Noah shook his head as he placed his hand over min "Then it's my turn to find you, Grace."

Not being able to hold it back any longer, I let my tea fall as Noah sat on the bed and gently lifted me up to ho me.

Feeling my mother's arms wrap around Noah and m I let reality in.

THREE MONTHS LATER

RIDING UP ON my horse Rocky, I slowly brought him to stop at the river's edge as I watched the water pass me b A cool Texas winter breeze blew the small strands of ha that fell from my ponytail around my face.

As I stared at the clear water rolling over rocks, I thought about the last few months since I'd lost the baby. At times I felt so broken I swore I was never going to heal. But today, today my eyes were open and I finally saw what I had been trying so hard not to see.

DRIVING BY A small country church that I've driven by since I was a little girl, something caught my eye and caused me to pull into the parking lot. As I parked, I looked straight ahead and saw several white crosses. Opening my car door, I got out and walked through the small metal gate.

As I walked around, I noticed none of the crosses had names on them. They were plain with no words written on them. Making my way down the path, I looked up and saw a preacher.

Smiling, I walked over to him. "Hello. I hope I'm not trespassing, but this little graveyard caught my eye and I had to come in."

Giving me a smile, he shook his head and said, "This isn't a graveyard my child. This is a place of healing. For those who feel lost and alone . . . you're walking among the cross."

Looking around, I noticed that the white crosses were all in perfect rows but they seemed to be making something. It didn't take me long to figure out the small white crosses made one giant cross.

"How have I never noticed this before?" I whispered.

Letting out a soft chuckle, the preacher said, "Sometimes our eyes don't see . . . until God reveals what we need them to see at the right time we need to see it."

In that moment, everything changed. The emptiness inside me disappeared and was replaced by hope.

CLOSING MY EYES, I let the sound of the water take me to a place I'd been so afraid to go to until today. A baby room painted in a theme of Winnie the Pooh. Noah, holding a baby in his arms as tears fell from his eyes. Me walking around the garden with a little girl with brown bouncy curls chasing after me.

Hope.

Hope of a future I was terrified of wanting. A future I was afraid I didn't deserve. Noah had kept me from totally drowning in the water that was slowly taking over my life.

No longer. I walked among the cross. The love I felt for our child would never be lost or forgotten. That love would be tucked safely away in a corner of my heart where he would never be forgotten.

Life started again today with the promise of hope.

Smiling, I patted Rocky on the neck and said, "You feel like running boy?"

Nodding his head up and down, I laughed.

"Let's go then."

Turning Rocky, we headed back to the open field where it only took a small amount of pressure from my legs to set Rocky free.

With each pounding of Rocky's hooves on the ground, I smiled bigger until I was screaming out in joy as we both ran free through the pasture.

Hello world.

I've missed you.

Thirty-Two

GRACE

"GRACE! WHAT IN the hell are you doing? I need to talk to you," Meagan called out.

Looking in the mirror, I stared at myself as I stood in my bathroom. Chuckling, I shook my head. "Dare I even dream?" It had been three weeks since my little walk among the crosses.

I think I knew then.

Taking a deep breath in through my nose, I exhaled it out and whispered, "Here goes nothing."

Closing the bathroom door, I chewed on my lip as Meagan continued to knock on my bedroom door. I couldn't concentrate with her banging over and over.

Letting out a frustrated sigh, I opened the bathroom door and marched over to the bedroom door and threw it open.

"Jesus H. Christ, Meg! What in the hell is wrong with you?"

Meagan pushed her way through and walked into my bedroom.

Turning around to face me, Meagan jammed her hands onto her side and glared at me. "Why is Gray here?"

Pulling my head back, I looked at her like she was crazy. "Um . . . he's Noah's cousin and family. Why?"

Meagan closed her eyes as she slightly shook her head. "He drives me crazy, Grace."

Wiggling my eyebrows, I asked, "In a good way or a bad way, Meg?"

"Fuck you, Grace," Meagan said as she flopped on my bed.

Laughing, I made my way over to her and sat next to her. "Meg, it's okay to like him. I know for a fact he's kind of into you."

Maegan shot daggers from her eyes at me. "He is like kryptonite, Grace. He is so bad for me, yet I can't seem to stay away from him."

Slamming my hands over my mouth, I widened my eyes. "You and Gray?"

"No. I mean, we have more of a stick and move method to our friendship."

My mouth dropped open as I said, "Stick and move method?"

Meagan shrugged her shoulders and said, "Yeah, you know we fuck, then I leave, then when we're both feeling lonely, we fu—"

Holding up my hands, I stopped Meagan from talking. "I get it, Meg. I. Get. It."

"I'm happy with that arrangement, but Gray keeps . . . he keeps . . . ugh! Men!"

Falling backward, Meagan let out a dramatic sigh.

"He keeps what?"

"Wanting more! I can't do more."

Lying next to Meagan, we both stared at the ceiling. "Why can't you do more, Meg?"

"Oh Grace. I want more than anything to do more, but I'm not good enough for him."

Sitting up, I hit Meagan in the leg. "What in the hell does that mean? Meagan, you are more than good enough for Gray. I'd have to say he isn't good enough for you."

Lifting her hands over her head, Meagan grabbed a pillow and pushed it over her face as she screamed into it.

Standing up, I stared at her as she dropped the pillow to her side. "Feel better?"

Sitting up, Meagan rolled her eyes. "No." Looking into my eyes, I saw Meagan's eyes glass over. "Grace, you know how I went through all that shit in college. The bullying and everything?"

Nodding, I said, "Yeah, how could I forget."

Swallowing, Meagan looked out the window and said, "There was one girl who seemed to just hate me. She was the one who started the rumors and shit."

"I remember. What about her?"

Meagan's eyes captured mine and I could see nothing but devastation. "She works with Gray. He took her to lunch the other day. I saw them together when I ran into them. I was taken back to college and I froze as she stared at me with that stupid bitch looking face of hers."

"Holy shit, no way, Meg. She lives in Durango?"

Nodding, Meagan said, "And I think Gray might be attracted to her."

Grabbing Meagan's hands, I pulled her up and said, "You have to tell him how vile she is, Meg. Gray needs to know what kind of a bitch she is."

Shaking her head, Meagan said, "No. If I do that then he's going to ignore her or worse yet, say something to her and she'll start up with something. I'll handle her on my own but—"

"But what?"

Worrying her bottom lip, Meagan closed her eyes and said, "I overheard Gray telling Noah there was a new girl at work that was hot. Noah asked if Gray had been out with her and he said once. He said he was tired of waiting for the one girl he wanted to wake up and realize what they had . . . so he had asked Claire to go out on another date when he got back into town. He said they were going to celebrate the New Year together."

Feeling all the air leave my body, I stood there staring at, Meagan. "So you're going to take a back seat to this bitch, forget the feelings you have for Gray and just let her walk in and take him from you? Aren't you tired of her taking something from you, Meg?"

Something moved across Meagan's face as her mouth parted open. She looked at me hard for a few moments and then said, "I am. She ruined my whole college experience and by God I'm not going to let her keep getting away with this. For shits sake, I council kids on this shit."

Smiling, I stood taller and said, "Hell yeah! Meagan, you are no longer that girl in college who let a bunch of cuntlickers bully her. You are Meagan fucking Atwood. You chew bitches like that up and spit them out!"

Meagan stood up and smiled. "Hell yeah I do! I . . . wait . . . did you call them cuntlickers?"

Nodding, I said, "Yeah. Why?"

Meagan stared at me for a few seconds before she busted out laughing. The next thing I knew, we were both on the bed laying down laughing our asses off. Noah walked through the door and looked at us as he let out a chortle.

"What's so funny?" he asked as Meagan and I finally got some composure and sat up. Glancing over to Noah, I quickly stopped laughing as my mouth dropped open as I looked at his T-shirt.

The white T-shirt had a black and yellow sign across the top that read *Oversized Load.* Under the words was a figure of man, like you'd see on a construction worker sign. Except there was something drawn between the legs signifying a dick. He was holding a yellow sign that said,

Caution.

Meagan busted out laughing again. She must have read the shirt. "You think highly of yourself, Noah," she said as she got up and continued to laugh as she left the room. I could hear her laughing all the way downstairs.

Standing up, I stared at the shirt. "W-where did you get that?"

Noah smiled like he was the luckiest man on Earth. "Your dad."

Closing my eyes, I whispered, "Holy hell. I'm going to kill him."

"Why? I like it," Noah said as I opened my eyes and shook my head.

"Okay, I can't deal with that right now," I said as I walked up and grabbed Noah by the hand and dragged him into our bathroom. Shutting the door, I turned to him and couldn't help but notice the smile on his face.

"Hell yeah! You in the mood for some quick sex, even though everyone is downstairs? I'm all about it, baby." Noah wiggled his eyebrows as he asked, "It was the T-shirt, wasn't it?"

Rolling my eyes, I picked up the pregnancy test and held it up in front of him.

Noah sucked in a breath and whispered, "Oh wow."

Smiling, I said, "Yeah. Oh wow is right. I missed my period last month and then again this month. I didn't want to get our hopes up, so I didn't say anything. But, this last month I've been feeling sick every morning. It usually hits around ten in the morning and lasts through lunch. My breasts are sore as hell and . . . well . . . I just feel it. I don't know how else to explain it."

Noah grabbed the box and ripped it open as he took out the test and said, "Pee, Grace. Pee like your life depends on it."

Laughing, I took the test and made my way over to the toilet. Pulling up my skirt, I pulled my panties down and sat. Noah dropped to his knees and just stared at my lady bits.

Tilting my head, I glared at Noah. "Um . . . I can't really pee with you staring at me like that, Noah."

Standing up quickly, Noah took a few steps back and said, "Shit. Sorry, baby. I'm kind of excited."

"Really? I couldn't tell with your face practically in my vajayjay."

Giving me a sexy smile and a wink, Noah leaned against the counter and whistled as he looked everywhere but at me.

Sitting there, I tried like hell to conjure up some pee to no avail.

Closing my eyes, I sighed. "Noah. Maybe you could just stand there and be quiet."

"Oh yeah, sure," Noah said.

Another two minutes went by with nothing. Then Noah turned on the faucet and it hit me.

Finally. My bladder was about to burst.

After I finished, I stood up and took a piece of toilet paper and put it on the counter as I laid the test on top of it. Noah grabbed my wrist and pulled me away from it.

"No matter what it says or what happens, we do it together. You and me."

Grinning from ear to ear, I nodded. "Always together always you and me."

Noah ran his finger along my jaw as I felt my insides tighten with need. "So beautiful," he whispered as he moved his lips across my neck.

Wrapping my arms around his neck, I let out a soft moan. Noah's hands slipped under my skirt as his fingers found their way to where I desperately needed his attention.

Two fingers slipped between my lips as I pushed my hips toward Noah. "Fucking hell . . . you're soaking wet."

"Oh God, Noah. I want you," I whispered as I quickly

unzipped his jeans. I didn't care that our friends and family were downstairs waiting on us. Or that the fireworks were set to go off soon. All I knew was that I needed to feel my husband's dick buried deep inside of me now.

I'd been horny before, but never this horny. Noah's dick sprang out from his jeans as I licked my lips.

"Fuck me, Noah. Now!" I said as Noah pulled my panties off and grabbed my ass as he lifted me up.

"Jesus, Grace," Noah said as he buried himself deep inside of me.

"Yes," I hissed through my teeth as Noah gave me exactly what I asked for. My stomach felt as if I was on a roller coaster. Noah had a way of bringing out every emotion in me. Every time we were together, it felt like the first time. My insides bloomed with desire as my orgasm quickly grew.

"So. Close," I panted as I felt Noah's dick grow bigger.

"Grace . . . oh hell, baby . . . come for me, Grace."

And just like that, I exploded as my entire body shook as my orgasm raced across my body from my toes to the top of my head. Not thirty seconds later and Noah was moaning as he had his own release."

When he finally stopped moving, he didn't pull out. We stayed as one as we both gasped for air like we had just run a marathon.

Leaning his head against mine, Noah chuckled. "Shit, I can't believe I just fucked the hell out of my wife with all our friends and family downstairs."

Giggling, I dropped my head back against the wall. "I needed that."

Noah kissed the tip of my nose as he said, "Me too."

My eyes glanced over his shoulder to the test sitting on the counter. Swallowing hard, I said, "The test."

Noah gently pulled out of me as he slowly set me back down. Reaching over, he grabbed my panties and motioned for me to step into them.

"I should wash up real quick," I said as Noah placed his hand on my stomach to stop me.

"No. I want your panties soaked with our cum. I want you to remember me pouring myself into your body."

My heart dropped in my chest as it felt like I needed to find air to breath. That had to be the hottest damn thing Noah had ever said to me.

"O-okay," I barely said as Noah slipped my panties back on. Standing up, he cupped my face with his hands and kissed me passionately.

Pulling his lips ever so slightly from mine, he whispered, "Are you ready?"

Squeezing my eyes shut, I nodded and said, "Ready."

Noah took my hand as we both made our way over to the counter and looked down.

Staring at the test stick, I wasn't sure what to say. Noah turned me toward him as he looked into my eyes.

"I love you, Grace Hope Bennet."

Wrapping my arms around him, I choked back my tears. "I love you the most, Noah Pete Bennet."

Thirty-Three

NOAH

HOLDING GRACE IN my arms, I looked up as the fireworks exploded in the night sky.

All you could hear were the ohhs and ahhs of everyone around as the different colored lights lit up the whole area.

Glancing around, I couldn't help but smile. Everyone I cared about was here including my sister, who held her daughter in her arms as her husband held onto their son. Em must have felt my stare as she gave me a quick smile before she looked up again.

Gray was standing on the other side of Emily with a couple of girls who were fighting for his attention. Chuckling, I shook my head and wondered how he was able to attract the women like he did. I wasn't sure who they were, all I knew was they were somehow related to Ellie and Jeff, but I never did catch how.

Luke stood with Libby in his arms as his hands rested on her pregnant belly as their daughter ran in circles

around them. Libby was due tomorrow and everyone wa
holding their breath she made it through tonight.

Will and Alex were next to her parents, Gunner an
Ellie. Taylor was standing next to her parents, Brad an
Amanda, as she kept pointing up and laughing. I think ou
of all the girls, Taylor was by far the most innocent, an
the one who had a heart of gold.

Meagan stood next to Grace and me as she shot dag
gers at the girls who were falling all over Gray. Laughing,
shook my head as I watched Meagan look away in disgus

Yep. This night was perfect.

When the fireworks ended, Grace turned around in m
arms and smiled up at me.

"Should we keep it our secret?" Grace asked as sh
lifted her eyebrows.

Letting out a quick breath, I glanced around at ever
one again. Shaking my head, I said, "I want to shout it fro
the rooftops, Grace."

Giggling, she nodded and said, "So do I."

"Let's do it then," I said as I pulled Grace over to m
truck. Lifting her up, I set her in the bed of the truck as
ran over and honked the horn.

Everyone turned and looked at Grace as she sai
"Ah . . . hold on. Noah?"

Jumping into the bed of the truck, I stood next to Grac
"Grace and I wanted to first say thank you to everyone fo
spending your New Year's Eve here with us and ringing i
the New Year. It meant a lot to us to have you all here."

Cheers erupted as well as some loud whistles.

"Second!" Grace shouted as she took my hand. "We fi
ured since we had y'all in one place, we'd share some new
we just found out today. It's a bit out of the normal, bu
we were both too excited not to share it."

"Jeff passed down his T-shirt collection to Noah"
Gunner shouted as everyone laughed. Laughing, I pointe
to Jeff who gave me a thumbs-up.

Grace chuckled and said, "No . . . but unfortunately I'm afraid my father has rubbed off some on my husband."

"I'm so sorry, sweetheart!" Ari called out.

Grace looked at me as she took my hand in hers and asked, "Are y'all ready to hear the news?"

My eyes landed on Ari and Jeff. They held each other as Ari wiped a tear from her eye and Jeff stared at Grace.

"Tell us already, Grace!" Alex shouted.

Grace laughed and then shouted out, "Noah and I are expecting a baby."

Cowboy hats went flying and cheers erupted as Jeff walked up and reached for Grace. Lifting her down from the bed of my truck, he held her tightly as Grace softly cried into his chest. I jumped down from the truck bed as Ari walked up to me and gave me a smile I don't think I'll ever forget. "Congratulations sweetheart." Taking me in her arms, she held me tightly.

Knowing this wasn't going to be easy, I tried to push my fears away. I was already scared to death for both Grace and our child. Grace had already told me she was nervous but wasn't going to walk on eggshells. We needed to have faith and that was what we were going to do.

It felt like our wedding day all over again. Everyone came up and gave each of us a hug and said congratulations. The last two people to approach us were Grams and Gramps.

Gramps hit me on the back and said, "Stop by tomorrow, son. We'll play a game of dominos."

Knowing I wasn't going to pass up the chance to spend time with Gramps, I nodded and said, "I'll be there, sir."

Grams cupped Grace's face and kissed her gently on the forehead. "I'm going to say it's a girl."

Grace chuckled. "What makes you say that?"

Giving Grace a wink, Grams smiled and said, "I have my ways." Laughing, I shook my head. Ari always said that Grams had a sixth sense when it came to knowing things before anyone else did.

Wrapping my arms around Grace, I said, "As long as he or she is healthy, I don't care."

Grace scrunched her nose up and said, "Me either. But I'm totally okay if Grams is right."

Laughing, I pulled Grace closer to me and kissed her as Luke yelled out, "Get your paws off my sister!"

For the next two and a half hours we told stories, laughed, ate s'mores and each person made resolutions for the upcoming year.

By the time Grace and I got up to our bedroom, we both face planted onto our bed and didn't move.

"Too tired to move," Grace said.

"Let's just sleep like this," I mumbled into the bed.

Grace giggled and said, "Or we could get naked and have hot sweaty sex."

Turning over onto my side, I stared at her. "How can you even think about sex? It's damn near four am. I don't even think my dick wants to wake up."

Giving me a sexy smile, Grace moved her hands into my pants and stroked me. The bastard came up and quickly started to throb.

Licking her lips, Grace sat up and pulled her shirt over her head and stripped out of her skirt and panties.

"Looks like your oversized load is ready to unload again."

I'd never taken my clothes off that fast before in my life.

The rest of the night, or what was left of it, was spent tangled up with Grace.

I was positive I'd never be able to bring in a new year like this one ever again.

Placing my lips on the top of Grace's head, I kissed her gently as she slept peacefully wrapped in my arms.

Moving my hand down, I rested it on Grace's stomach as a smile grew across my face.

It had been a long road traveled . . . but it was worth every twist and turn we had to face. As long as Grace and I were together, we'd never be lost again.

My eyes grew heavy as I finally gave in and drifted off to sleep, dreaming of a little girl with bouncy brown curls being chased by a dark-haired little boy with a giant toad in his hands.

Life didn't get any better.

Epilogue

MEAGAN

WALKING TOWARD MY rental car, I glanced over and saw Grayson leaning against a car, talking to one of the girls he met tonight.

Ugh. Man-whore.

Pulling my eyes off of Grayson, I focused on getting to the car and heading back to my parents' house. I made it through the holidays intact. All I needed to do was get back to Colorado, immerse myself in my job, and push everything else away.

"Meg?"

Closing my eyes, I sped up and tried to pretend like I didn't hear Grayson call out to me.

"Meg! Stop!"

Shit. Keep walking, Meagan.

Reaching for the handle on the car, I went to pull it open when I felt Grayson pull on my arm. Turning me to face him, I prepared myself.

Cue the cold black heart.

Looking up at Grayson's smile, I ignored how it made me feel. "Meg, before you leave, I was wondering if we might be able to talk?"

My eyes glanced quickly back over to the girl who was sitting in her car now, but watching every move Grayson made.

Not looking directly at Grayson, I asked, "What in the world would we possibly have to talk about at three in the morning, Gray?"

Focusing on his earlobe, I waited for his response. His hand lifted as he rubbed a piece of my hair through his fingers. I had died my hair brown three months ago and Grayson had made it clear to me he loved the new color. A lot. "What's the matter, Meg? You can't even look me in the eye when you talk to me?"

My eyes snapped up to his. *Don't get lost in them, Meagan.*

Letting out a nervous laugh, I rolled my eyes and said, "Don't be ridiculous, Gray. I'm tired and ready to go home." My eyes looked back over to the girl who was still sitting and watching us. Motioning with my head toward her, I said, "Looks like your new friend is waiting for you. Have fun tonight, Gray."

Turning, I went to open my car when Grayson used his hand to shut it. Leaning in closer to me, his body pressed against mine as I came alive and took in a deep breath.

He's only good for sex.

Amazing, mind blowing, incredibly hot sex.

That's it.

Grayson's mouth moved toward my neck, stopping just below my ear. Thank God my parents had already left. The last thing I wanted to do was explain any sort of relationship with Grayson to my father.

Grayson's hand swept my hair away as he pressed his lips against the sensitive skin behind my ear. My body trembled and I cursed under my breath for letting him get to me.

"The only person I want to have fun with tonight is you, Meg."

Swallowing hard, I looked into Grayson's eyes. "Gray," I whispered as he flashed that smile at me. My cold black heart quickly melted away as I felt my lower stomach pull with the idea of being with Grayson. His deep-blue eyes had a way of making me forget everything and everyone around me. His broad chest demanded my hands run gently over it as I kissed every inch of his muscular body.

Must.

Stay.

Strong.

Placing his hand on the side of my face, Grayson never broke eye contact with me. "Get in the car, Meg. I'll drive."

Before I even knew what was happening, I was walking around the front of my car and getting into the passenger seat. Grayson got in, pushed the start button, and began driving away from Grace and Noah's house.

Glancing out the window, I couldn't help but notice the pissed off look on the girl's face. Forcing myself not to smile, I turned to Grayson. "Where are we going, Gray?" I asked as my stomach jumped with the touch of Grayson's hand over mine.

With a purr in his voice, Grayson said, "To my hotel in Fredericksburg." Turning to look at me, Grayson's eyes burned with a fire I'd seen many times before. Smiling a smile that would easily cause a nun to give in to his demands, Grayson gave me a wink. "It's been far too long, baby."

Looking back out through the front window, I closed my eyes and made a silent vow.

One last time.

Thank you's

EVERY TIME I sit down to do my thank you's I have a million different people running through my head that I need to thank. So many people play a part in this dream I get to live and I wish I could list every single one of them.

For now, I'll start here.

Darrin and Lauren—As always, thank you for you never ending support. It means the world to me. I promise someday I will get this time management thing down! I love you both so very much.

Danielle Sanchez—Seriously I don't know what I would do without you. You do so much behind the scenes to help me do what I do and I appreciate every single thing you do. Thank you for all of your hard work, your amazing ideas, and most importantly, your friendship. #KickAssPublicist

Kristin Mayer—Thank you for your friendship and for reading my books as I write them. Your honesty and input mean the world to me!

Laura Hansen—Thank you so much for always taking the time to beta read my stuff! You are the best and your input is amazing!

Nikola Siervert—Thank you for being the last eyes on this book before it goes out to the world! You're the best!

Elizabeth Thiele and Nancy Metsch—Thank you for doing a last minute read on this for me! You'll never know how grateful I am to you both!

Molly McAdams, Vilma Gonzalez, Anna Easter, and Danielle Sanchez (AKA—the lunch crew)—I love you girls to the moon and back!!!!

My readers—There could *never* be enough words to say thank you for your continued support and love that you show me every single day. If it wasn't for y'all I wouldn't be able to take the story that is floating around in my head and bring it to life on paper. For that I say THANK YOU! I hope you enjoy Grace and Noah's story. I had so much fun writing it. We are that much closer to saying goodbye to the WANTED gang. Happy reading y'all!

Playlist

Kelsea Ballerini—Love Me Like You Mean It
Noah standing on Grace's front porch.

Sam Hunt—Take Your Time
Noah singing to Grace

Ashley Clark—Greyhound
Noah and Grace walking along the river.

Dierks Bentley—Here on Earth
Noah and Grace talking in parking lot of Target

John Mayer—XO
Noah and Grace before Grace meets Noah's mother

Rascal Flatts—Hurry Baby
Noah admitting he has a problem with prescription drugs.

Jake Owen—What We Ain't Got
Noah going through withdrawls.

Colbie Caillat—Hold On
Grace fighting to hold on to things as Noah goes through withdrawls.

Chris Young—The Man I Want To Be
Noah at the end of his withdrawls telling Grace he needs time alone.

One Republic—Good Life
Jeff and Noah talking on the porch.

Haley and Michael—Giving It All To You
Grace walking down the aisle

Tim McGraw—My Best Friend
Noah singing to Grace at their wedding.

Mickey Guyton—Safe
Grace and Noah after she loses their baby.

Lady Antebellum—Hello World
Grace riding in the open field.

Lady Antebellum—Can't Take My Eyes Off You
Noah holding Grace after New Years Eve.

Florida Georgia Line—Sippin' On Fire
Epilogue

piatkus